PRAISE FOR THE NOVELS OF RHONDA WOODWARD

THE WAGERED HEART

"A very likable heroine and historically accurate writing that shines . . . enjoyable."
—All About Romance

"Remember the name Rhonda Woodward, because this author is developing into a topflight Regency favorite." —*Romantic Times* (4 stars)

A SPINSTER'S LUCK

"Woodward gives romance readers much to enjoy. . . . The tale flows smoothly and naturally, with several refreshingly different plot twists, and the ending is thoroughly satisfying." —Romance Reviews Today

"Talented newcomer Rhonda Woodward penned an enjoyable tale with a mix of mischief and matrimony."
—*Romantic Times*

Moonlight
and Mischief

Rhonda Woodward

A SIGNET BOOK

To Heidi Owens
for believing

SIGNET
Published by New American Library, a division of
Penguin Group (USA) Inc., 375 Hudson Street,
New York, New York 10014, USA
Penguin Group (Canada), 10 Alcorn Avenue, Toronto,
Ontario M4V 3B2, Canada (a division of Pearson Penguin Canada Inc.)
Penguin Books Ltd., 80 Strand, London WC2R 0RL, England
Penguin Ireland, 25 St. Stephen's Green, Dublin 2,
Ireland (a division of Penguin Books Ltd.)
Penguin Group (Australia), 250 Camberwell Road, Camberwell, Victoria 3124,
Australia (a division of Pearson Australia Group Pty. Ltd.)
Penguin Books India Pvt. Ltd., 11 Community Centre, Panchsheel Park,
New Delhi - 110 017, India
Penguin Group (NZ), Cnr Airborne and Rosedale Roads, Albany,
Auckland 1310, New Zealand (a division of Pearson New Zealand Ltd.)
Penguin Books (South Africa) (Pty.) Ltd., 24 Sturdee Avenue,
Rosebank, Johannesburg 2196, South Africa

Penguin Books Ltd., Registered Offices:
80 Strand, London WC2R 0RL, England

First published by Signet, an imprint of New American Library,
a division of Penguin Group (USA) Inc.

First Printing, December 2004
10 9 8 7 6 5 4 3 2 1

Chapter One

1816

"*B*y damn. Queens, you say," Lord Haverstone drawled, tossing down three jacks with a flick of his wrist.

Across the table, Lord Brampton stared down at the playing cards with a dumbstruck expression. Swallowing several times, he slumped back in his chair with his mouth open.

"I won?" Even with the evidence before him, Lord Brampton could not quite believe that he had finally come out the victor in this intense game of chance.

Leaning casually back in his chair, Lord Haverstone looked past Lord Brampton to the awed expressions of the keenly attentive gentlemen standing around the table. They, like Brampton, continued to stare in surprise at the haphazardly splayed cards.

Picking up a heavy crystal goblet, Lord Haverstone drank the last of a very fine brandy. Soon, a murmur grew among the small crowd of bucks crammed into this corner of White's. No one could recall Stone, as he was familiarly known, ever losing a significant amount of money at cards.

And it is a rather significant sum, he thought, disliking the unfamiliar feeling of self-disgust. His luck and wits had rarely failed him, but he had to own that he had been reckless in the last few hands. *Well, good fortune cannot run forever,* he mused, philosophically dismissing his disappointment over the loss.

"I really won?" Brampton asked again. His bushy gray eyebrows came together in surprise.

An ironic smile came to Stone's lips as he pushed his chair back and rose from the table. "It would appear so, Brampton. May I call upon you in the morning to settle the matter?"

Not surprisingly, Stone did not have the prodigious sum of seventeen thousand pounds on his person.

Brampton dragged his gaze from the cards still resting on the highly polished table to look at the earl with shock-glazed eyes.

"Pardon? Oh! Yes, at your convenience, Stone," Brampton said, turning his dazed attention back to the table.

Some of the blades who had witnessed this unprecedented event laughed a little in understanding of Brampton's reaction.

Giving a jaunty salute, Stone moved through the parting crowd, noting wryly that it looked as if the entire membership of the club had witnessed the last few hands.

The ever-alert majordomo met him near the door with his hat, walking stick, and gloves.

Taking his time, Stone pulled on his gloves and made sure his hat rested upon his head at his preferred angle before leaving the club and stepping into the misty night.

He was several strides down the narrow, dimly lit street when his senses alerted him of footsteps approaching from behind.

After a few more yards, he whipped around to confront whoever had the nerve to sneak up on him on the darkened street.

Beneath the yellowish glow of a streetlamp stood a startled young man. Although Stone found the younger man's face familiar, he could not quite recall his name.

"My apologies, my lord, I-I was about to announce

my presence," the young man said in a quick, nervous voice.

Stone perused the young man's features for another moment. Now he recalled him standing among the bucks who had watched the tensely charged battle of skill and luck several moments ago.

If memory served, this nervous-looking buck was the son of a wealthy tradesman. Town seemed to be full of such creatures this Season. However, this young man had not seemed such an encroaching mushroom as some of the others.

"You wanted to speak to me?" Stone did not bother to keep the edge from his tone. He was in no humor to give consequence to overly familiar pups.

"Y-yes, my lord. I wanted to say that I am sorry that you lost."

Stone allowed his frown to deepen. "Your name, sir?" He watched as the younger man swallowed hard.

"I am Steven Thorncroft, my lord," he said as he performed a passable bow.

Stone shifted to casually lean on his ivory-tipped walking stick, and his cold gaze held Thorncroft's for a silent moment. "Permit me to give you a bit of advice, Mr. Thorncroft. Never console a gambler on his losses."

Even in the poorly lit street, he could see the flush come to Thorncroft's cheeks. Although Stone was satisfied with the wince that crossed the younger man's features, annoyance flashed through him when Thorncroft made no move to depart.

"Thank you. I will remember."

Despite the exceedingly late hour, a few other pinks of the *ton,* on horseback or in carriages, passed them. Stone turned to take his leave when the young man quickly spoke up.

"There was one other matter that I would speak to you about, my lord, if you would be so kind as to give me another moment."

Stone's innate politeness halted his progress. "Yes?"

"The Season is almost at an end, and although I

have no doubt that you will be occupied in the coming months, I would like to extend an invitation for you to come to a house party at my parents' estate in Chippenham."

At Mr. Thorncroft's rushed speech, a dark, finely arched brow rose over one of Stone's light blue eyes. Examining the younger man more closely, Stone had a strong suspicion that he was holding his breath.

"Egad, are you foxed?" Stone drawled, mentally recanting his earlier assessment that Thorncroft was not an encroaching mushroom.

The younger man gave a choked, nervous laugh. "I am a bit, or I would never have the nerve to ask you. You see, my lord, when I saw you lose such a vast sum, I immediately thought of my sister."

At this odd comment Stone almost guffawed. "Why? Does she go about losing fortunes as well?"

"No. She hates gambling," Mr. Thorncroft said quickly. "I thought of her because not only is she quite pretty, but my father has settled an enormous sum upon her. More than enough to recoup a fortune lost in gambling."

At this singularly unique explanation, Stone so forgot himself that his usually unreadable mask slipped. He found himself staring at Mr. Thorncroft in complete astonishment.

"Damn me, are you offering your sister as a way to save me from ruin?"

"Not until the two of you have a look at each other," Thorncroft said, taking the question seriously. "Under the circumstances, I did not think it would hurt to ask. But I beg your pardon if you feel I am overstepping myself."

The sheer unabashed, yet somehow self-effacing, cheek of the invitation disarmed Stone completely. Suddenly his chest began to rumble with laughter. At the baffled look that came to Thorncroft's features, Stone tried to restrain his amusement, but he failed. He could not recall finding anything so droll in recent memory.

Deep, genuine laughter shook his shoulders for some moments before his mirth subsided enough to respond to the young man.

"Thorncroft, our encounter has been an unexpected pleasure. Unfortunately, I have plans for the next few months, but I will be hosting a house party of my own at Heaton in the fall. It would be my greatest pleasure if you would bring your sister and stay for the whole six weeks." He suspected that Mr. Thorncroft would prove quite an antidote. No doubt his friends would find the pup as amusing as he did.

The look of shock and joy that came over Thorncroft's face softened Stone's amusement. He thought the younger man looked the way old Brampton had some minutes ago.

"We—we would be truly honored, my lord. This is most kind of you," Thorncroft stated in a rush.

"Excellent. I shall take my leave of you, Thorncroft. I look forward to seeing you at Heaton the first of October."

With his look of surprised pleasure increasing, Thorncroft made a flourishing bow. "Thank you, my lord. Until October."

Lord Haverstone turned and strode up the street before Mr. Thorncroft had the time to complete his bow.

Chapter Two

"*A*nd then he called me 'Thorncroft,' just as a friend would."

Suppressing a vexed sigh, Mariah Thorncroft looked up from her embroidery to glare at her brother's pleased face as he lounged on the sofa across from her. She had lost count of the number of times she had heard him repeat this utterly dull story. Looking down, she stabbed the needle into the hoop; her mood rebelled against hearing it yet again.

Even with the retelling, she always had the feeling that Steven left something out. It did not make sense to her that an earl would suddenly strike up a conversation with her brother—a definite nobody in aristocratic circles—and invite the Thorncrofts to a house party at his country estate.

Especially the Earl of Haverstone.

An image of his lean, angular face with intense blue eyes and a proud expression immediately came to mind.

She had had the dubious honor of being introduced to the wickedly handsome earl while visiting friends in Bath last spring. The encounter had been extremely brief. She recalled how the earl's light blue gaze had passed over her without a flicker of expression crossing his bored features.

Mariah could come up with no plausible reason for the earl to have invited them. Steven had not even made the trip to Bath. She strongly suspected that

Steven had mistaken the earl's meaning, or had highly exaggerated the connection.

Over her embroidery, she contemplated her older brother with a suspicious eye as he twirled a chair pillow between his hands.

Besides, her thoughts continued, the Earl of Haverstone—known as Stone among the *ton*—would not find her family at all interesting. From all she had heard of him, the earl's world was as different from the Thorncrofts' as chalk and cheese.

"But, Steven, that was months ago, and we have yet to receive a formal invitation. He has probably forgotten all about it. By all means, go if you do not care about embarrassing yourself, but I have no intention of showing up on the earl's doorstep."

"But you must!"

Mariah raised her brow at her brother's vehement tone and opened her mouth to argue.

"Indeed, you must, young lady."

Mariah closed her mouth and turned at the sound of her mother's voice. The petite lady marched into the room, looking quite lovely in her morning gown of cream-colored silk.

"I have great hopes that eligible gentlemen from illustrious families will also be guests of the earl. This is a gift from heaven," Mrs. Thorncroft proclaimed. Seating herself next to her daughter, she sent a smile to her son.

Mariah shook her head in a hopeless gesture. "Oh, Mama, are you still determined to buy a title? I have managed to evade such a fate these last three Seasons, and I am determined to last three more if need be."

Mrs. Thorncroft's smile faded into a frown as she addressed her daughter. "Have I not taught you that it is as easy to marry a peer as a plain mister? Sometimes I think you are determined to see me miserable. Do you not wish to give me and Papa grandchildren?"

Mariah sighed. Setting aside her embroidery, she gave herself a moment to marshal her response to this oft-repeated argument. "Well, I certainly do not need

to have a title for that. What about Steven? He can
give you grandchildren, but he is not even close to
getting near an altar. Why are you not haranguing him
to marry?"

Mrs. Thorncroft waved a dismissive hand toward
her eldest son. "Yes, Steven will give me grandchildren someday, but only you can give me *titled* grandchildren. Just think—me, the grandmother of a future
baron or even an earl," she sighed, a dreamy look of
delight coming to her pretty features.

"Oh, Mama." Any endeavor to dissuade her mother
from daydreaming about Mariah wearing a coronet
would be hopeless.

"Do not 'Oh, Mama' me. We shall be going to Heaton in two weeks. A verbal invitation is good enough.
I am just concerned that some of your gowns will not
be completed in time."

Mariah made no response and sat silently as her
mother and brother excitedly discussed the impending
journey to Heaton. After some minutes, Mariah felt
her temper rise, and she turned her annoyed gaze on
her brother.

"You are no help at all. You used to be on my
side," she said in an accusatory tone. "Now you are
helping Mama put me on exhibition in front of a
bunch of strangers. They will look down their noses at
us. That is, if they let us pass through the front door."

Stephen ran impatient fingers through his wavy
brown hair. "Of course they will. Let us past the front
door, I mean, not look down their noses. Do not be
a widgeon. Stone invited us outright."

"Well, I will manage to get out of it. Just you wait
and see," she stated, ignoring her mother's outraged
gasp.

"You can't, scamp." Steven slouched farther down
in the chair and sent her a rather smug look.

"You keep saying that. If you want to go, then go.
Why put me through what will prove to be a humiliat-
ing experience?"

Steven sighed heavily and looked from his sister to

his mother, then back again. "As our departure draws near, I might as well tell you both the whole of it."

Mariah felt an immediate sense of dread at her brother's words. "I have had the feeling you were hiding something!"

"Do not speak in riddles, Steven. Out with it," Mrs. Thorncroft commanded, leaning forward with a frown.

"I told the earl I would bring Mariah."

Mariah's breath caught in her throat, and she clutched the chair arm reflexively.

"He lost a fortune that night," Steven continued, sitting up straight, his tone no longer smug. "Seventeen thousand pounds."

Mariah gasped and felt her mother's hand clutch her arm.

"Seventeen thousand pounds!" the ladies exclaimed in unison.

"Yes," he confirmed, looking at Mariah. "Later, I mentioned that you had an enormous dowry. He seemed delighted. I did not want to say this earlier, especially to Mama—I would hate to get her hopes up—but this might be your chance to land a plum title."

Mrs. Thorncroft vigorously fanned her cheeks with her hand. "Such a fortune! Why, that sum would keep a family well housed for twenty years! He lost so much in one night?" she asked with dismay.

Mariah stared at her brother, unable to formulate any coherent words to express her own astonishment.

"What?" she finally whispered in horrified anger. She could not quite believe that she had heard aright. How could her brother have been so crass?

This really is the outside of enough, she thought, clenching her hands at her sides.

Quite possibly, this could be the most mortifying moment of her life. Even enduring the ignominy, Season after Season, of having her mother practically trip her in front of any remotely suitable gentleman paled in comparison to hearing this.

An instant later she drew her arm back and threw

the pillow right at her brother's head. As it hit him on the forehead, she only regretted that it had not been a rock.

"I will not be joining you on your trip to Sussex," she stated in a surprisingly calm voice and left the room without a backward glance.

Two days before the dreaded visit to Heaton, Mariah determined to try once more to convince her papa to put a halt to this ill-conceived journey.

As she walked down the main hallway, she made her way through the jumbled mass of her mother's antiques and bibelots.

Thorncroft Manor, as her mother had styled it years ago, was a large, handsome house in the rambling Tudor fashion. However, Mariah often felt almost suffocated by the sheer number of *things* stuffed into every corner and taking up almost every inch of wall space.

Papa had recently grumbled about the price he had paid for the wallpaper when it could barely be seen beneath the expensive clutter. Mariah agreed with his complaints as she passed yet another old portrait of a member of someone else's family.

Shaking her head as she sidestepped an enormous urn, she despaired over her otherwise sweet mama's obsession with the trappings of nobility.

For as long as she could remember, her mother could not resist purchasing anything gilded and costly. No matter how Papa threatened to cut off her credit with the local tradesmen, odd items still arrived almost monthly. Papa would seethe and occasionally rant, Mama would coo and cajole, the item would stay, and the house grew ever more stuffed.

Mariah had long ago concluded that her mother's overspending had a direct correlation to her father's tightfisted behavior with the rest of the family. He agonized over the pennies his children and servants spent, while ignoring the crowns his wife threw away.

She found him, as she usually did, working away on

his papers in the large library—the library he had refused to allow Mama to decorate for him.

"Ah, Mariah, love, come in," he called as she poked her head through the partially open door.

She sent him a hesitant smile before stepping in. "Good morning, Papa. May I harangue you a little more about this ridiculous trip?"

"If you must," he said, a twinkle coming to the hazel eyes very like her own. He rose and came from behind the desk to sit with her on the overstuffed sofa by the fireplace.

Settling in next to him, Mariah gave her father a beseeching smile. "Now, you must know that I am terribly serious about refusing to go to this awful house party. I do not even have an assurance that we are truly invited. Steven and Mama do not seem to care that we could arrive and be turned away in an instant."

Papa nodded in understanding as he tugged the bottom of his deep green waistcoat down over his trim stomach.

"It's no use, my love. Your mother and Steven are utterly determined. Even George seems quite excited about the prospect of going."

"Of course he would." Mariah rolled her eyes at the mention of her ten-year-old brother. "But Papa, my wishes are not even being considered. Mama has ordered the servants to pack all my clothes, even things I would never take, just so I will have nothing to wear if I refuse to leave! I have never seen her so ruthless."

Her father chuckled sympathetically. " 'Tis no point in gainsaying your mother when she is this determined to have her way. She considers this a golden opportunity to present you to the right sort of people."

"I could not help noticing that you have gotten out of having to join us," she pointed out, her tone only half teasing.

"You know I have too much to do here. I can barely keep up with everything going on at the mills.

With the fluctuations in wool prices, I have to be extremely careful. No, there will be no haring off to country house parties for me. But you might as well make the best of it, Mariah, love, for you will be in the traveling coach two days hence."

Mariah felt the weight of her father's prediction settle upon her and sighed deeply. "I suppose so, but I have no intention of cooperating with Mama's plan to dangle my dowry in front of any titled gentleman under the age of eighty."

A frown furrowed his brow. "Now, Mariah, your mother does not expect you to wed an old man. I understand the Earl of Haverstone is young. Since his pockets must be to let after losing such a vast sum of money, you may have a little luck bringing him to scratch," he offered in a hearty, encouraging tone.

Sinking into a feeling of hopelessness at ever making her papa see reason, Mariah watched his determined expression for a moment before deciding to lay down her trump card.

"There really is no reason for such a vulgarly large dowry, Papa. Just think how much money you can save if you reduce the amount by half." Mariah watched his strong features closely, hoping to see some sign of softening.

Everyone knew of Mr. Thorncroft's penny-pinching ways. How he could resist the temptation to hold on to some of his hard-earned money?

He frowned and wagged a finger at her. "We are not going to tread this ground again. Since your birth, your mother and I have been planning for your future. That fancy governess who taught you how to speak and act like a lady retired in luxury on what I paid her. It would be foolish to waste everything we have done for you on anyone less than a peer."

"I know, Papa, but do you not see how you have consigned me to a tenuous fate?"

"I do not see it that way at all," he stated, looking a little hurt. "I have ensured that you will have the best of everything. You shall be fully accepted in Society and treated with respect by everyone."

"How can you believe what you say? There is no assurance that I will wed a man of honor. If, by the greatest good luck, I am fortunate enough to wed a man of good reputation, how will I ever know for certain if he truly cares for me?"

At her father's closed expression, she continued, her tone almost pleading for understanding. "Worse yet, it is most likely that he will see me only as the goose that laid the golden egg. It's too dreadful to contemplate."

"What's this? Do not be silly, Mariah. Any man fortunate enough to have you as his wife could not help but adore you."

Mariah threw her hands up in frustration. "What guarantee do I have of that? Only fortune hunters and wastrels will be attracted to me. Gentlemen of good character do not want to be seen in that light."

Her father continued to look stubborn. Long ago, Mariah had tired of arguing with her parents on this subject. Wearily, she gave reason one more try.

"You should know that I intend to make myself quite disagreeable to any titled gentleman who comes within ten yards of me."

"I do not intend to quarrel with you, my dear," Papa said, rising from the sofa. He went back to his desk and pulled a small object from a drawer. Returning to the sofa, he dropped the leather drawstring bag next to her.

"There is a little something to take care of the servants and for any trips to the local village. Do not spend it all at once."

Gently hefting the bag in the palm of her hand, Mariah seriously doubted the bag held enough coins to tip the servants, never mind for shopping.

With a resigned inward shrug, she rose from the sofa and kissed her father's smooth cheek.

"Thank you, Papa."

"That's a good girl," he said, patting her shoulder. "Now, no more pouts about leaving, hmm?"

"No more pouts," she said with a sigh.

Two mornings later, in defiance of her mother's strict instruction to be ready to leave for the two-day trip within half an hour, Mariah lingered over her breakfast. This might be her last peaceful morning for many weeks.

Her enjoyment of the solitude disappeared the moment she saw the door open and Steven enter.

After one look at his sheepish countenance, she turned her gaze away.

Without a word he prepared a plate from the sideboard and then seated himself next to her at the long mahogany table.

Tense silence filled the air for several minutes. Setting her napkin aside, Mariah pushed her chair back to leave.

"Dash it, Mariah!" Steven put his fork down with a clatter. "You cannot still be angry with me."

Mariah halted her movement and sent her brother a scathing look. "Of course I am, you dolt."

Steven sat back, deflated. "Well, I guess I cannot blame you. In truth, at the time it seemed like such a good idea to mention your dowry to the earl."

She relaxed, leaning against the seat back. "Really? Why would you think such a stupid thing?"

A flush rose to his cheeks. He pushed his plate away and sent her another pained look. "Because I was rather deep in my cups that night."

At least he had the good sense to seem ashamed, Mariah reluctantly conceded. Beneath her anger she realized that she felt more sad and disappointed than angry. She and Steven had always been close, so it hurt that he would be as eager as Mama and Papa to offer her to the highest title willing to have her.

"I am sorry, Mariah. I never should have said anything about you to the earl," Steven said.

"No, you should not have," she said softly, knowing

he would sense her impending forgiveness. What was the point of being angry with her brother? He was only following Mama and Papa's lead.

Steven smiled. "You might not find it so bad at Heaton. Everyone says it's an impressive estate."

"Well, it should be." Her tone was dismissive as she refolded her napkin.

"You know, there may be an eligible gentleman attending the house party you might actually like."

She glared at him again. "You do not fool me. You would go to Heaton with or without me."

His sheepish look returned. "The Earl of Haverstone's set is all the crack. It would certainly be a feather in my cap to be taken up by them. But even if you don't meet a worthy young man, you may make some friends and receive a few invitations to balls and such in Town next Season."

Mariah shrugged dismissively. If she never went to London again it would suit her fine. Being dragged to Town, Season after Season, with Mama growing less hopeful and more desperate, had made each year more miserable than the last.

This year she had finally received a respite from the tedium of a Season. Seeing the futility of driving up and down Rotten Row every day, Mama had given in to Mariah's persistent entreaties to avoid London, and they had spent the Season in Bath instead.

Unfortunately, Mama's dream of Mariah attracting a titled gentleman had been ignited anew upon being introduced to the Earl of Haverstone and some of his friends while visiting Julia Allard and her cousin Lady Farren.

But once again nothing came of it, and they returned to Thorncroft Manor, Mama defeated and Mariah relieved.

"I care nothing for London," she told Steven in a firm tone. "I would like, above all things, to remain here with my sketchbook and the parish school to keep me company."

"You are talking like an old maid. You are a very

pretty girl. I can't imagine why you haven't had dozens of offers."

"Because Mama reaches too high. Plum titles are not thick on the ground, you know."

Steven picked at his food. "I don't like to hear you sound so bitter."

Mariah smiled wryly. "Oh, it doesn't bother me as much as it used to. I rarely rail at Mama and Papa anymore. I have learned that arguing is a waste of energy. I shall do what I have done for five years— ignore any men Mama manages to present to me. It has worked quite well so far, and Mama will eventually have to give up."

Steven looked little surprised. "Do you truly never wish to marry?"

Mariah met her brother's serious gaze with an intense gleam in her hazel eyes. "The thought of being tied to a man who only wants Papa's money is completely repugnant to me. Wouldn't it be to you?"

Steven contemplated the question for a moment. "I, too, would prefer that my spouse care for me over my money."

"Then please cease bandying about the size of my dowry to all and sundry."

"I will never mention it again," he vowed.

For the first time in days, the two smiled at each other.

Chapter Three

"*E*xcuse me, my lord. A Mr. Thorncroft and family have arrived."

Stone, seated at his desk in the library, looked up from his papers in mild surprise. "Mr. Thorncroft?"

"Yes, my lord. I have placed them in the gold salon."

Stone laid his pen aside. "Did I invite a Mr. Thorncroft and family?" Frowning, he noticed the usually unflappable butler's face looked a little pinched.

"I do not have them on the list Mr. Willoughby gave me."

Leaning back against the leather squabs of his chair, Stone searched his memory for a Mr. Thorncroft. "My secretary is a very efficient chap, so I must have forgotten. Didn't think I knew anyone named Thorncroft."

"They seem respectable."

Stone's eyebrows rose at this neutral-toned comment. He found it very telling that Jarvis would even comment on a person's respectability. Pushing back his chair, Stone stood and walked to the door.

"How do my other guests fare?"

"No one has come down for breakfast yet, although Lady Charlotte rang for chocolate a little while ago."

"Very good. I will go have a look at our mysterious visitors and decide if I shall escort them out myself or have you do the job," he said, grinning slightly at his butler's alarmed expression.

Leaving his library, Stone walked along the painting-lined corridor toward the gold salon. When he came to the wide staircase, he hesitated. Looking down at his riding attire, he debated whether to change into something a little more formal.

Shrugging, he continued to the salon, wondering who the devil were Mr. Thorncroft and family.

With a gesture to the footman indicating not to announce him, Stone opened the door and strode into the room. His gaze swept the four people inside, who quickly rose at his entrance.

The instant he saw Steven Thorncroft, Stone hazily recalled a late-night conversation on a London street. He also recalled tossing out an invitation. Gad, he never thought the pup would take the offer as anything more than politeness.

Next to Steven Thorncroft stood two women and a young boy who looked about ten years of age. The older woman, obviously his mother or some other close relative, smiled widely. By their likeness, Stone knew the young lady and the boy must be Mr. Thorncroft's siblings.

"Good morning, Mr. Thorncroft. How very good to see you. Welcome to Heaton. Won't you please introduce your friends?"

"Gladly, my lord," Steven responded with a bow, his smile widening. He presented his mother, an attractive woman with green eyes, light brown hair, and a prodigious amount of jewelry for so early in the morning. Mrs. Thorncroft curtsied deeply and began to speak in a rushed, breathless voice before completing her bow.

"Your lordship is too kind to invite us to your house party. I arrive with my husband's regrets that he cannot partake of your generous hospitality, for business at his mills keeps him terribly busy."

Stone found himself momentarily mute at Mrs. Thorncroft's speech. He must have truly been in his cups to invite the entire Thorncroft clan without quite realizing he had done so.

"I understand perfectly. Perhaps he shall be able to join us at another time."

Steven Thorncroft then presented his sister, who curtsied with lowered eyes and flushed cheeks. Though she was unadorned with jewelry, an expert hand had obviously cut her moss green traveling costume. Out of sheer habit, he allowed his eyes to discreetly sweep her face and figure as she rose from her curtsy. Slim and above average in height, Miss Thorncroft had a pretty, heart-shaped face and wavy light brown hair. He had no notion of her eye color, for she had still not raised her gaze to his.

Mrs. Thorncroft finally brought the boy forward and introduced him as George Thorncroft. After bowing stiffly, the youngster quickly scurried back behind his mother.

"I am delighted that all of you could come to Heaton. Lords Stothart and Mattonly arrived some days ago," Stone stated, gesturing for everyone to be seated. "I am sure, Mr. Thorncroft, that you must be acquainted with them."

Steven swallowed nervously. "Ah, no, I have not had the pleasure."

Stone felt another jolt of surprise at Thorncroft's words. All the bucks in Town knew Bart and Mattonly. "We will have to rectify that. Mr. Woburn and the Walgraves will be with us for the next few weeks. They must be known to you?"

Noting Mr. Thorncroft shifting in his chair, Stone waited patiently without allowing his polite expression to slip. The rest of the Thorncrofts remained mute.

"No, we have not been introduced, my lord."

"Well, I have a whole house full of people. You must be acquainted with someone. Let us see. Mr. and Mrs. Spence-Jones? Mr. Elbridge? Lady Davinia Harwich?" Lud, Stone thought, it seemed this odd lot did not know anyone. How tedious.

At that moment Miss Thorncroft spoke up in a surprisingly clear and well-modulated voice.

"I have had the pleasure of meeting Lady Davinia,

my lord. We met this past spring in Bath. My mother and I spent several pleasant evenings in her company."

Stone's gaze moved to Miss Thorncroft's features as she made this announcement. Her unusually golden hazel eyes sparkled beneath dark lashes.

"Bath? I, too, visited Bath last spring. I wonder how we missed each other. It is not a large town—especially if we have a mutual acquaintance."

At his words, he saw her expression instantly close. She inclined her head but made no reply.

"Excuse me, my lord." The little boy spoke up. "May I take a closer look at the suit of armor I saw in the grand hallway? I promise not to touch."

"Now, George, watch your manners," Mrs. Thorncroft admonished, her cheeks growing pink with embarrassment.

Stone smiled at the sturdy little boy. "Not at all, Mrs. Thorncroft. Young George can look at the armor with my blessing. In fact, another room holds a suit of armor that is quite small. It may still be too big, but you may have some fun trying it on. My steward, whose family has been with mine for generations, knows the way of getting into it."

"Thank you, sir," George said, his eyes shining in barely contained excitement.

Mrs. Thorncroft sent Stone a beaming smile. "You are very good, my lord."

After a brief inclination of his head, Stone gave a smile that encompassed them all. "I must beg your indulgence. I have a number of matters to deal with this morning. I shall leave you to the capable hands of Mrs. Billings, my housekeeper. We are quite informal here. We have breakfast in the morning room, unless you prefer to partake in your rooms. I shall next see you at luncheon, where I will be able to introduce my other guests. And you, Mrs. Thorncroft, Miss Thorncroft, will be able to reacquaint yourself with Lady Davinia. I again bid you welcome. Please do not get up."

With another polite smile, he rose and left the room. Reaching the grand staircase, he took the steps two at time, allowing his features to relax into the amusement he felt. Of course, once he had a look at Mr. Thorncroft he remembered their brief encounter in London some months ago. It had been on the street after he had a bad night at the tables.

The details of their conversation were a little sketchy. It had been late, and he recalled that he had finished a bottle of port with the last few hands. He did recall that Thorncroft had been rather amusing.

Stone did not doubt that he had invited the pup to Heaton. Four more guests would go unnoticed by the servants. However, he would never have invited a child or a country miss to this particular house party. Some of his past parties had become legend among the *ton* for their sophisticated revelry.

The Thorncrofts would no doubt put a damper on the freedom he and his guests had grown used to enjoying.

What an odd lot, he decided. Beautifully dressed, fine manners, yet patently awkward and ill at ease. They glaringly lacked what the *ton* called polish.

He could only hope that the Thorncrofts would soon realize that they did not belong at such a gathering and go home to whatever backwater they had obviously come from.

Upon entering his vast bedchamber, he saw Stolt, his valet, overseeing the footmen pouring hot water into the large copper tub in front of the fireplace. Even though autumn had arrived in full and the weather had turned bitter of late, he would not forgo his morning bath.

"Good morning, my lord. I trust you enjoyed your ride," Stolt intoned as he bowed.

"Yes, quite bracing. I expect we shall have a hard frost soon," Stone said as the valet helped him out of his snuff-colored riding jacket.

"I noticed we have some new guests this morning, my lord."

"Yes. The Thorncrofts. I am hoping that their visit shall at least prove amusing."

"I wonder that we did not meet in Bath," Mariah drawled, making her voice as deep as possible. Though it was inaccurate, Steven and George laughed at her imitation of the earl's low, smooth tones.

"The Earl of Haverstone is utterly insufferable," she stated, resuming her normal voice. She moved to a chair in the beautifully appointed sitting room adjacent the bedchamber her mother had been given. She could hear Mama in the next room, directing the servants while they unpacked her trunks.

"I sat down to dinner with him at Lady Farren's townhouse in Bath. We actually exchanged a few pleasantries across the table. I do not believe he finds me even vaguely familiar. And"—she snapped her fingers—"I would lay odds that he did not recall inviting you to this house party, Steven. From the look on his face when he entered the salon, I would also bet that it took him through the introductions to even recall ever having a conversation with you."

Steven shrugged, sliding farther down into the overstuffed chair. "The Earl of Haverstone is a busy and important man. I do not wonder that he did not instantly recall meeting me. Nevertheless, he was awfully kind to invite us. Besides, you can't accuse him of being a fortune hunter if he does not even remember that I told him about your dowry."

"You can be assured that Mama will have no trouble throwing that last bit of information into the dinner conversation. Dash it, I just want to go home."

"I don't care what you say, Mariah. I like the earl," George piped up from his place at the window seat.

"What do you know?" She waved a dismissive hand in her little brother's direction. "You only say so because he will let you play with the armor."

George sent her an impudent look.

"Don't you think Heaton is grand, Mariah?" Steven asked.

"Well, I confess that as we came up the drive I thought the grounds lovely in all their autumn glory. And the house, if one can call such a vast place a house, is impressive and beautiful. It does not seem the least bit drafty, especially compared to the Inn last night. But we do not know anyone here, and you know Mama's overt matchmaking will only put me to the blush."

Steven shrugged. "I can understand your frustration. However, I am looking forward to spending a few weeks in these splendid surroundings. We have not been here above a few hours, and I have already received a note from the earl inviting me to join the hunt tomorrow."

"Lovely," Mariah pronounced with a sarcastic edge. "The men will be hunting all day, enjoying this bracing weather, while the ladies stay trapped indoors with nothing to do but gossip."

"Didn't you bring your needlework or sketchbook?"

"Yes, I did. Maybe I will take my sketchbook to the lake I saw in the distance from my bedchamber window."

"We can always explore the house," George suggested.

"Yes, that should take days, at least. For now, I wish to explore the grounds." She rose and left the room with both her brothers frowning after her.

After several hours Mariah felt she had had a good stretch of her legs. Under any other circumstances she would have certainly enjoyed a visit to this amazingly beautiful place.

As she slowly strolled along a meandering gravel path that led from the house to a lake and woodland, she hugged her leather sketch case to her chest against the biting chill.

If she found Heaton this hauntingly beautiful beneath gray skies and with half-dead leaves rattling in the wind, then what would it look like in the budding of spring, the abundance of summer? Mariah fairly itched to pull out her sketchbook and pencils, for at every turn some new prospect or angle would inspire her to another page.

Dejectedly, she knew that little time remained before she would need to prepare for dinner. With dread, she forced herself to contemplate the evening ahead.

If entertaining at Heaton followed the fashion of other country house parties she had attended over the years, everyone would gather in one of the salons before dinner. This would give the guests a chance to visit before being paired up at the dinner table.

Those moments always made Mariah feel awkward because her mama usually started throwing out none-too-subtle hints about the size of her dowry.

Now that Mama knew the earl had lost a fortune gambling last Season, Mariah feared that her mother's inferences would be even less subtle.

In addition, Mariah felt nervous about the stultifying sense of shyness that sometimes overcame her. Despite feeling at ease among her family and close friends, she tended to be shy among strangers. She found it rather odd, because her parents were both wonderfully open and gregarious.

Papa, although not as verbose as Mama, fancied himself as something of a local squire and loved nothing better than the local assembly balls. The parties at home often lasted until the wee hours.

Mariah had never been blessed with easy manners among company. Occasionally, she struggled with a certain paralyzing self-consciousness that nothing seemed to ease. In cases such as tonight, she usually tried to attach herself to a lively older woman. Lively older ladies loved Mariah because they listened to their gossip with avid attention and never spoke of herself.

Of late, she had pondered the reason for her shyness, for it caused her no end of distress. She had known since childhood that her parents loved her dearly, but they had always intended for her to marry very well. Not just a respectable gentleman from a good family—no, her parents, especially her mama, wanted nothing less than a title.

Papa, the son of a farmer, had worked long hours for decades to make his business endeavors successful. Her parents had made it clear to her from an early age that they expected to move among superior society, and for that desire to be fulfilled Mariah must marry a well-connected gentleman.

As Mariah grew and her promise of beauty came to fruition, Mama expanded her goals. Nothing less than a peer of the realm would suffice.

Mariah was always painfully aware of her mother's eagle eye upon her, and every social gathering became a test of her poise. If she spent too much time in conversation with a young man who was insufficiently pedigreed, Mama would swoop in and pull her away.

Soon friends began to avoid her—all except Julia Allard, who had remained her closest friend all through those difficult years. Mariah missed Julia terribly, but happiness overrode her sadness, for Julia was now blissfully wed to the Duke of Kelbourne.

Mariah determined to sit down soon and write a letter to Julia apprising her old friend of her stay at Heaton, the home of the Duke of Kelbourne's good friend. Maybe Julia would have a bit of advice for her.

The fact that Julia Allard had married so astoundingly well had only fueled Mama's desperate hope that Mariah would do the same. After all, her mother had often pointed out, Julia had not had the added advantage of a large portion.

Shaking off these depressing thoughts, Mariah continued her tour of the grounds.

Despite the fading day and the looming dinner, Mariah wandered farther, to the stand of trees on the south side of the lake. A chill wind rustled the burnt orange leaves of several ancient-looking chestnut trees. Breathing in the crisp air, she halted by a fallen tree and set her leather case upon it.

Turning slightly, she saw the imposing north-facing

edifice of the mansion with its striking gate tower. Perfectly situated on an expansive rise, Heaton seemed to stretch to the horizon. The late-afternoon sun cast a silver gleam over the gray, age-mellowed stone.

The place exuded an air of imposing elegance and a sense of history. Mariah could easily envision knights in shining armor, with colorful banners waving in the wind, riding toward the porte cochere.

In spite of all of this grandness, a deep peacefulness emanated from the ancient house and grounds.

Sitting on the fallen log, with the trees around her intermittently dropping their vivid leaves, she continued to contemplate the Earl of Haverstone's home. She wondered if a man like the earl could really appreciate such a place, or if the beauty constantly around him went unnoticed.

As the shadows grew and the chill deepened, she realized that she could no longer delay returning. She would probably be late, and Mama would ring a peal over her head. Rising from the log, she picked up her leather case.

Hang dinner, she thought. *I am not rushing back.*

Chapter Four

"*S*o you and your family live in Chippenham? How sweet. I believe there are lots of sheep in Chippenham," Lady Walgrave said, leaning across the massive dining table, her blond hair burnished gold in the candlelight.

"Indeed. Probably more sheep than people," Mariah replied dryly, reaching to pick up her crystal wine goblet.

Casting a quick glance up the table, Mariah felt relief that Mama had not heard Lady Walgrave's comment. If she had, she would probably have announced that the Thorncrofts owned most of those sheep.

Mariah shifted anxiously in her chair, feeling completely out of her element. Ever since she sat down to dinner, it had been utterly apparent that she had nothing in common with these people. The earl had obviously invited friends from his set: all of them sophisticated, brittle, and witty.

After an hour in their company, only the sheer beauty of the room and the excellent food kept her from yawning with boredom.

As she gazed around, she secretly hoped some of the understated style would rub off onto her mother. The room proved a serene contrast to Mama's overwrought taste in furnishings. The coved ceiling, painted with a realistic pastoral scene, made Mariah sigh with admiration.

As the chatter of the guests swirled around her, she

looked across the table to her brother. She could see by his expression that he was enjoying himself immensely. She knew Steven loved this world. He found it exciting and challenging—challenging because he wanted to prove himself a real gentleman.

Mariah knew that part of the reason Steven had managed to wheedle an invitation from the earl had nothing to do with helping her find a titled husband. He wanted the chance to spend time with the aristocracy so that he could learn their modes and manners. Steven wanted to be a part of this world.

An intense feeling of love and exasperation tugged at her heart. *Why does he care so much?* she wondered. But she knew why. From birth, they had been taught that it mattered terribly to be accepted by the right people—the important, powerful people. Having money was not enough. Being part of the beau monde, the beautiful world, was what really counted.

Tonight Mariah refused to allow herself to ruminate on this old subject. Instead, she continued to observe her dinner companions.

Steven, seated next to the lovely Lady Davinia Harwich, looked relaxed and happy, no doubt because of Lady Davinia's wonderful company.

To Mariah's surprise and pleasure, Lady Davinia had indeed remembered her from their brief time in Bath. Before dinner she had greeted Mariah with great warmth, asking after her health and their mutual friend, Julia, the new Duchess of Kelbourne. Lady Davinia had also introduced Mariah to her cousins Mr. and Mrs. Spence-Jones, an engaging young couple whom Mariah liked immediately. Unfortunately, Lady Davinia was sitting too far up the table for Mariah to converse with her easily.

For some minutes she picked at her food and allowed the conversation to roll over her without really hearing the words.

She had given up trying to chat with the gentleman to her left, a corpulent man introduced to her as Lord Stothart. From the moment they sat down at the long table, Lord Stothart had focused his complete attention on each perfectly prepared dish the footman set before him.

The gentleman to her right, whose name she had forgotten, had been in deep conversation with the woman on his other side for most of the evening. This left Mariah to quietly take in the rest of the guests. Fifteen people graced the earl's table. She knew this because, out of sheer boredom, she had counted heads between the first and second courses.

As she slowly ate tender bites of roast grouse, she shamelessly listened to bits of the conversation above the clinking of glass and the splashing of wine.

At the head of the table, the ladies seated on either side of the earl caught her attention. Elegant and beautiful, both seemed to laugh quite a bit at whatever he said.

To his left sat Lady Charlotte, a petite, delicate blonde. Before dinner, Mariah had met all of the guests, and Lady Charlotte had greeted her with nothing but a dismissive smile.

The lady to his right, Mrs. Ingram, had deep red hair piled high atop her head. From half-heard snippets of their chatter, Mariah surmised that both ladies were widows.

For his part, Lord Haverstone did not appear as enthralled with his table companions as they were with him.

As she examined him over the rim of her glass, Mariah grudgingly conceded that no criticism could be made of him as a host. He gave supreme attention to everything going on around him. From the way he had greeted her family earlier, she realized that he was much too polished to let his mien of politeness slip. He was also better-looking than she had thought him when they had met in Bath. Though his face was rather long, his high cheekbones and square chin combined to be more dashing and striking than classically handsome.

After discreetly watching him for some minutes,

Mariah decided that the earl represented exactly the kind of man her mama wanted her to marry—titled and with loads of cachet among the beau monde. The fact that he was in need of money did not make him less desirable in her mother's eyes.

Thank goodness social standing did not obsess her the way it did her mother, Mariah mused. Of late, Mama would often become pettish and frustrated as a result of her fixation with the aristocracy.

The thought of marrying a man for social status utterly repulsed Mariah. Nonetheless, she knew her mama would not give up her hope of the earl showing an interest in her only daughter—or, more accurately, in her only daughter's dowry.

By the opulent luxury evident around every corner, the earl's money troubles had not yet become evident. Mariah knew little about gambling or the managing of money, but she knew that the loss of seventeen thousand pounds would ruin even a wealthy man.

Disguising her actions while sipping her wine, Mariah watched the earl for another moment.

Plainly, he had never known anything but privilege and extravagance. She also knew that many men of his rank felt they had a duty to marry a fortune. Papa said that was how the rich got richer—fortunes combining with fortunes. She also knew that breeding and family name were held in even higher esteem among the *ton.*

Mariah watched the widows on either side of the earl shower him with their laughter and praise. They vied for his attention in such an obvious way that she wondered how they fared in the running for his coronet.

With her splendid gown and jewelry, Lady Charlotte was obviously not only gorgeous but also wealthy. Mariah admired her cool blond beauty, which complimented the earl's dark good looks.

Mariah's attention shifted to the redheaded lady to the earl's left. Mrs. Ingram, although not as bejeweled as Lady Charlotte, was also exquisitely garbed. Mariah found her flashing, intelligent gaze more attractive than Lady Charlotte's somewhat overblown splendor.

Setting her glass down, Mariah shifted her gaze to the earl again. Even though it first appeared that he gave the widows his full attention, she now noticed his interest seemed elsewhere.

Occasionally he would throw out a witty comment in response to something said across the table, sending his adoring ladies into transports of mirth, but Mariah sensed that there was something missing in his enjoyment of the dinner.

Watching his face during one of these exchanges, Mariah saw that he did not appear to be the least bit flattered by the fawning praise lavished upon him by the lovely blonde and redhead.

Mariah again thought him quite handsome, particularly his lean, chiseled features and dark hair. She wondered why dark hair and blue eyes gave some men such a devilish appearance.

Once or twice, she noticed his lips tightening ever so slightly in what she interpreted as irritation. *Goodness, I seem to be making a study of him,* she thought with an inward smile.

Her impression that the earl had grown irritated solidified into certainty as dinner stretched through the evening. As each course appeared, the earl's expression grew increasingly bored. Mrs. Ingram seemed to sense something amiss and became less talkative. Lady Charlotte, however, became even more effusive as the earl grew more distant.

Laughing to herself, Mariah thought it rather ironic that the earl found himself the hunted, instead of the hunter.

At that moment he turned from the blonde and his clear blue gaze locked with hers.

Against her best efforts, the laughter bubbling inside must have shown upon her face, for his eyes held hers as his brows went up in query. Trying to school her features to reveal nothing of her inner struggle, Mariah found herself unable to look away. Suddenly,

the urge to laugh died, and her heart began to beat
in an oddly breathtaking rhythm.

His questioning look intensified, so much so that
the redhead turned to look down the table to see who
held the earl's attention.

Wouldn't that be awful? she thought, nervous laughter rising again. It would be too horrid to have the
earl think her one of his admirers. At that, she pulled
her gaze away, but the beating of her heart remained
staccato for some moments. Something in the intensity
of his sharp, perceptive gaze unnerved her.

Mariah took a sip of wine as Lady Walgrave leaned
forward to address her again.

"So, Miss Thorncroft, do you and your family plan
to stay at Heaton long?"

"I am not sure, my lady." Oddly, she found the
prospect of staying awhile at the lovely place slightly
less objectionable than she had only hours ago.

Lady Walgrave only said, "Oh," and turned back
to her husband.

With an inward sigh, Mariah felt her stomach twist
with self-consciousness. She and her family did not belong here, she thought again with growing anxiousness.

Determined to avoid the earl, she glanced up the
table and watched her mother converse with the handsome young Lord Mattonly. At least he did not look
as bored as the earl did. Mariah would say one thing
about her mother—despite being a dreadful social
climber, she had a well-deserved reputation as a con-
versationalist.

Mariah watched Lord Mattonly throw his head back
and laugh at something Mama said.

Her mother had an innate ability to ask the right
questions of her companion and a subtle way of making people, especially men, feel utterly fascinating. It
was an ability that Mariah envied.

A little while later, as she finished the dish of delicious peaches in brandy sauce, Mariah sighed with relief that the meal would soon be over.

At the head of the table, Lady Charlotte and Mrs. Ingram both rose from the table at the same time.

Mariah watched, fascinated, as each glared at the other, as if willing her rival to disappear, or at least sit down.

The redhead opened her mouth to speak, but Lady Charlotte jumped in quickly.

"My lord, I believe the ladies will leave you gentlemen to your port and talk of hunting."

Mrs. Ingram flushed hotly at being trumped in her obvious desire to act as hostess. Mariah again felt a gurgle of laughter rise at the drama unwittingly being played out before her. Although her dinner companions had barely addressed her, she had certainly not found dinner dull.

Setting her napkin next to her plate, Mariah rose and glanced toward her host, who had risen with the rest of the gentlemen. To her surprise, she found his vivid blue gaze directed toward her once again. Hastily she looked away, lest he realize that she found his behavior with his dinner companions vastly amusing.

Curtsying, she stepped away from the table and followed the other ladies out of the room. A footman led them down the hall to a smaller but no less charming salon. Mariah lagged slightly behind the group, pausing in the doorway to admire the beautiful décor as the others laughed and chatted.

"How like the earl to direct that my favorite dishes be served," Mrs. Ingram pronounced as she seated herself on a chair next to the sofa. Mariah watched Lady Charlotte flush with anger at the smug look Mrs. Ingram sent her way.

As the other ladies settled themselves in various chairs and settees, Lady Charlotte quickly moved to the bellpull. A moment later the butler stepped into the room.

"Please have tea brought in, Jarvis," Lady Charlotte directed in an imperious tone.

The look of annoyance on Mrs. Ingram's face at

being beaten to addressing the butler was comical. Mariah covered her laugh with a cough and seated herself near the hearth.

She looked across the room to see Lady Walgrave and Mama sharing a settee, apparently settling in for a nice coze.

"So, Mrs. Thorncroft," Lady Walgrave began in a clear tone, "I am curious to learn how you became acquainted with the earl. The earl and my good husband have been the dearest of friends for ages. I thought I knew all of Stone's friends, but he never mentioned that anyone else would be joining our merry party this week."

Mama's smiling, guileless green eyes met Lady Walgrave's cold blue gaze without hesitation.

"My daughter and I met the earl in Bath this spring. Mariah is the great good friend of Julia Allard, who, as I am sure you know, is the new Duchess of Kelbourne. My son also became acquainted with the earl in London, and—well—here we are." She finished this vague explanation on a happy little laugh.

Mariah noticed that Mrs. Spence-Jones and Lady Davinia had broken off their tête-à-tête to attend to Lady Walgrave and Mrs. Thorncroft.

"The Duke and Duchess of Kelbourne?" Lady Walgrave drawled with the merest hint of disbelief and suspicion in her voice. "I attended their wedding some months ago. Stone stood as the duke's supporter. I am surprised I did not see you or your daughter at the ceremony or the breakfast that followed."

Mrs. Thorncroft shrugged. " 'Tis not a wonder to me, my lady. It was such a large affair, after all. My husband, our eldest son, and I attended. Mariah, alas, was unable to join us. I thought it would fair break her heart, for she was to be Julia's chief attendant. However, Mariah caught a vicious cold at the last minute and had to cry off. Julia wanted to postpone the nuptials until Mariah recovered, but my daughter would not hear of it, especially with the guests practically on the doorstep. It was a lovely affair, though. Don't you agree?"

Lady Walgrave stared at Mama for a moment, seemingly nonplussed by her rambling speech.

"Yes, lovely," she finally said.

Mariah admired how her mother blithely ignored the attention some of the other ladies directed toward her. Glancing around the room, Mariah noticed with relief that Lady Davinia and the widows now seemed involved in their own conversation.

Lady Walgrave's firm voice recalled Mariah's attention.

"Miss Thorncroft, your mother says you spent the Season in Bath this year. I would have thought that an attractive young lady like you would have gone to London for the Season—or perhaps London does not agree with you?"

Mariah did not like the sly tone in Lady Walgrave's voice. "No, my lady, I quite enjoy London and have spent some time there in previous Seasons."

"Indeed?" the lady replied. "I wonder that we never met at any balls or at Almack's."

Mariah would rather have eaten glass than admit that she had never, in three Seasons, received her vouchers to Almack's. Mama had never been able to wangle a strong enough acquaintance with any of the patronesses for there to have been hope of a coveted voucher to the near-sacred—to Mama—assembly rooms.

"It is a curiosity. May I ask what part of the country you reside in, my lady?" Mariah really did not give a fig where Lady Walgrave hailed from; she just hoped to divert the subject.

At that moment a plump little maid opened the door wide, allowing a footman carrying a huge tea tray to enter. The maid quickly darted in front of him and cleared a vase from the large low table in the middle of the room so that he could set the tray down.

Lady Charlotte and Mrs. Ingram reached for the teapot at the same instant.

Mariah noticed that the rest of the ladies ceased their conversations to watch the two women glare at each other over the teapot.

After a tense moment, Mrs. Ingram finally released the bottom part of the handle. "Do pardon me, Lady Charlotte," she said sweetly.

"Not at all, Mrs. Ingram. May I pour you the first cup?"

As much as Mariah found this spectacle amusing, she had no intention of continuing to be the target of Lady Walgrave's pointed questions.

Rising, Mariah said, "Please excuse me, Mama, ladies. I find I am rather fatigued and would seek my bed early this evening."

Mama looked a little disappointed, no doubt because she hoped the gentlemen would leave their port soon and join the ladies, but she did not press Mariah to stay.

Amid murmurs entreating her to have a good evening, Mariah executed a swift curtsy and left the ladies to their tea and gossip.

Taking her time, she chose a meandering route to her room, admiring the restrained, exquisitely appointed public rooms before heading upstairs.

Upon entering her room, she found Harris already laying out her night things.

"You're quite early, miss," the maid said as she put a pair of pink slippers next to the bed.

"Yes, and I am not ready to go to sleep yet. I believe I shall read for a while, Harris, but there is no need for you to wait up for me."

"As you wish," Harris nodded. "Would you like me to bring your breakfast at your usual time, or would you prefer to go downstairs in the morning?"

"I would like breakfast here, please. And thank you, Harris." Mariah smiled at the older woman as she finished fluffing the pillows.

With one final pat to the pillow, Harris bid her mistress good night and left the room.

Retrieving a book from her nightstand, Mariah

moved to a comfortable chair by the glowing fireplace and lost herself in *Emma,* by the very insightful and entertaining author of *Pride and Prejudice,* a book she had thoroughly enjoyed a couple of years ago.

Some time passed before Mariah put the book aside. Not feeling the least bit sleepy, she left the cozy warmth of the fireplace and crossed the room to the large window.

The intricately carved wood on the diamond-shaped window frames held dozens of pieces of glass in place. Lightly, she touched a pane and felt icy coolness but no draft.

Glancing upward, she saw the large moon, bright and full, spilling wavering shadows across the garden below.

"How lovely," she said aloud.

How beautiful would Heaton be, bathed in the silver-blue glow?

An instant later she pushed away from the window and went the wardrobe to grab her heavy green redingote. Suddenly she desired nothing more than to experience the beauty of this place in the moonlight.

Chapter Five

*U*pon gently closing the arched door behind her, Mariah breathed deeply of the chilled evening air and paused, allowing her eyes to adjust to the dimness.

After a moment or two she moved into the formal garden before her, noticing the low, sculpted evergreen hedges laid out in a Roman key design.

Walking farther, she saw dormant vines, stripped of their leaves and twined in ghostly shapes up stone arches. With a sigh of satisfaction at the sculptural beauty before her, she continued along the stone path between the hedges, past little sheltered places that she would like to explore during the day.

For now, she wanted to get away from everyone, to get far enough from the house to see the full moon. Just the thought of the moonlight bathing Heaton in its silvery glow caught at her heart.

She would try to remember the details and attempt to sketch them tomorrow. She had to admit that the overwhelming loveliness of Heaton had cast a soft spell over her senses.

Mariah desired to see the house in every light and to examine every angle to take in fully the splendor of this unexpectedly magical place.

Taking a turn between the hedges, she caught sight of the moon through the bare tree branches overhead. Pausing, she allowed her senses to absorb the mysterious, romantic beauty of the silvery orb. The moon and the stars had fascinated her since childhood. Could other worlds possibly be floating around in the heavens? She pondered this mystery often.

As she continued along the path before her, it opened to a wide area where a number of stone benches squatted beneath still more leafless trees. She paused to breathe deeply of the cool air, not caring if she caught cold again, as she had before Julia's wedding. A moment later she thought better and paused to fasten the last few frogs on her heavy woolen coat before continuing her moonlit walk.

This was the first moment of real peace she had experienced in many days. She savored the feeling as she strolled along the shadowy, wind-rustled path.

The sudden sight of a man and woman embracing closely a short distance away halted her movement as if she had been thunderstruck.

For an instant she wondered if the figures could be a statue.

The doubt instantly dissolved when she saw the man run his hands up and down the woman's back. A moment later, she recognized his height and profile to be that of the earl.

As his hand moved to caress the small of the woman's back, Mariah stared, feeling mesmerized and unable to move.

With a sinuous movement, the earl pulled the woman even closer against the length of his body. The breath caught in Mariah's throat as she watched the woman rise on tiptoe to snake her arms up around his neck.

Standing silently in the pale moonlight, her chest aching from holding her breath, Mariah continued to stare at the entwined couple.

A warm, fluttery feeling traveled up from the pit of her stomach and into her chest. She remained motionless for several moments.

Without conscious thought, her gaze shifted to the

movement of powerful muscles flexing beneath the earl's coat sleeve. Mariah had no doubt that he could pick up the delicate-looking blonde and carry her off.

So this is what passion looks like. This startling thought—and the sudden awareness of the sheer impropriety of just standing there staring—finally shook her from her frozen stance.

Whirling, Mariah sent up a quick prayer that she would be able to leave before they saw or heard her.

In her haste, her foot caught on something hard, and she took several long—and loud—stumbling steps before regaining her balance.

A feminine gasp reached her in midstride. Mortified, Mariah refused to look back. Somewhat hindered by the swirling length of her coat, she moved as quickly as she could up the path, the night air cooling her hot cheeks.

Moments later, over the pounding of her heart, she became aware of footsteps behind her.

"Miss Thorncroft."

It did not seem possible, but her heart pounded even faster at the sound of the earl's deep voice speaking her name. Slowing, she turned, grateful for the shield of moonlight shadowing her flushed face.

The earl approached, and she could see that his partially revealed expression seemed unperturbed. With great effort Mariah tried to catch hold of her belabored breath.

The earl reached her side. "Please allow me to escort you back to the house."

Straining to discern his half-hidden features, Mariah suspected a hint of amusement beneath the polite offer.

"I know the way." Tilting her head, she looked past his shoulder to see if the lady had come with him.

"She took another way back to the house," he supplied.

Mariah felt a flush of warmth rush again to her cheeks. "Oh. I am sorry, my lord. I never would have . . ."

"Don't give it another thought. I am sorry if you were embarrassed."

At the droll amusement in his voice, some of Mariah's embarrassment abated, replaced by an inexplicable flash of annoyance. *All in an evening's work,* she thought acerbically. Being caught in such a compromising situation obviously did not discomfit him in the least. Never had she encountered such unabashed arrogance.

"I would be careful, my lord. The lady might expect you to come up to scratch." She could not resist the temptation to goad him a little.

His deep velvet laughter filled the silvery darkness.

"Not likely. That was Lady Walgrave. You really are an innocent." His tone, though amused, did not make the words a compliment.

Her spine stiffened. *How utterly insufferable!* She spared a sympathetic thought for Lady Charlotte, whom she had assumed was the earl's companion, and Mrs. Ingram. She wondered if the widows knew that they had more competition than each other for the earl's favor.

"I am not so very innocent—I am just not completely jaded." She strove for a tone of indifference as she hurried up the path.

Evidently her words missed their mark, for she heard his rumbling laughter again as he walked in step next to her.

"Well said, Miss Thorncroft. You are not what I expected after spending dinner in your company."

As much as she did not want to ask, she could not help herself. "How so?"

"My first impression was that you were one of those typical, perfectly polished misses who would have had a fit of the vapors at the sight of a man kissing a woman. You surprise me."

Mariah pulled the hem of her coat away from a low flower bed. "I am so pleased. Do I rise even higher in your esteem for not fainting over the fact that your companion is a married woman?"

"Undoubtedly," he said, catching her elbow as she stumbled slightly. "Nothing is more guaranteed to insult the sensibilities of a delicately brought-up miss than the evidence of adultery. You have shown remarkable restraint in not reaching for the hartshorn."

A definite tease laced his words, causing her blood to boil. Furthermore, it annoyed her no end that he did not even have the grace to be pricked by her sarcasm.

"Forgive me for correcting you, my lord, but today is not when you formed your first impression of me. We did meet in Bath. We sat down to dinner together at Lady Farren's party. My dearest friend, Julia Allard, has recently married your friend the Duke of Kelbourne."

He stopped beneath a stone arch, and she perforce stopped as well.

Looking down at her with an expression of mild surprise, he said, "You don't say? Were you at their wedding?"

"Unfortunately I was too ill to attend."

"Hmmm . . . I do recall Miss Allard being quite upset that her chief attendant was too ill to witness the nuptials. Were you the young lady she was referring to?"

"Yes."

The earl bowed briefly. "My apologies for not recalling you, or at least your name, Miss Thorncroft. My only excuse is that I was so bored during my brief visit to Bath that I stayed half-foxed most of the time."

"I had noticed," she said, her tone dry. As if in accord, they resumed walking toward the house.

"I will have to restrain from indulging to excess from now on. I must have been impaired if I do not recall such a pretty face as yours," the earl continued in a conversational tone.

Mariah burst out laughing and turned her head to peer up at him. "Spare me your compliments, my lord. I have the measure of you. Your flirting is quite wasted on me. In fact, I am sure you would prefer that my family and I leave. I shall arrange our departure tomorrow."

The earl halted on the cobbled pathway. After a few steps, Mariah's curiosity slowed her progress as well. She turned toward him.

"That is not what I want at all," he stated firmly, moving to stand in front of her. "I would be quite disappointed if you did not accept my hospitality for the duration of my house party. I know that your mother and younger brother may feel out of place now, but in another week or so some other family members will be arriving. I have younger cousins George's age and aunts your mother's. There is no reason to leave, especially not over the little dalliance you just witnessed."

Beneath the moon's glow, Mariah studied the angled, handsome planes of his face and found his expression sincere. Knowing how difficult it would be to talk her family into leaving, she reluctantly gave in.

"Thank you for reassuring me of our welcome," she said in a stilted tone. "Please know that I shall not discuss what I witnessed this evening."

"You are too kind."

Again, the amusement in his voice set her back up, but this time she did not feel true anger. "You really are incorrigible, aren't you?" she said softly, feeling his arm brush against her shoulder. It was strange the way his warmth seemed to permeate the thick material of her coat.

"So I have been told. But it is too late for you to revert to the vaporish miss I thought you to be. Odd, but I find it quite refreshing that there is at least one person in my home with whom I do not have to pretend to be something I am not."

They continued to walk side by side while Mariah contemplated what he had just said.

"Were you pretending to be something you are not with Lady Walgrave?" she could not help asking.

"Of course, and she would not have it otherwise."

Mariah took her time digesting this startling comment. She could not believe for a moment that he had not thoroughly enjoyed kissing Lady Walgrave. "But what were you pretending?"

"That I find her utterly irresistible, for one thing."

Mariah only half suppressed her disbelieving laugh. "It certainly looked as if you found her irresistible."

Mariah felt, rather than saw, him shrug. "For the moment I find her amusing and accommodating."

"How horrid. In what other ways do you pretend?" She knew her tone did not have its previous sting. Admittedly, she found this conversation quite fascinating—when would she ever again have the chance to speak candidly to an unmitigated rakehell?

"With most women I pretend to be brooding and dangerous. I have discovered that ladies respond quite delightfully to brooding and dangerous."

A frisson of awareness traveled down her spine as the memory of his arms tightening around Lady Walgrave came to mind.

"But you *are* brooding and dangerous." It surprised her that he would say otherwise.

"Do you think so?" he asked, his tone untroubled. "I would not hurt a flea. Although I am a dab hand with the foil, if I say so myself."

Throwing her arms up impatiently, Mariah said, "Not *that* kind of danger—not physical danger. You are the kind of dangerous that mamas warn their daughters about. You are the kind of man who will attempt to steal a lady's heart for sport. Once the thrill of the hunt is over, you will toss the lady aside, uncaring of her heart or her reputation."

"Egad." His deep, mild voice reached her as they came to a halt within the moonless shadow of the house. "I hope I am not that callow. Besides, I only dally with married ladies."

"Well! Then that makes everything just fine."

"You are quite attached to sarcasm, aren't you?"

Mariah shrugged. "Yes, to my mother's lament. I try not to indulge in front of strangers."

"So with me you can set aside your demure façade and be yourself as well. Odd as it seems, I believe we have come to an understanding, Miss Thorncroft."

She realized, to her surprise, that she felt the same. "I believe we have," she replied softly.

They resumed walking until they had reached the double doors that she had used earlier. Hesitating, for she felt strangely disappointed that their conversation was about to end, she said, "I shall bid you good night, my lord, and thank you for a most interesting conversation."

Reaching down, he lifted her hand to his lips. "The pleasure was mine. Pleasant dreams, Miss Thorncroft."

Pulling away, she slipped past him through the open door and rushed to the staircase.

As she ascended the steps, she rubbed her hands vigorously over her arms, feeling the gooseflesh beneath the heavy sleeves. With a little shiver, she knew that the condition had nothing to do with the chilly autumn evening.

Chapter Six

Walking through the hushed, dark halls, Stone bypassed the staircase that led to his bedchamber and continued on to the library.

Shutting the doors behind him, he crossed the room to a large burled walnut cabinet and poured himself a shallow brandy.

With a contemplative frown, he replaced the crystal stopper, then moved to the massive fireplace. Resting his foot on the brass fender, he stared into the flames, watching the massive logs burn. His well-trained servants always kept this room at the ready for him.

"Well, I am a bit surprised to see you still up. Mind if I join you, Stone?"

Stone turned to see Roger Spence-Jones' tall frame filling the doorway.

"Come in, Roger," he said to his old friend. "Care for a brandy?"

"Please," Roger said, approaching. "I must not have gotten enough exercise today. Can't seem to sleep." With the ease of an old friend, the blond man moved to one of the overstuffed leather chairs in front of the fireplace and seated himself, stretching his legs before him.

Pushing away from the fender, Stone went to the cabinet and grabbed another glass. "I'm looking forward to a good day of hunting tomorrow," Stone said over his shoulder as he poured the brandy. After putting away the decanter, he handed Roger the snifter and settled in the opposite chair.

"I am, too," Roger said, before taking a sip.

Getting comfortable again, Stone loosened his neckcloth and crossed his ankles. A few moments of silence ensued before Roger cleared his throat.

"Amelia and I were surprised that you had not mentioned there would be any more guests arriving. Although I had not the opportunity to converse with Miss Thorncroft, her brother and Mrs. Thorncroft were excellent company. Your new guests certainly helped make dinner more interesting."

And the rest of the evening as well, Stone thought, taking a substantial swallow of brandy before responding.

"They are an interesting family." Stone chose to ignore Roger's implied question about the Thorncrofts' unheralded arrival. Although he and Roger had shared confidences since their days at Harrow, Stone did not feel comfortable sharing information about the somewhat awkward circumstances of how the Thorncrofts came to be at Heaton.

Roger did not press him on the matter and continued his observations about the new guests. "Steven Thorncroft's manner, though a little tentative, grew more engaging and pleasant as the evening passed, and I found Mrs. Thorncroft, despite the fussiness of her attire, charming."

Stone nodded his agreement. "I must give her credit. Although she was the oldest person at the table, she did nothing to stifle the exuberance of the evening."

"Did you happen to notice that by the end of the meal Mattonly seemed quite enthralled with the pretty matron? I found it rather fun to watch that little drama unfold," Roger said, chuckling.

A smile came to Stone's lips as he remembered their friend's unusual behavior.

He and Roger relaxed into companionable silence

over their drinks, slouching further into the warm leather chairs.

Stone admitted to himself that after meeting the Thorncrofts this morning, he had expected them to behave in a provincial and amusingly gauche manner. Obviously his judgment had been completely wrong.

As he continued to stare into the leaping flames, he pondered the new arrivals, Miss Thorncroft in particular.

Roger broke into his thoughts by saying, "For all her charm, I got the distinct impression that Mrs. Thorncroft is on the hunt for a husband for her daughter."

Stone shrugged. "In my experience, all mamas with daughters of a certain age are like bloodhounds when it comes to hunting a husband."

Roger chuckled at Stone's acerbic observation. "You would know better than most. But Miss Thorncroft is an attractive young lady. Maybe Mrs. Thorncroft will be successful. After all, you, Stothart, Elbridge, and Mattonly are all unattached."

"I shall leave the field open for the others," Stone offered in a dry tone.

He did think Roger correct in his assessment of Mrs. Thorncroft's intentions. However, she might have a problem on that front, for Miss Thorncroft's unique personality could prove off-putting to a potential suitor.

Miss Thorncroft had certainly been the biggest surprise of the evening, he thought, taking another swallow.

At first he had given her little notice. As they all sat down to dinner, he had observed her perfect posture and composed expression and dismissed her as missish and dull.

But as Charlotte and Lydia, the merry widows, had grown more tedious in their attentions toward him, Miss Thorncroft had caught his notice.

The mischievous laughter in her eyes had taken him by surprise. The cheek of the girl to look so amused at his predicament! Usually it took only his direct gaze to quell even the sturdiest constitution. But Miss Thorncroft had met his stare without flinching. Quite unexpected.

Later, when she had interrupted his liaison with Felicity Walgrave, he had done his best to discomfit the chit. Her eyes had sparkled even in the moonlight, despite the fact that he could discern that her sensibilities had been truly shocked by what she had seen.

He smiled at the memory of their walk through the moonlit garden. It really had been bad of him to tease her, but to her credit, she had given as well as she got.

Truthfully, he had wanted to hear what she would say next. He would never have guessed that such a sheltered miss would be so quick-witted.

To his surprise, he had enjoyed their brief conversation, although her comment about his being dangerous had perplexed him. "You are the kind of man who will attempt to steal a lady's heart for sport," she had stated boldly. He had been about to dismiss her assessment out of hand, but something in the conviction of her tone had silenced him on the subject.

Plainly, Miss Thorncroft did not think him quite a gentleman. Frowning, he lifted the snifter. He watched the flames in the grate twist and distort through the glass.

How absurd. For if Nicholas Edward Charles Morley, fifth Earl of Haverstone, was anything, he was a gentleman. *What an opinionated little minx,* he thought mildly, taking another sip of brandy.

That comment had not been the last of the evening's surprises. As he had said good night to her in the open doorway, the glow from a nearby wall sconce had revealed her features. Her startling beauty had suddenly struck him. Odd that, for during dinner he had not thought her more than passing pretty.

However, Miss Thorncroft's beauty was not to his usual taste. He'd always been partial to lush blondes, lush brunettes. . . . All right then, he'd always been partial to *lush*, he conceded with a lopsided smile.

Miss Thorncroft might not be lush, but she certainly was prettier than he had first thought. With sparkling, intelligent eyes, a heart-shaped face, and that elegant figure—well—it was a mystery such loveliness had escaped his notice during dinner.

Perhaps it was because he rarely bothered conversing with unmarried misses. They usually had nothing of interest to say and often went off in gales of giggles for no apparent reason.

No giggling from Miss Thorncroft. And no fit of the vapors. She had not even launched into a priggish sermon on morality. She was certainly an unusual young lady.

Although her shock at finding him with Lady Walgrave had been evident, he admired her attempt to behave with aplomb. For all his teasing, truth be told, he felt a little embarrassed that Miss Thorncroft had caught him in such roguish behavior.

He would have preferred not to reveal his companion's identity, he thought, frowning at having done so. Then, shrugging pragmatically, he dismissed the concern. Better to disclose all to the unpredictable Miss Thorncroft than chance her doing something silly—like apologizing to Lady Charlotte for the interruption. He certainly did not need the headache that situation would cause!

Now here he sat in his library with good old Roger, instead of lying in his bed with Felicity Walgrave.

"You know, Roger," he said to his old friend, "tomorrow might turn out to be quite an interesting day." It rather surprised him to realize that he was looking forward to it.

The next morning, wrapped in a heavy robe and nestled in the large window seat carved out of the thick stone wall, Mariah raised her cup of chocolate to her lips and sipped with satisfaction. Outside, a bank of low black clouds rolled in from the west. Rain streaked down the windowpanes, and the nearest clouds intermittently glowed with flashes of lightning. The sound of rumbling thunder grew nearer by the minute.

Mariah knew that mere rain would not discourage the gentlemen from hunting, but she wondered if the lightning would prove too dangerous for them to venture outdoors.

She felt bad for Steven, for she knew how much he had wanted to join the grouse shoot.

After another nearby rumble of thunder, Mariah swung her legs off the window seat and set her cup and saucer on the tray the maid had placed at the foot of her bed.

Her thoughts, for the countless time, returned to the earl. She did not know what disturbed her more—stumbling upon him kissing Lady Walgrave, for never before had she seen passion so boldly displayed, or her unexpected conversation with him afterward.

Despite her initial shock, she realized that she had felt a certain daring thrill at their frank discussion. As close as she and Steven were, she could never imagine openly discussing the ways of men and women with him.

She had fully expected the earl to dismiss her, and now she felt ashamed that she had been flattered that he had not.

As her deeply ingrained sense of propriety pricked her conscience again, she admitted to herself that she should have done the proper thing and returned to the house as quickly as possible. Mama would have apoplexy if she knew what had happened, but Mariah did not intend to enlighten her.

It did surprise her that the earl had taken her direct speech so well. Shaking her head, she had to admit that her stay at Heaton had begun in a completely different manner than she had expected.

Having finished her breakfast of hothouse fruit and toast, Mariah decided to have a bath before starting her day.

Standing, she pulled her robe close against the morning chill. Just then she heard a tap at the ornately carved door.

"Come in."

The door opened, and Harris, her maid, entered the room.

"Good morning, miss. I thought you might like a nice hot bath on this dreary morn. There's a tub ready for you in the chamber beyond." She gestured toward the door on the other side of the room.

Mariah smiled at the older woman. "Thank you, Harris. Sometimes I suspect that you are clairvoyant, for I was just wishing for a bath."

"My grandmother was fey, miss, so I might have a touch of the second sight."

"No doubt," Mariah said with a laugh.

As she passed the window, she saw that the clouds had grown blacker and lower across the expanse of rolling countryside.

"It is too bad about the filthy weather. I dearly wanted to continue my exploration of the grounds. I am itching to sketch one of the views," she said, conceding to herself that the exercise would have the added benefit of keeping her out of the house and away from the other guests.

"My bones tell me we are in for bad weather for a few days, at least," Harris said, moving the tray to tidy the bed.

"Your bones are never wrong, Harris. Please rest your legs as much as possible," Mariah said as she crossed the room.

"I'm not in my dotage, Miss Mariah, and if I'm too idle, I stiffen. But thank you."

Mariah smiled at the woman's stubborn tone. Harris had been her maid for almost ten years, and Mariah had learned early on that the good woman had a very wide obstinate streak and took great pride in her position in the Thorncroft household.

Closing the door behind her, Mariah thought the

room appeared even smaller with the enormous copper bathtub taking up so much space.

After removing her robe and nightgown, Mariah gingerly dipped a toe into the tub. Though hot, the water felt deliciously inviting. Stepping in, Mariah lowered herself, shivering slightly as the steaming water warmed her faintly chilled skin.

To her delight, the bathtub was so large she could recline fully. Leaning her head back to rest against the tub, she closed her eyes for a moment and savored the cocooning warmth.

She knew she could linger over her bath, since she had likely awakened before most of the other guests. It had always been her habit to rise unfashionably early.

Opening her eyes, she noticed a flannel cloth and a cake of soap on a small table next to the tub. Trying not to slosh water, she leaned forward and picked up the soap. As soon as her wet fingers caressed the cake, the scent of wisteria assailed her senses. Rubbing it between her hands, Mariah inhaled deeply as a wave of spring suddenly enveloped her.

She found it rather ironic that after dreading the visit, everything about Heaton enchanted her eyes and senses.

Except the thought of her next encounter with Lord and Lady Walgrave. Never before had she been confronted by such an awkward situation. She prayed she would be able to comport herself in a normal fashion when next she encountered the earl's paramour and her cuckolded husband.

Another low thrum of thunder penetrated the silence of the antechamber. If she could not explore the grounds, she decided, she would ask the housekeeper to give her a tour of the house.

Despite the storm—and the dreaded encounter with the earl and Lady Walgrave looming ahead—Mariah realized that she was actually looking forward to the day.

* * *

Some time later, after making her way to the morning room, Mariah discovered that Steven, George, and Lady Davinia, as well as Mr. and Mrs. Spence-Jones and Lady Charlotte, were already present.

Relief mingled with her pleasure, because neither the earl nor Lord and Lady Walgrave were in the room. Facing them could be avoided a little longer, at least.

She assumed the rest of the guests were late risers like her mama.

After bidding everyone good morning, she sat on the sofa next to her younger brother.

Lady Davinia, looking sunny in pale yellow despite the dreary weather, smiled at Mariah. "You are just in time, Miss Thorncroft. Young George was just about to share some very exciting news."

"Oh?" Mariah looked down at George's smiling face.

"You'll never guess, Mariah! The Master of Arms is going to show me the armory! I will not only get to try on a suit of armor but he will show me the swords and shields and maces."

By his expression Mariah could tell her little brother felt very near to heaven. "How very exciting."

"I would not mind taking a look at the armory myself," Mr. Spence-Jones put in. "Would you mind if I joined you on your tour, young man?"

Mariah smiled at the fair, solid-looking man, liking his indulgent attitude toward her brother.

"I would like that, sir," George replied.

"Why don't we all have a look?" Mrs. Spence-Jones chimed in, her dark eyes alight with interest.

"I think it would be an excellent way to spend this dull morning. Besides, I take the greatest interest in everything about Heaton," Lady Charlotte proclaimed from her seat by the window.

"I think it would be great fun," Lady Davinia agreed, looking to Steven with a warm smile.

Taking note of the partiality Lady Davinia showed

her brother, Mariah smiled. She had instantly liked the beautiful young lady when they had first met in Bath. Though it was too soon to hope for anything truly romantic, she hoped that this budding attraction between the lady and Steven would continue to flourish. She knew her brother well enough to tell that beneath his cordial demeanor he was more than a little attracted to the lovely Lady Davinia.

"I wonder where Stone is." Lady Charlotte pouted, fretfully smoothing the skirt of her russet-colored morning gown. "I do hope he will join us, for the earl always tells me the most interesting stories. Alas, I know that he often reserves his mornings for the care of estate matters."

Looking at the elegant blonde, Mariah could almost feel sorry for her. By the possessive, proprietary tone that she used regarding the earl's activities, it seemed clear that the beautiful widow felt that the earl belonged to her.

Even if Lady Charlotte managed to bring the earl up to scratch, any chance of happiness would no doubt be ruined. His faithlessness and indiscretions would cause her nothing but heartache.

On the other hand, Lady Charlotte might be of the temperament to ignore that kind of behavior. Mariah had met a few such women over the years and never understood their willingness to tolerate a husband who could disrespect them so grievously. She knew her attitude could never be so accepting toward marital infidelity.

The others rose in preparation for George's tour.

"Will you be joining us, Mariah?" Steven asked, as she remained seated.

"I beg you all to excuse me, but I believe I would prefer to write a few letters this morning."

It was true. She did want to write letters, but she also wanted to put off meeting the earl until the last possible moment. It had been one thing to speak so frankly with him in the veil of moonlight, but it would be a completely different proposition in the clear light of day. Maybe if she stayed in this smaller salon she could avoid him for a little while longer.

After the others left, Mariah wandered to a small desk on the other side of the room. It stood in front of a multipaned window that afforded an expansive view of the parkland. She watched a few moments as the trees and shrubs swayed and bent in the raging storm.

As she had suspected, there were writing supplies in the desk, and she set her hand to a long letter to her friend Julia, the Duchess of Kelbourne. Mariah began to describe almost every detail of what had already occurred during her visit to Heaton.

Soon time lost its measure as the rain rapped against the windowpane in rhythm with the scrape of her quill across the foolscap.

At the sound of the door opening, Mariah turned to see Mrs. Ingram, Lord and Lady Walgrave, and Mr. Woburn stroll into the room.

With a sinking heart, Mariah pasted a smile to her lips.

"Ah, Miss Thorncroft, you seem to have found a productive way to spend this gloomy morning," Mrs. Ingram called as she and her companions settled themselves comfortably in the overstuffed furniture.

Rising, Mariah bobbed a quick curtsy. "Good morning." Her smile encompassed them, and her eyes briefly met Lady Walgrave's confident gaze. Then she resumed her seat at the desk.

Lady Walgrave, elegant in a dove gray gown and paisley cashmere shawl, yawned delicately and watched Mariah for a moment.

"You make me feel guilty, Miss Thorncroft. I, too, should be attending to my correspondence. I owe so many of my friends a letter that I do not know where to begin. Therefore I shall put it off another day. Am I not shockingly lazy, my love?" the lady said, sending this last comment to her husband.

Lord Walgrave, his portly frame lounging in a wing chair by the fireplace, responded with a harrumph as he opened his newspaper with a crisp rattle.

Trying not to stare, Mariah could only marvel at Lady Walgrave's nonchalant demeanor. Obviously Mariah's presence did not disturb her in the least. How on earth could someone betray her husband and then refer to him as "my love" the very next day?

"This blasted weather has certainly curtailed our hunting," Mr. Woburn lamented from his stance by the window.

"Quit blubbering, Woby," Mrs. Ingram chided. "We will have a perfectly lovely time indoors. Now, let us get to know Miss Thorncroft a bit better. I did not have a chance to converse with her last night." The redhead turned her gaze to Mariah.

"That is a good idea, Mrs. Ingram," Lady Walgrave quickly agreed. "I, too, would like to learn more about Miss Thorncroft."

Mariah could not miss the arch smile the lady sent her way.

Out of politeness, Mariah turned from her letter to listen to the women. At least the gentlemen appeared to have no interest in learning more about her, she noticed with some measure of relief.

"So, Miss Thorncroft, which balls have you attended in past Seasons?"

Mariah fiddled with the silver inkwell lid while she searched for a proper answer. She did not intend to tell these women that she and her mother had only hovered on the fringes of Society.

"I particularly enjoyed Lady Farren's entertainments. And of course the theater and the opera are always diverting."

Mrs. Ingram and Lady Walgrave exchanged glances.

"I do not believe I know Lady Farren. Do you, Lady Walgrave?"

"No, I am not acquainted with Lady Farren," Lady Walgrave quickly replied.

"Lady Farren is a relation of the new Duchess of Kelbourne," Mariah siad.

"Ah, I see. What of Almack's? My memory must be failing me, for I do not recall meeting you there."

Mariah decided she liked Lady Walgrave even less than she had last night. The lady knew very well that there would be little chance for someone like Mariah to receive approval from any of the patronesses, and to quiz her about it revealed the lady as patently disingenuous.

Even Mr. Woburn turned from the window to gaze at Mariah with sudden interest.

Feeling a flash of anger, Mariah looked directly at Lady Walgrave. "I never attempted to gain vouchers."

Lady Walgrave's blond brows rose in surprise. "How singularly unique. I have never met anyone who did not wish to attend the assemblies. I believe Miss Thorncroft is an original," she finished on a girlish titter that set Mariah's teeth on edge.

Making no reply, Mariah turned back to her letter. After carefully dusting it with fine sand, she picked it up and rose to leave. Giving everyone her most polite smile, she said, "Please pardon me. I should have joined my mother some time ago." Without waiting for a response, she dropped a shallow curtsy and left the room.

Chapter Seven

"*T*his engraved silver goblet was given to the third Baron Morley by King Charles the Second in 1678. Baron Morley was my lord's great-grandfather several times over." Mrs. Billings picked up the goblet and held it up for Mariah's interested inspection.

"There is a very good painting of him on the other wall, miss," the housekeeper said, replacing the goblet and moving farther down the great hall. "You can see the goblet depicted on the table next to him."

Mariah followed the housekeeper, her slippered feet whispering along the polished floor. Glancing around the vast room with pleasure, Mariah owned that she was thoroughly enjoying her impromptu tour of the earl's home—even more so because, to her immense relief, the rest of the guests appeared to be otherwise occupied.

Moving closer to the large portrait the housekeeper indicated, Mariah studied the earl's ancestor with great interest.

The man in the painting wore a long, curly wig, and lace fell from underneath the wide cuffs of his fancy blue coat.

Her gaze traveled back up to the face. The current earl bore little resemblance to the man in the painting. Lord Morley had a rather plain face. The only resemblance to his descendant was the proud expression and the blue eyes.

"If you will come this way, miss, I will show you

several interesting portraits that explain the importance the Morleys have played in the history of our country. There is also a lovely painting and miniature of Alice of Surrey."

Feeling curious at the note of pride in Mrs. Billings' voice, Mariah turned from the portrait to follow the knowledgeable housekeeper.

As they moved farther down the hall, Mariah continued to marvel at the multitude of artwork and fascinating objects—all on display to show the illustrious history and extreme wealth of the Morleys.

How the earl could put all of this in jeopardy by gambling away fortunes made Mariah shake her head in dismay.

On the verge of asking Mrs. Billings a question, Mariah heard footfalls echoing from the other end of the hall. Turning, she saw Lady Walgrave and a few other houseguests approaching—including the earl.

With her heart pounding furiously, Mariah did not know where to look. Feeling a blush come to her cheeks, she tried to smile politely, praying that this encounter would not prove embarrassing.

The earl, walking ahead of the others, smiled at Mariah with complete ease. She envied his aplomb. She also admired the way his dark blue coat molded perfectly to his shoulders and highlighted the clear blue of his eyes.

"Evidently Miss Thorncroft has found a distraction from the furious weather outside. We have come to join you on your tour of my house," the earl said with a sweeping gesture that took in the room.

So much for avoiding him this morning, Mariah thought wryly.

"How delightful." Mariah smiled at the earl before turning to Mr. and Mrs. Spence-Jones. "Did you enjoy the armory?"

"Indeed we did," Mr. Spence-Jones stated, and his wife concurred.

"We enjoyed ourselves so much that we are continuing the tour of Heaton, with an expert guide," Mrs. Spence-Jones said, sending a smile to the earl.

Steven and Lady Davinia, who had trailed behind the rest of the group, stepped forward. "I think exploring the house is a lovely way to spend such a dark and dreary day," Lady Davinia said.

Mariah thought Lord Stothart, Mr. Elbridge, and Mr. Woburn appeared more resigned than pleased to be part of the tour. Lady Walgrave stood at the earl's elbow, looking sublimely satisfied.

Mariah wondered why Lord Walgrave and the merry widows had not joined them, but she decided not to ask.

"Mrs. Billings, I thank you for conducting the tour thus far, but I shall continue from here." To Mariah's surprise, the earl moved to her side as he spoke to his housekeeper.

"Of course, my lord." Mrs. Billings curtsied. "His lordship is much more knowledgeable about Heaton than I ever hope to be," she said to Mariah.

"You have been most informative, Mrs. Billings. Thank you for taking the time to show me around."

"My pleasure, miss." The housekeeper curtsied again before taking her leave, her chain of keys jingling with every step.

"I say, Stone, if we must gawk at all your riches I would rather not have to listen to a dry-as-dust history lesson on top of it," Mr. Elbridge opined, causing the other gentlemen to laugh.

"I think it will be vastly fun to have Stone give us the real stories," Lady Walgrave said, sending the earl a blatantly intimate smile.

Mariah caught the knowing amusement in the look that passed between Lady Davinia and Mrs. Spence-Jones. But what could have been an extremely awkward moment passed with ease since the other guests joined in expressing their desire to hear the earl.

"I will share with you the story of my favorite ancestor. Hopefully, I will not bore anyone with the telling." He sent a dry look to his friend Mr. Elbridge.

The little group followed the earl to the end of the hall, where a large portrait framed in heavy gilt hung on the huge expanse of wall.

Stopping before it, they all gazed up in unison, waiting for the earl to speak.

"This is Alice of Surrey." He gestured at the painting.

Standing behind the others, Mariah tilted her head to study the painting. The note of affection and pride in the earl's deep voice could not be missed.

The woman in the portrait faced the painter full on. Mariah got the impression that the lady had been tall. Her gown, depicted in rich hues of burgundy and gold, looked almost lifelike. Ropes of pearls hung beneath a large ruffled collar, and her fingers were covered in golden rings.

Mariah had always been of the opinion that Elizabethan clothing looked decidedly uncomfortable, but the earl's ancestor wore the odd garb as regally as any queen.

Alice of Surrey had an oval face, a complexion pale as ivory, large dark eyes, and dark hair. The face was that of a young woman, but the expression showed maturity, and there was a hint of humor to the set of her mouth.

Mariah felt a spark of interest and wanted to learn more about the mysterious lady—especially why the earl and his housekeeper referred to her in such awed and respectful tones.

"Alice was a fascinating, tenacious lady," the earl began, as everyone turned to listen to him. "As the fifth daughter of a poor knight, Alice had few prospects of bettering her circumstances."

" 'Tis her poor father you should feel sorry for. What a chore to find husbands for five daughters," Lord Stothart offered with a guffaw.

"Actually, there were seven daughters," the earl explained with a chuckle, gazing up at the portrait affectionately.

"I would hate to have so many sisters. How did she ever rise to such glorious heights?" Lady Walgrave asked the earl.

"The true making of Alice began when she somehow managed an invitation to Queen Elizabeth's court. Alice had no dowry to speak of, but she was a fetching little thing with a keen intelligence. She had the good fortune to become the bosom bow of the redoubtable Bess of Hardwick and spent her time at court very wisely. Bess shared her knowledge of politics, the law, and how to avoid palace intrigue. Alice caught the attention of Robert Morley. Robert was a relation of the Cavendishes and much favored by the queen. Robert and Alice married after a very brief courtship, and she cleverly aided Robert's rise in power at court. Alice had just as good a mind for business as Bess, and I am sure she would be just as well known as the famed Countess of Hardwick if she had had as many husbands." He finished with a wry smile, as everyone laughed.

Smiling, Mariah turned back to the portrait, marveling at the power this long-dead woman had held. How in the world had she managed it? How surprising and . . . and wonderful that the earl so obviously admired his ancestor, Mariah thought with the oddest catch in her chest. Her own papa, as kind as he was, would no doubt show nothing but disdain at the idea that a mere woman could have a good head for managing money.

"Did she only care for business matters?" she asked, still gazing up at the portrait.

"Indeed not," the earl said, stepping to her side as some of the others moved on to other objects of interest.

"Alice was fond of dancing and playing the harp," he explained. "She also loved to travel in an era where travel was not as easy as it is now. She adored receiving jewels and wore rather too many at once—thus piquing Queen Elizabeth's annoyance, for she liked to be the most bejeweled woman at any given occasion."

Mariah laughed at the image the earl had conjured. "Then Alice was a brave woman on many fronts."

"Yes, a fascinating character altogether. Despite her varied interests, her greatest passion had been the creation of Heaton. From the size of the windows to the stables, Alice oversaw the smallest details. Her husband, Robert, who became the first Baron Morley, soon realized that it was useless to try to withstand her desires. As I wander the rooms, I often think that he was right in letting her have her way."

"Indeed." Mariah gazed up at the fan-beamed ceiling, then around the well-designed mahogany-paneled room. "I have rarely encountered a more beautiful, perfectly appointed house."

"Thank you." The earl bowed slightly. "Over the years I have read and reread her diaries. Alice has taught me much of the intricacies of life. Because she was quite educated for a woman of her era, she knew there could be more to our existence than struggle and strife. She longed for beauty and had the indomitable courage and intelligence to go out and create what she desired."

At the deep, unexpected inflection of love and admiration in the earl's voice, Mariah felt a swift rush of emotion well up in her chest. Going over what the earl had just said, she continued to stare at the woman in the portrait.

Suddenly a keen longing rose from the deepest recesses of her soul. A yearning for a different life than the one she saw before her. She closed her eyes for a moment against the unexpected prickle of tears.

Mariah had received a very fine education as well. But what was the point of an education if she could not go out and use it as Alice had done? She raised her tear-filled gaze to the blurring portrait once more.

Instantly Mariah felt an affinity with the earl's long-dead relative. She understood Alice's yearning for independence and beauty. Mariah realized that she had the same desires but had never fully faced them until this moment.

The years of learning had opened new vistas in her imagination. Education had created longings for more experiences and dissatisfaction with the limitations her parents had put on her future.

If only, if only. Her heart whispered the lament over and over. The earl's story about Alice tapped into a well of yearning within her that she had never suspected existed. She blinked several times as the tears threatened to spill over.

"How lucky she was," she began with a fierce half-whisper. "How lucky not to have been hemmed in by convention and fear. How truly blessed she was to have been able to pursue her dreams." Mariah heard the fervency in her voice and glanced around quickly, nervous that she was making a spectacle of herself. Relaxing with relief, she saw the others were scattered around the room. Mariah quickly turned away as Lady Walgrave looked back with a fierce frown twisting her lips.

The earl looked down at her, a dark brow raised in curiosity. "Don't we all pursue our dreams, in some fashion, Miss Thorncroft? Is that not our nature?"

"Maybe the nature of *men*, my lord. Nevertheless, few women, no matter in what station in life they find themselves, are ever as blessed as Alice. No matter how capable, intelligent, and intrepid, a woman would rarely be *allowed* to follow her dreams." She looked up into his surprised blue gaze and marveled at the words she heard herself speak. Where had she developed the temerity to voice such outrageous opinions?

"You are very unusual, Miss Thorncroft. I would not have thought that a sheltered, gently brought up young lady would have the opportunity to develop such strong views." This time his voice held no tease.

"Even gently brought up young ladies manage to experience some of life's darker aspects, and that breeds strong opinions." She sent him a wan smile, grateful that her tears were receding.

He continued to hold her gaze, frowning slightly. "If you have a great desire for something, as Alice did, why not throw caution to the wind? We all have shackles that bind certain areas of our lives, but why not tempt the Fates and follow your dreams?"

Unnerved by the intensity of the earl's piercing blue gaze, she turned her eyes from his, feeling confused. It took her a moment to formulate her response.

"You have given me much to think about, my lord. But I know that I could never completely throw caution to the wind, as you say. What one discovers—what *I* have discovered—is that life is difficult enough without any interference from us. Why add to it?"

"I am curious to know what the Fates have thrown at you that has made life so difficult."

Mariah could not bring herself to answer his question. The unanticipated emotions swirling within her were too raw for her to reveal. Biting her lip, she looked away.

"I see that I ask too much," he said softly. "Then tell me this. You are obviously intelligent and capable—what prevents you from doing what you wish, as Alice did?"

Mariah shrugged in dejection and turned back to the portrait. "I am neither so brave nor so foolish as to emulate your ancestor. A woman can do little on her own, and I do not have an indulgent husband, as Alice did."

The earl stood silently next to her, and the chatter of the other guests suddenly seemed far away. Mariah wondered if he were trying to think of a polite way to extricate himself from this strange conversation.

"I cannot argue with your opinion, Miss Thorncroft. And I will say that I can empathize with your point of view."

At this unexpected comment, Mariah looked up into his eyes. "You can?" She tried to keep the note of skepticism from her voice.

"I know you will find it hard to believe, but I, too, have not been able to pursue my dreams unfettered."

A doubtful frown furrowed her brow. "Indeed? But you are a peer of the realm. You have the means and the power to do whatever you wish."

"I know it would seem so. But the harsher realities of life often interfere with the best-laid plans. For instance, my deepest desire had been to join the fight against Bonaparte. It went against my every instinct—my every desire—to stay home. As much as it stung, I stayed and took my seat in the House of Lords and managed my estates."

She found it hard to believe that a man like the Earl of Haverstone had ever faced any kind of disappointment. He seemed so supremely confident and at ease with himself.

Nevertheless, the lingering disappointment in his expression told her clearly how difficult it must have been for him to stay home during the war.

"But surely you performed an extremely important service to our country?"

"It was what needed to be done," he shrugged dismissively. "The troops needed clothes and food. War is expensive. I could never have ignored my duty and joined the guards, leaving my estates and all my tenants to fall into unproductive disorder."

He lifted his shoulders briefly and continued. "I share this information only to show you that I do understand your views and that they don't apply just to the fair sex."

Mariah considered his words. Her judgment of him as an utterly selfish libertine no longer seemed to fit quite as well.

"It seems that none of us are truly free." She spoke softly, looking back up to the portrait.

The earl did the same. "I believe that Alice had the right of it—we will find freedom if we strive to pursue the beauty and passion we desire, no matter what else life has in store for us."

"I like the sense of that, my lord."

A cozy, warm feeling spread through her body. It suddenly felt as if she and the earl were old friends sharing deep intimacies. She quite liked the feeling.

Now that she felt better, her earlier emotionalism embarrassed her. Wanting to clarify her statements, she spoke quickly. "I didn't mean to sound as if I have anything to complain about. Indeed, I know my existence is more comfortable than most."

The earl sent her a perceptive smile. "I have not forgotten that you have not answered my question about what has caused you to suffer. Maybe another time you will feel that you can."

"I confess I did not think that you would be interested, my lord." She kept her tone light.

"I am surprised myself," he said. "However, you have brought up some interesting points of view. I own that I am curious as to how you have developed them—especially since you cannot be more than nineteen or twenty years of age."

Mariah smiled, suspecting him of flummery. "I am almost four and twenty."

"So old? A woman who admits to her real age is a rare creature."

Mariah could not miss the dry tease in his tone and smiled up at him.

"I may not start lying about my age until I am as old as you, my lord."

He sent her a look of feigned disapproval. "I am not yet one and thirty."

"So old?" she teased back.

Their gazes met and held. A blatantly alluring smile slowly spread across his features.

Fascinated by the sudden change that came over him, Mariah felt her breath catch in her throat. How could she ever have thought, even for a moment, that they could be "old friends"?

The smile lingered on his lips as he gazed into her eyes. For no reason she could discern, Mariah's heart began to thump heavily within her chest.

"You know, I believe I am quite pleased that you came out for a moonlit walk last night, Miss Thorncroft."

Shocked, Mariah glanced around, praying no one had heard his comment.

"You really are rather bad, aren't you?" she stated softly.

"I would not think you know me well enough to make such a sweeping statement."

Mariah almost snorted. "Maybe witnessing your liaison with a married woman has something to do with my hasty conclusion about your character."

"That's what has prejudiced you against me? And here I thought it was my lax table manners," he drawled.

Mariah could not help finding him amusing, but she would much prefer that he did not know it. "Does it not matter to you at all that your behavior is quite beyond the pale?"

"Not at all. Besides, what am I doing that is so bad? I just do what's expected of me."

Mariah thought the grin he shot her said that he was thoroughly enjoying himself.

She shrugged. "You do not strike me as the kind of man who does things just because they are expected."

"You are correct. I should have said that I enjoy doing what beautiful women expect of me—otherwise I am quite willful."

Meeting the mischief in his gaze with speculation in her own, she said, "I suspect that statement is not completely accurate. You enjoy doing what beautiful *married* women expect of you."

He laughed. "How astute, Miss Thorncroft. I find the desires of married women much easier and more pleasurable to fulfill than the expectations of unmarried misses."

"I should imagine so. All your married ladies cannot expect a proposal."

"Well, not a marriage proposal at any rate."

Suppressing her laughter at his outrageousness, Mariah said, "Do I need to remind you that I am a gently reared young lady? I am unused to speaking so plainly on such indelicate subjects." Her voice was not as firm as she would have liked.

"I would apologize if I thought that I had offended you. However, I will confess that I have never had such frank discussions with an unmarried young lady."

"I won't say that I am flattered, my lord," Mariah said, doing her best to keep her expression severe.

"You really are bad, aren't you?" he said, laughingly using her words against her.

Just then, the butler entered, his sonorous tones carrying throughout the gallery. "Luncheon is served, my lord."

The earl had not taken his eyes from Mariah's during this pronouncement. "We must continue this fascinating discussion another time, Miss Thorncroft," he said, a slight smile still on his lips.

Mariah only nodded. For some reason, she was finding it difficult to speak above the racing of her heart.

Chapter Eight

*T*hat evening, as he dressed for dinner in his sumptuous green-and-gold bedchamber, Stone found himself in a most inexplicable mood.

He had almost finished tying his neckcloth when Stolt approached with his black dinner jacket and helped his master on with the snug-fitting garment.

"That will be all, Stolt. Thank you," he said, wanting a few moments of privacy before joining his guests.

"Very good, my lord." Stolt, his features impassive, bowed and left the room.

Stone frowned at his reflection in the cheval mirror. Again he asked himself the same question that had been rattling in his brain all day. What had possessed him to share such personal information with Miss Thorncroft?

Never had he spoken so frankly to anyone, much less a young woman he had only just met.

His frown deepened as his long fingers worked the intricate folds and knots of his neckcloth. The foreign feeling of embarrassment pricked him anew.

He again went over what had occurred in the gallery earlier. When he told her the story of his ancestor, he had witnessed a startling change come to Miss Thorncroft's eyes. The intensity in her gaze and voice had resonated with something unidentifiable within him. The profound emotion gripping her for those few moments had made him want to reach out to her in some way—to let her know that despite the differences in their backgrounds he understood how she felt.

His hands stilled. Why did he care what Miss Thorncroft thought or felt? Something was definitely wrong. Had he grown so bored of late that an unsophisticated, sarcastic little nobody could cause him to behave in this completely uncharacteristic manner?

After their encounter last night, his only intention regarding Miss Thorncroft had been to engage in a mild flirtation. Nothing serious in the least—he had never developed a taste for sullying virgins. So how had flirting turned into something else entirely? He did not deny that he found her attractive and intelligent, and he enjoyed trading quips with her, but that did not explain his completely baffling behavior. Even though it made very little sense to him, those few moments in front of the portrait of Alice of Surrey had felt more intimate than kissing Felicity Walgrave in the garden.

Again, embarrassment sent a faint flush up his neck when he recalled telling her how he had hated staying home during the war. Why bring that up? The subject was one that he had spent little time mulling over of late. He had thought that he had set aside his disappointment some time ago.

He did not like the idea of Miss Thorncroft being privy to such personal information about him, but unfortunately he could not take his words back.

From this point on, he must behave with much more circumspection around Miss Thorncroft. His inexplicable foolishness could easily give her the wrong impression. He certainly did not need three women vying for his title this month, he thought with a humorless smile. Somehow, this attempt at levity did not improve his mood. It was not that he did not wish to marry; he would just prefer it to be later rather than sooner. He intended to follow his father's example and hold on to his very satisfying bachelorhood for many years to come.

The wisest choice would be to keep a polite distance

from the disarmingly charming Miss Thorncroft. Since she seemed to have an odd effect upon him, he did not want to chance baring any more of his deepest thoughts to her.

Shaking off his frown, he finished tying his cravat and left his bedchamber.

Tossing one last glance at her reflection in the large looking glass next to the dressing table, Mariah readjusted the drape of her blue-green India silk shawl before declaring herself satisfied with her appearance.

"The gentlemen downstairs would have to go a long way before finding another young lady with your looks," Harris stated, standing back to admire her mistress.

Sending her maid a wry smile, Mariah picked up her reticule from the bed. "You are certainly biased, Harris, but thank you. I will confess that I feel like a plain sparrow compared to some of the ladies here. They are as lovely as swans."

"Humph. Sometimes being too modest about your looks won't help you find a husband."

"Oh, Harris, you sound like Mama," Mariah called over her shoulder as she left the room.

Heading down the hall toward the grand staircase, Mariah took a deep breath and chided herself for her nervousness.

Nothing she did seemed to dispel the odd feeling fluttering in her chest since her conversation with the earl. Now a keen sense of anticipation warred with a feeling of dread regarding the evening.

She hated feeling so nervous. She had even changed her mind about which evening gown to wear, something she had not experienced since her first Season. Finally, she decided on her new cerulean blue gown with the pin-tucked sleeves that capped her shoulders. She also wore the demi-parure of diamonds and aquamarines set in silver that her parents had given her for her eighteenth birthday.

Instead of taking the wide staircase down, she continued along the corridor to the other side of the house.

A sturdy young maid carrying a tray was coming out of George's room as Mariah approached. "I am just going to peek in and say good night to my little brother." Mariah knew she was really telling herself this to justify delaying her next encounter with the earl.

The middle-aged maid curtsied. "The young man has just finished his dinner and is playing with some of his lordship's old toy soldiers before going to bed."

Mariah thanked the maid and pulled open the door. The room, handsomely appointed in deep blues and browns, was large and held sturdy, comfortable-looking furniture. She found George, already dressed in his nightclothes, sitting on the rug before the fireplace and putting little toy men into formation.

"Mariah! See what I have?" he said, lifting up a soldier as soon as he saw her.

"Yes. You look as if you are enjoying yourself." She sat in a low chair next to him.

"Oh, I am. Is not Heaton fun? Home is not like it is here. I could stay forever."

Mariah laughed at his enthusiasm and leaned forward to affectionately tousle his sandy hair.

George grinned and peered at her attire. "You look pretty, Mariah. Are you going down to dinner?"

"Yes. I just wanted to say good night before you went to sleep."

"I wish I could stay up and have dinner with the earl. Don't you think he's a rum 'un?"

Mariah smiled at his cant and said, "He is a very nice gentleman, especially to let you play with his little soldiers."

"I know. I am practicing for when I am in the guards," he said, moving around some of the toys.

"Has Mama been in?"

"Yes. She said I could play in the stables tomorrow if the earl says that I may. I want to see the earl's horses."

"It sounds as if you will be having another full day. Do not stay up too late, scamp."

"I won't. Have a good dinner."

He rose from his knees to kiss her on the cheek, then scrambled back to the soldiers.

Leaving the warmth of the cozy fire, Mariah smiled down at her brother. Sometimes he could be very sweet, she thought fondly. Reaching the door, she turned back at his call.

"You do like the earl, don't you, Mariah?"

The anxiety in his large eyes caught at her heart. "I really don't know him very well. Why do you ask?"

"Because if we like him and he likes us, maybe he will invite us back."

A tender smile curved her lips at his hopeful little face. What a blessing to see the world in such an uncomplicated way.

"Maybe he will, scamp. Sleep well."

Slipping out of the room, she shut the door behind her and walked back down the hall.

Pausing before the staircase, she frowned. Thinking of the earl left her bewildered and strangely agitated. She told herself their earlier discussion and his generosity toward George did not change what she had seen in the moonlight. Besides, rakes *had* to be charming. And one as successful as the earl most likely had more than his fair share of allure.

Trying to shake off her doubt, she went down the stairs, a vague feeling of trepidation still lingering. Catching a glimpse of herself in the large gilt-framed mirror next to the bottom of the staircase, Mariah admitted to herself that her gown and shawl were extremely fashionable and her simple hairstyle flattered her large eyes and heart-shaped face. She felt grateful for this much-needed boost to her confidence.

Checking her posture, Mariah took a moment to steady her breathing before nodding to the footman to open the door.

Upon stepping into the warm, wood-paneled room, she was enveloped by the sound of happy chatter. She was greatly relieved to find that dinner had not yet been announced.

Pausing, she scanned the guests for her mother and Steven. Her gaze alighted on the earl first as he stood with the widows and Lord Mattonly. The fluttering in her chest sped its tempo at the sight of his tall, lean frame and dark hair.

He really was devilishly handsome, she thought as he smiled at something Lady Charlotte said. *I've met any number of handsome men. There's no reason to get the vapors,* she cautioned herself.

Her heart continued to be uncooperative. Could the moonlight somehow have enchanted her last eve? This flight of fancy caused her to smile as she dragged her gaze from the earl.

At that instant, Mariah saw her mother waving from her stance by the fireplace. Moving across the room, Mariah greeted some of the other guests before reaching her mother's side.

"Gracious, Mariah! I thought you would never come down. I'm sure dinner will be announced any moment."

"I am sorry to be so late, Mama."

"You are forgiven," Mrs. Thorncroft said quickly. Mariah now caught the twinkle in her mother's eyes and the flush on her cheeks.

"What has you in such high color, Mama?" Mariah hoped her mother was not hatching another match-making scheme.

"I am so excited about what I have just heard! Some of the ladies have persuaded the earl to have dancing after dinner! As we speak, the grand salon is being prepared. Is that not wonderful?"

Dancing did indeed sound wonderful to Mariah. "I wonder what we shall do for music. Perhaps one of the ladies is proficient at the pianoforte."

Mama waved her fan impatiently. "Do not be so provincial, Mariah. The earl keeps a small orchestra for just such spontaneous occasions."

"Of course he does. How silly of me," Mariah responded dryly, wondering how much longer the earl would be able to maintain such extravagances.

"I am so glad you are not too late, Mariah, for I would have another word with you before we go in to dinner."

"Yes, Mama," Mariah said in a distracted tone, for she had just noticed Steven standing nearby with Lady Davinia and Mr. and Mrs. Spence-Jones.

"I wish you to converse with Lord Stothart if you are seated next to him at dinner again."

"Lord Stothart?" Mariah turned back to her mother in alarm. "Heavens, why? He barely looked in my direction last night. In truth, I do not find him the least bit appealing."

"Do not be silly, Mariah. I am sure he noticed you. Just now, before you came in, he asked after you."

"Did he? Perhaps that was because you managed to slip the size of my dowry into the conversation?"

Mariah watched her mother's eyes go wide with offended innocence. "Of course not! Not right out, anyway. However, a subtle hint cannot hurt. After all, I am no longer in the least hopeful of securing the earl's interest in you, so we must move on to other pastures."

Mariah laughed. "What a dreadful thought, Mama. I was never *in* the earl's pasture. But why are you suddenly casting your hopes for him aside?"

Frowning, Mrs. Thorncroft sent a quick glance around the room. Satisfied that they were relatively private, she explained. "I have been hearing some rather wild stories about him, even worse than his gambling away such vast sums. And Lady Charlotte shared certain things with me this afternoon that leave me to suspect that they will be making a match of it soon."

"Really?" Mariah did not believe it for a moment. Even if she did not have firsthand evidence of the earl's dalliance with Lady Walgrave, she had seen how dismissive he was of Lady Charlotte's fawning. Nevertheless, she would not enlighten her mama, for if she would leave off trying to throw her daughter at the earl's feet, then so much the better.

"Even so, I have no interest in Lord Stothart," Mariah said flatly.

"I am fatigued with your protests. He is a perfectly wonderful young man. Smile at him this evening. And after dinner, when the dancing begins he will have all the more reason to admire you, for you are such an accomplished dancer. I can just see you, snug and happy in the baronial splendor of his estate, Tilton. I understand that the rents alone are seven thousand a year!"

At that moment the butler opened the double doors that led to the dining room, saving Mariah from having to respond to her mother.

Trailing behind the others, Mariah hoped to avoid Lord Stothart. To her dismay, the guests sat in the same places as they had last night, leaving Mariah no choice but to be seated next to him.

Taking her time unfolding her napkin, Mariah kept her eyes on her lap. From the corner of her eye, she noticed Lord Stothart watching her closely.

"So, Miss Thorncroft, do you enjoy whist and piquet?"

Before she could answer, the footman stepped forward to fill her wineglass. "Not particularly, sir."

His pale brows rose high. "Eh? Why not? Nothing better than a good game of cards."

"So I have heard. Nevertheless, I never developed a taste for cards. Although I do enjoy chess."

"Chess?" he snorted. "Dashed dull game, if you ask me. To each his own, I guess. I understand your father owns a mill of some sort."

Nonplussed at his quick change of subject, Mariah took a sip of wine before replying. "Yes, sir, a woolen mill." She was not about to add that Papa also owned herds and herds of sheep.

"Excellent, excellent." He raised his glass and finished off the wine in two gulps. The footman stepped up to refill it a moment later. "And I understand your father quite dotes on you?"

Next, he will be asking the exact amount of my portion, Mariah thought cynically, affronted at his unsubtle attempt to find out just how fond her papa was of her.

It was not only his blatant fishing about her dowry that made her dislike Lord Stothart; his pasty face and pudgy fingers caused her a definite shiver of revulsion.

"I am sure my father is no fonder of me than most fathers are of their daughters."

The look of disappointment that came over his bloated features gave her a small measure of satisfaction.

At that moment Mrs. Spence-Jones distracted Lord Stothart's attention, leaving Mariah relieved to be free of his pointed questions.

Mr. Elbridge, seated on her left, addressed her politely and briefly before turning back to Mrs. Ingram.

Picking up her wineglass, Mariah saw that Steven again sat next to Lady Davinia. Smiling to herself, Mariah looked farther up the table and saw handsome Lord Mattonly gazing at her mama with an enthralled expression.

Good heavens, she thought with some alarm beneath her amusement. Mrs. Thorncroft certainly did not appear to notice the effect she seemed to have on the young man.

The doors opened, and the servants brought in the first course. The volume of chatter softened, and Mariah decided to concentrate on her food.

After cutting into her grouse, she became aware of a prickly sensation and could not prevent herself from glancing at the head of the table. For an instant she felt the disturbing intensity of the earl's gaze on her.

A moment later his gaze became shuttered, and the polite smile he sent before he turned away caused her rapidly beating heart to lurch to its normal pace.

Returning her attention to her meal, she wondered why the evening suddenly seemed so flat.

*   *   *

Almost three hours later, Mariah took her place opposite Lord Stothart for the first dance, a quadrille, and allowed her attention to wander around the lovely room.

Garlands of fir boughs draped the heavily carved mahogany mantel. The rugs had been removed, and the floors gleamed with an almost mirrorlike finish. In the far corner, the members of the six-piece orchestra sat tuning their instruments.

She could not imagine a more pleasant room in which to spend an evening.

Some of the other guests were forming another set at the other end of the floor. It did not surprise her a bit to see her brother standing up with Lady Davinia. Mariah watched as the young woman laughed at something Steven said and suddenly realized she was glad, for Steven's sake, that they had come to Heaton.

Anything could develop from the spark so evident between her brother and the beautiful, petite blonde. Mariah owned that the enveloping beauty of Heaton could easily inspire romance in almost anyone.

The music began and Mariah crossed in front of Lord Stothart.

Hearing a familiar musical laugh, Mariah glanced around to see her mother, among the dancers in the other set, crossing in front of Lord Mattonly, who beamed down at her.

A vague alarm again went off in the back of Mariah's senses. Back home, everyone knew that Mama was a practiced, but innocent, flirt. None of the gentlemen at the assemblies and other parties had ever taken her subtle flattery and eyelash batting seriously—until now.

No, surely she mistook young Lord Mattonly's attention toward her mother, Mariah thought, tamping down her concern. Lud! He could not be much older than Steven!

The music pulled Mariah's attention back to the steps of the dance. Though keenly aware of Lord Stothart's gaze continually upon her, she refused to pay him any heed. Despite her mother's entreaties, she did not intend to show him any particular consideration.

In her desire to avoid making eye contact with Lord Stothart, she kept her attention on the other guests as she performed the steps of the quadrille.

As she moved through the line of dancers, she noticed the earl standing by the fireplace with Lord and Lady Walgrave.

Lord Walgrave, despite his paunch and receding hairline, still managed to appear proud and superior.

Mariah wondered if he had the slightest notion that his wife was having a liaison with his good friend.

Lady Walgrave, golden hair swept up *à la Grecian,* looked stunning in a gown of carmine silk. Mariah's chest tightened as the blonde smiled intimately up at the earl.

The beau monde was certainly a different world from her own, she mused. Most of the time she found its modes and manners confusing and hard to follow.

All the people born to the *ton* seemed to know the unwritten rules instinctively. Discretion, it seemed to her, was considered one of the essential morals among the beau monde. Therefore, it would not surprise her if Lord Walgrave did suspect his wife's betrayal—and thought little of it.

No matter the conventions of the *ton*, Mariah mused, she could never tolerate her husband being unfaithful to her. The thought was unbearable. Unless, of course, she did not love him.

Casting a quick glance at Lord Stothart as they made a turn, Mariah wondered if he were her husband, would she care if he had a mistress? No, she decided instantly, it would not bother her at all. However, she could not imagine being married to Lord Stothart.

She knew herself well enough to be certain that if her emotions were engaged, the thought of her husband so casually breaking their marriage vows would be devastating.

But what choice would she have if she married someone like the earl? *No choice but to become a shrew, that's what,* she thought honestly as she made another turn. No, it would be better to become an old maid than to become the nagging, embittered wife of a man who saw her only as a means to fill his coffers and nursery.

She met Lord Stothart in the middle of the set and sent him a polite smile.

He smiled back, his gaze lowering to her bosom. She swung away from him with a feeling of disgust. *He may be a gentleman by birth but certainly not by nature,* she thought with scorn.

When the quadrille finally ended, she swiftly crossed the room toward her mother, uncaring whether Lord Stothart escorted her or not.

Before she had the opportunity to speak to her mother, Mr. Elbridge approached and bowed.

"I understand that several waltzes will be played this evening. Will you do me the honor of dancing the first one with me, Miss Thorncroft?"

Mariah looked at the sturdy young man with some surprise. She could not help noticing how stiffly he spoke, his dark brown eyes barely meeting her gaze. They had scarcely shared a dozen words, and here he wanted to waltz with her! She found it rather strange.

Finding no polite way to decline, she smiled graciously. "I would be delighted, Mr. Elbridge." Besides, she loved to waltz.

Without a word, Mr. Elbridge bowed and strode off.

When he was far enough away, Mama turned to Mariah excitedly, with shining eyes. "Oh, Mariah, did you know he is heir to an ancient baronetcy! Wouldn't that be lovely? I am becoming quite chummy with Lady Walgrave. I will quiz her about Mr. Elbridge's circumstances."

Mariah looked at her mother in mortification and put a staying hand on her arm.

"No, Mama! Please do not! Especially not Lady Walgrave."

Mrs. Thorncroft halted, looking at Mariah with surprise. "Why ever not? She is a most charming lady and seems to know everything about everyone. Who better to ask?"

Casting about desperately for something to say that would make her mother reconsider her plan, Mariah stammered for a moment. "Please trust me on this. What if Lady Walgrave carried tales back to Mr. Elbridge about your questions? He might think it odd, and we have not even had our dance yet."

Mama sent her a doubtful look. "Well, maybe you are right. I will wait to see how your waltz goes before I make any discreet inquiries."

Thinking that it would be the first time her mother had ever practiced discretion, Mariah said, "That makes sense."

"But do try to be agreeable."

"I will do my best," Mariah said, intending to do nothing of the sort. "Excuse me, Mama. There is Lady Davinia, and I wish to have a word with her before the next set begins." It was the first thing she could think of to escape her mother's presence.

As she moved across the room, from the corner of her eye she saw the earl separate from Mr. Woburn and Lord Mattonly and approach her. Taking in how his dark hair and light eyes showed to advantage in his black evening clothes, her heart again clutched in that strange way.

She stopped. Obviously, he intended to speak to her.

"So you shall give Elbridge the honor of a waltz."

Startled, she said, "Yes, why?" instantly suspicious of his tone.

A half-smile curved his lips, and he shrugged slightly. "Although your virtue won't be in any danger, I advise you to be careful of your toes and your dowry."

Gasping in shock, she stared up into his amused eyes.

Beneath her sputtering, startled anger, Mariah felt

a stab of hurt. Even though she had no interest in Mr. Elbridge, the earl could not know that. Was he suggesting that the only thing a man like Mr. Elbridge would find attractive about her would be her dowry? This attack took her completely by surprise. After all, despite her awareness of his rakish ways, she had begun to feel that she and the earl had an understanding, even the beginnings of an odd sort of friendship. *Good heavens,* she chided herself, *my judgment must have gone begging to think such a thing.*

Lifting her chin, she tried her best to appear disdainful and strove to say something cutting. "My toes, dowry, and virtue are none of your affair."

Before he could respond, she turned on her heel and moved to where Lady Davinia stood with Mr. and Mrs. Spence-Jones.

Feeling flushed and upset, Mariah concentrated on the light chatter circling around her. Praying that no one would notice her flustered demeanor, she deliberately avoided looking in the earl's direction again.

By the time the notes of the first waltz filled the room, she felt so tense and troubled that she had lost her desire to dance. Thank goodness Mama was not close enough to notice something amiss.

She scoffed at herself for being so upset over the earl's comment. After all, what did she expect? She knew very well that he was an insensitive rogue. But such a charming one, her heart betrayed in a whisper.

As Mr. Elbridge approached, Mariah straightened her shoulders and took her wayward emotions in hand.

Silently, he led her to the middle of the room. As he put his arm lightly around her waist, Mariah experienced a hint of alarm. He began to lead her, a half step behind the tempo, without lifting his gaze from his feet.

Feeling a bit panicked, Mariah glanced around the room. She caught sight of her mama on the other side of the room, staring with her mouth slightly agape. From the corner of her eye, she saw the earl dancing with Lady Charlotte at the opposite end of the floor. A moment later, Mr. Elbridge—still concentrating on his feet—almost pushed her into Lord and Lady Walgrave.

Valiantly, Mariah struggled to follow her partner's lurching steps, with little success.

Her cheeks burning with mortification, she watched the other couples giving them a wide berth as they circled the impromptu dance floor.

"Do you like dogs, Miss Thorncroft?"

Startled that Mr. Elbridge had finally taken his eyes off his feet long enough to address her, she took a few measures to answer him.

"Dogs, sir? Why yes, I do."

Evidently Mr. Elbridge could not speak and dance at the same time. He lost completely what little sense of rhythm he had and now just moved her around in a swaying two-step.

"I have one of the finest kennels in all of Leicestershire. No one breeds finer foxhounds than I do."

Mariah could not help smiling at the pride so evident in his voice. "That must be quite gratifying," she offered, not knowing what else to say.

He must have realized that they had stopped dancing, for he suddenly pushed her into a turn and trod squarely on her left foot.

"M'apologies," he mumbled, helping steady her balance.

Trying to ignore the pain, Mariah sent him a tight-lipped smile. "Quite all right, Mr. Elbridge."

They resumed their awkward attempt at waltzing. "I am making plans to expand my kennels."

"Ah. That must keep you very busy."

"Yes indeed. Breeding foxhounds is much more complicated than you could imagine."

"No doubt." She winced as his knee bumped into hers.

"It takes a lot of capital to maintain a first-rate kennel."

"I am sure it does," she replied, praying the dance

would end before she found herself bruised from head
to toe.

"Your father owns a woolen mill."

It was a statement, not a question. *Mama!* Mariah
thought in silent accusation.

Suddenly she recalled the earl's warning to be careful of her toes and her dowry. He had predicted Mr.
Elbridge's behavior.

"Yes, he does," she said flatly.

"Does he like foxhounds?"

Good heavens! How was she supposed to respond
to that? Mariah wondered a little desperately. While
she wracked her brain for a reply, they continued to
sway clumsily on the floor for some moments. To Mariah's eternal gratitude, the music finally ended. She
immediately stepped back from Mr. Elbridge and sent
him a bright smile. "Thank you, sir."

Looking a little disappointed, Mr. Elbridge began
to escort her back to her mother. To her dismay, Mariah again saw the earl approaching, his black brows
pulled together in a fierce frown.

The earl stepped in front of her before they had
reached Mrs. Thorncroft. Ignoring Mr. Elbridge, he
said to her in a firm tone, "Miss Thorncroft, since you
so enjoy history, I would like to show you a painting
on the wall over here. It is a rendering of how Heaton
looked more than a century ago. I believe you will
find it interesting."

Solemnly, Mariah looked at the earl and realized
that unless she wanted to be unspeakably rude and
give him the cut direct in front of most of his guests,
she had no choice other than to go with him.

Thanking Mr. Elbridge again, Mariah took the
earl's arm.

He led her to the far side of the long salon. As the
other guests appeared to be occupied with conversation or dancing, they found themselves relatively
private.

Standing next to him in front of the large painting,

Mariah felt intensely aware of his tall body very close to hers. With the memory of his earlier words still stinging, she refused to look at him.

After a moment, the earl turned to her and said in a low voice, "It would seem that I am the one to have inadvertently stepped on your toes before Elbridge even had the chance. I would like you to know I meant my comment only as a friendly warning. Everyone knows Elbridge is on the hunt for a plump dowry and can't dance to save his life."

Mariah felt her cheeks grow hot. After the torturous waltz, she could not disagree with him, and could—almost—see the humor in the situation. Torn between laughter and embarrassment, she said nothing for a moment. However, something about his original remark still vexed her.

"I realize it is known that I have a large enough portion, but why would you think my virtue is so safe?"

Even though she knew her question to be shockingly unladylike, she could not help asking him. Inwardly, she cringed as she waited for his answer.

Dawning understanding cleared the frown from his brow.

"Now I see." His deep laugh rumbled through her body. "You must be aware that you are dashed fetching, so don't be a goose. Everyone knows that Elbridge only cares for gambling and his hounds—that is why your virtue is safe with him. It is an old joke among his friends. Nevertheless, I am deeply sorry that you were insulted by my maladroit attempt to tease."

His apology was so simply sincere and unexpected that she could say nothing for a moment. What a fascinating man. One moment his supreme arrogance shocked her, and the next, his gentleness disarmed her resistance.

"Thank you," she said softly, her defenses completely collapsed. "I know I should not be so sensitive, but I have sometimes encountered gentlemen who have found my dowry more attractive than they have found me."

"Then they are complete sapskulls and beneath your notice. However, I can empathize with you. My title is often the attraction, instead of my sterling character." His tone was light and full of amused self-deprecation.

A little laugh escaped Mariah's lips. "You have given me a new way to view your situation, my lord. You have the luxury of being just as horrid as you wish, and unmarried misses will still flock to your side."

A smile came to his lips. "Including you?"

"Me?" Mariah flipped open her fan, sending him a startled glance. "Never. I am learning too much from you to want to ruin our friendship by fawning over you."

"Then learn something else from me—learn to be horrid as well."

Mariah's eyes widened at his words. Beneath his light tone, she could discern that he was serious. "Whatever for?"

"If men are going to flock to your dowry, as women flock to my title, then make them work for it."

Looking up into those disturbing blue eyes, Mariah contemplated his words for a moment. "Even though I have no interest in Mr. Elbridge, I would not wish to be horrid to him."

She watched one beautifully arched brow rise. "Why not? He is only interested in your dowry."

"True," Mariah agreed slowly. "But that is what Society expects of him. It is almost his duty to marry a fortune."

"You are very generous in your attitude. But what of your sensitivity to being wanted only for your dowry?"

Struggling for the right words, she took her time before answering. "I *am* very sensitive about it, but that does not mean I don't understand why it happens.

Besides, even though Mr. Elbridge may be a fortune hunter, his innate good manners would make marriage bearable if I were inclined to settle."

The earl sent her a sharp look of amusement mixed with scorn. "I agree—good manners are preferable to passion."

Mariah, sensing he was trying to shock her, refused to look away.

"Is there a reason I cannot have both?"

The change that came over his features at her words caused her heart to skip. She supposed that her question could be taken as provocative or flirtatious, but she meant it seriously.

Somehow, they had established that they could speak frankly to each other. He was so sophisticated and experienced; she wanted him to answer her question honestly.

He said nothing and only gazed down at her with an odd expression.

A long moment passed. Mariah felt a strange, swirling tension building within her as his searing blue gaze held hers. Holding her breath, she waited for his response. Somehow, the answer felt vitally important to her.

"Miss Thorncroft, I believe—"

"Stone." Lady Walgrave's carrying tones cut through the earl's words. "Come dance with us. They are going to play a reel and you promised to be my partner."

Chapter Nine

*T*he next afternoon, Mariah wandered through the halls feeling restless and confused. She did not encounter any of the other guests, thankfully, before finally discovering the library.

At the sight of the two-story bookshelves lining the walls, she sighed with deep satisfaction. Loving books so much, she felt she had found a treasure trove.

In the middle of the room stood a beautifully carved, ancient oak table, obviously placed there so that the heavy tomes could rest on its polished surface and be perused at leisure. Walking around the table, she let her hand trail along its curved edge. Under the table, numerous portfolios nestled in rows of racks.

At the opposite end of the room, situated in the alcove of a large bow window, were two low, deep leather chairs. A small table stood between them. Next to the window, resting on an elaborate brass stand, was the largest globe she had ever seen.

How utterly perfect, she thought. Moving to the window, she set her leather case upon the small table, then moved to look at the bookshelves.

The earl's library was one of the most impressive features of an extremely impressive house. Her fingers skipped across history books and others on art, philosophy, and architecture. There were tomes in Greek, Latin, Italian, and French. The room held enough books to last an entire lifetime of constant reading. She sighed again, imagining herself sitting in one of those impossibly comfortable-looking leather chairs with a cup of tea and her pick from the shelves.

Even if she did not have a cup of tea, she could at least enjoy one of those impossibly comfortable-looking chairs.

Sinking into the buttery soft leather, she paused to pull her case onto her lap, thinking that she might draw a little to distract herself from her muddled thoughts. Gazing out the window, she tried to concentrate on the beautiful prospect of the lawn sloping down to the ornamental lake and the wooded area beyond.

It was a clear, cold day with a band of clouds edging the horizon. Dead leaves skidded across the lawn, and a breeze swayed the barren branches of a few chestnut trees in the distance.

At that moment, her heart leapt as she saw the earl and the rest of the male guests, including George, strolling toward the house across the damp, dead grass. Servants hurried ahead, carrying guns and baskets full of what looked to be dead grouse. Her little brother walked next to the earl, skipping to keep up with their host's long strides.

The earl, wearing a bark brown Carrick coat with several shoulder capes, smiled down at George. The earl was close enough for her to see, beneath the deep collar of the coat, his simple, loosely tied stock. He was hatless, his almost black hair swept back in the wind. His hunting clothes made him seem less formal, revealing a raw masculinity that caused a melting warmth to settle in the pit of her stomach.

She thought he looked even more striking than he had in his evening clothes last night.

Last night.

Dash it! What had he been about to say? she wondered for the thousandth time that day. She recalled the expression on his face the instant before Lady Walgrave had approached. Why did that dreadful woman have to interrupt them at that moment?

She caught hold of her tumbling thoughts and tried

to think in a more logical manner. Why did it matter so much what the earl had been about to say? Although refusing to examine why, she could not deny that it did matter. Very much. Putting her fingers to her hot cheeks for a moment, she felt bemused and completely unlike herself.

It was too bad that he was so dashed handsome and charming. No, she swiftly amended; it was too bad he was such an unrepentant rakehell. She closed her eyes, frustration mixing with her confusion. *Saint or sinner, what does it matter?* her heart whispered, betraying her best intentions to protect herself. He would never look at her the way he looked at Lady Walgrave. Why, she asked herself, did he have the ability to disturb her so easily?

Looking out the window again, she saw that the group had moved closer to the house now. George picked up a stick and waved it around in a parody of swordplay.

With the ends of his coat flapping in the wind, the earl looked down at George's antics with amusement. Gripping the sill, she leaned closer to the windowpane, looking intently at the earl. Tingling warmth constricted her heart as her gaze stayed riveted on the pair.

The earl stopped and held his hand out to George. The other men continued until they were almost beneath the window and out of her field of vision.

George handed over the stick, smiling up at the earl.

Lifting the stick, the earl made a slicing flourish in the air before assuming the stance of a fencer. An instant later, George imitated the earl—legs spread, left arm arcing behind.

Nodding approval, the earl handed the stick back to George and then picked up another thin branch from the windswept lawn.

For the next half hour, Mariah's gaze remained fixed on the earl and her brother, enchanted, as the earl gave the boy a very thorough lesson in the art of fencing.

George appeared to be getting the hang of it, and by the end of the lesson they engaged in a little swordplay.

George "pinked" his tutor, causing Mariah to smile at the earl's generosity. Then the earl patted George on the back, and they resumed their walk to the house, the impromptu lesson over.

Mariah turned away from the window, staring blankly at the bookshelf on the other side of the room, and considered what she had just witnessed. Had there ever been a more contradictory personality than the earl's?

This man, so patient and fun-loving with a little boy, bore little resemblance to the selfish libertine she knew him to be.

Moreover, she did not think that she had ever felt so torn in her opinion of anyone.

Hearing a noise, Mariah dragged her thoughts from the enigmatic earl and looked up to see one of the housemaids approaching.

After curtsying, she said, "Beggin' your pardon, miss. May I bring you a spot of tea? Or is there anything else you might like?"

Smiling at the pleasant-looking young woman, Mariah said, "Tea would be lovely. Thank you."

"My pleasure, miss. Would you like me to stoke up the fire? 'Tis a bit chilly."

"No need. I am quite comfortable. The tea will be warming me soon."

"Very good, miss. I will bring it straightaway." With another quick curtsy, the maid left the room.

Mariah watched her go, marveling at how happy and attentive all the earl's servants seemed to be. Alone again, she turned her attention to the leather case on her lap. She scolded herself for spending so much time thinking about the earl. Her contemplation of him was ridiculous as well as pointless, and she was much too intelligent to waste any more time on him. *There! That should take care of that,* she told herself sternly.

After untying the straps that held the case secure, she opened it and pulled out a few clean pieces of paper and a pencil. She closed the case, turned it over, and placed the paper on its smooth back.

Looking out the window, she studied the beautiful landscape before making her first line. As she had since childhood, Mariah soon lost herself in the intense feelings of creativity that always gripped her when she drew. She had done several sketches when she heard the maid approaching again.

Her smile froze when she saw that it was not the maid standing before her.

"I had no idea that you are an artist, Miss Thorncroft," the earl said, his brow arched in curiosity.

Except for the Carrick coat, he was dressed as she had seen him a little while ago—bottle green coat, tan waistcoat, buff leather breeches, and Hessian boots.

Gasping with surprise at his unexpected appearance, Mariah tried to gather up her sketches and rise at the same time.

"I am not! An artist, that is—"

He stepped forward quickly. "Please do not get up. I should apologize for interrupting your solitude. But, I confess, when I walked by the open doorway and saw you in such deep concentration, my curiosity forced me to barge in."

Flustered by his unexpected—and overwhelmingly masculine—appearance, Mariah did not know where to look. "It is nothing, really. Just something to pass the time."

Without asking her leave, the earl moved to sit in the chair next to hers.

"Art is never just something to pass the time. It is a higher form of thought and self-expression and worthy of the utmost respect."

Shoving the sheets back into the case, Mariah glanced at the earl in surprise. "I have never thought of it in that light before." She relaxed back into the chair, the desire to flee having vanished.

"Although I am being eaten alive with my desire to

see what you have drawn, I have surmised that you have no intention of showing me. Perhaps you feel as if you would be casting your pearls before swine?"

"Oh no, my lord!" she gasped, horrified that he would think such a thing. Then she caught the teasing gleam in his piercing eyes.

"I take great pleasure in drawing and painting as well," he continued. "Perhaps if I show you some of my work, you might in turn take pity on my curiosity and show me what you have been drawing."

Tilting her head to the side, Mariah considered his offer. "Maybe," she said in a noncommittal tone. "But I would truly like to see what you have created."

Smiling at her cautious reply, the earl rose and went to the oak table in the middle of the room. Squatting before it, he rolled out one of the racks and pulled a portfolio from it.

He returned to his chair and said, "Here is a watercolor I did while touring Italy some years ago." Sorting through the sheaf, he handed over a large, thick sheet of paper.

Accepting it with surprise, Mariah thought that she would never have guessed the earl had an interest in art. She had assumed that he cared for nothing but gambling and philandering. Yet she felt strangely honored that he would share something so personal as his artwork with her. Without saying a word, she careful examined the watercolor.

Her gaze traveled over the paper, taking in a blazing sunset over an Italian villa nestled on a hillside. The colors conveyed the vibrancy of a summer day. An amateur could not have created the play of shadow and light on the rooftop and hillside. She could almost feel the movement of the sun sparkling on the sapphire ocean in the background. A tabby cat lounging on the steps of the villa raised a smile to her lips.

She examined the watercolor for several minutes, feeling as though she held a beautiful work of art in her hands—one created by someone who obviously cared deeply for the subject matter.

Finally, she looked up at him, her hazel eyes glowing, and softly said, "You are an amazing artist, my lord! You have taken me from the cold English countryside to the radiant Mediterranean. If you were not a lord, you could make your living with such a gift. I am now even less inclined to show someone of your prodigious talent my paltry efforts."

Her last comment was not exactly true. She had never met a real artist before and already had a dozen questions for him on the tip of her tongue. Nevertheless, the thought of him being condescendingly kind about her meager scribblings still made her hesitate.

As if sensing her vacillation, the earl did not press her.

"Thank you. I hope my ability has improved through practice and study. But the greatest challenge I face when painting is to effectively convey the mood of the subject I am attempting to capture."

Eyes alight with pleasure at his insight, Mariah said, "I very much agree with you, my lord. I am always disappointed that I am unable to convey the *feeling* of the scene I draw."

Their eyes held in a moment of understanding before the earl continued. "Perhaps all artists struggle with this problem. My father was also something of an artist. That is one of his paintings." He gestured toward the far wall. "A small portrait he did of my mother shortly after their marriage."

Mariah gazed across the room to the simple yet obviously loving portrayal of a young, pretty woman.

"It's beautiful. Is it very like your mother?"

"Yes, even though it was done more than five and twenty years ago. I feel my father captured something elusive in my mother's expression, especially around the eyes, that reveals much about the humor in her personality. You will be able to judge for yourself next week when my mother and some of her friends arrive."

"I look forward to it. Did your father do many more paintings?"

"A few. There is one in my mother's drawing room

of me when I was a boy. I recall being prodigiously bored sitting for him. My father died when I was seventeen, so I treasure his paintings and sketchbooks."

Mariah looked back at him, her eyes clouded with sympathy. "So young? How tragic to lose your father in his prime. I am sorry, my lord."

He sent her a slight smile, his left brow quirked into an arch. "Father was past seventy and broke his neck riding while foxed."

"Oh!" Mariah struggled to suppress a shocked laugh at this revelation. Raising her hand to her mouth, she covered the laugh with a cough. *It really is not funny,* she chided herself.

"Do not be embarrassed. I was extremely sad to lose him, but I, too, shake my head and smile at the thought of that old man getting on a horse, drunk. My mother has never completely recovered from his death. Despite the vast difference in their ages, they had an extremely successful marriage."

"That is a blessing indeed."

"Yes. And I will always be grateful that he instilled in me his love of art."

A comfortable silence held them for a moment as Mariah continued to gaze at the portrait of the earl's mother.

Coming to a decision, Mariah opened her leather case and pulled out the sheets she had stuffed into it only moments ago. Giving herself no time to reconsider, she laid the stack on the table between them and pointed to the sheet on top, saying, "I tried for a little more detail with this one. I am not happy with the proportions of the trees and lake in comparison to the lawn and sky."

His features were expressionless as he picked up the first sheet and examined it carefully. Mariah watched his blue eyes scan each section with seemingly serious interest. She found it difficult to remain relaxed in her chair. This was the first time she had ever discussed her passion with another artist, and she found herself growing tense waiting for his opinion of her work.

He picked up the other sheets and examined those just as carefully. Finally, when she had almost reached the point of snatching the papers back, he spoke.

"There are a few techniques I can show you to help with your use of depth and proportion." His eyes stayed on the sheet he held in his long fingers.

Finally, he placed the paper on top of her leather case and looked at her, his expression serious and direct.

"Miss Thorncroft, you are an extremely gifted artist. I cannot express to you how impressed I am with what I have seen so far."

Ever uncomfortable with any kind of false flattery, Mariah could not hold his gaze. Looking down at her hands, she said quietly, "You are being too kind, my lord." She heard the flatness in her own voice.

"My dear," he said after a sharp laugh, "you should know me well enough by now to know that I am quite frank in my opinions."

She raised her gaze to meet his, a smile coming unbidden to her lips. "I will own that you do not hesitate to speak your mind."

"Then believe me. You are much more naturally talented than I am. I have just had better instructors."

Mariah laughed at this. "Considering that I have never been taught anything about drawing, I must concur with you."

His black brows rose in an expression of surprise. "I am even more impressed. To produce this quality of work with no instruction on the basics of drawing is amazing. I do have a number of books on the subject you will find interesting."

He pushed himself up from the chair and went to one of the enormous bookcases on the other side of the room.

Staring after him, Mariah gripped the armrests of her chair. *You have much more natural talent than I have.* So much for her judgment of him as insufferably arrogant. The men in her world would never admit that a woman had more talent than they did on any subject.

With her eyes riveted on his broad back, she wondered why her heart felt so strange.

This disturbingly handsome, completely unpredictable man elicited the most powerful feelings she had ever experienced. Unthinking, she rose from the chair and went to stand next to him as he pulled books from the shelves.

"Here are several books that I am sure you will find informative."

Her heart swelled at his praise of her talent. She kept her gaze riveted on his chiseled profile as he selected another book. Suddenly, a strange and overwhelming awareness of him caused her breathing to become tremulous and shallow. The quiet room felt warm. Inhaling deeply, she took in the faintly smoky, woodsy scent of him and savored it for a moment.

From the remainder of her good sense, a distant warning bell sounded. It cautioned her to think carefully, but she ignored the alarm, too enthralled and curious about these new sensations. With her eyes traveling over every inch of his finely wrought profile, she wanted him to look at her.

Her heart clenched again when a moment later he did. His contemplative frown cleared as their eyes met and held. Without taking his eyes from hers, he put the thick book down on the table next to them. Then he took a step closer.

"You have done something that few people have been able to do, Miss Thorncroft."

"I have?" Her husky whisper sounded strange to her ears. "How, my lord?"

"You have surprised me. Repeatedly."

"How very strange. I was just thinking the same thing about you."

She watched, fascinated, as a hint of a smile creased the corner of his mouth. With a subtle movement he drew closer.

Almost unthinking, she took a small step forward, her senses besieged by the sheer masculine beauty of his strong body and arresting eyes. Feeling herself tremble, she realized that she had never felt anything like the intense, yet languorous heat spreading through her limbs.

The room seemed to recede, leaving only her deep awareness of disturbing, yet welcome, new feelings that were wholly connected to him. Instantly, she knew that if he kissed her, she could not, would not, be able to resist.

Taking his time, he reached out and put his right hand on the curve of her waist. The warm strength of his fingers sent an exquisite shiver racing through her body. She swayed toward him.

The smile faded from his lips as his hand moved to the small of her back and gently tugged her closer.

With their bodies barely brushing together, Mariah opened her mouth to speak. As his other arm circled her body and drew her inexorably against him, she completely forgot what she had wanted to say.

Feeling herself pressed against his ironlike hardness, Mariah raised her arms and twined them around his neck. Taking an unsteady breath, she allowed herself a moment to absorb the heat of his body enveloping hers.

As she gazed into the depths of the earl's blue eyes, the feeling drugging her senses seemed mirrored in his gaze. *This must be desire,* came the distant thought.

Pulling her tighter against him, he lowered his head toward hers. An instant before she was sure his lips would meet hers, she closed her eyes, savoring the anticipation of his touch.

Feeling his warm breath on her lips, she heard him whisper her name. "Mariah."

At the passion-filled ache in his tone, she made a small movement, and the space between them, no wider than a sigh, disappeared.

As his firm lips met hers, there was a moment of shock at the strangeness of his touch, but the moment quickly crystallized into one of searing beauty. His arms tightened around her body as his lips moved over hers in a sensual tug. A feeling of wonder at this ever-increasing awareness caused her to press even closer to him.

Then, without warning, a loud, crashing clatter penetrated her sensual haze.

Instantly, they both turned their heads to see the maid, on her knees, picking up pieces of a broken teacup. Beet-red, she looked up at them with a mortified expression that matched how Mariah suddenly felt.

"I beg your pardon! I am so sorry, your lordship! I am ever so sorry." Frantically, the flustered maid began to mop up the spilt tea with her apron.

Briefly, Mariah closed her eyes. Passion's haze vanished in an instant, leaving her shocked and unable to look at the earl.

For a moment she could not move. Then his arms fell away from her. Stepping back, she walked across the room, circumnavigating the puddle of tea and the distraught maid. Trying her best to hold on to what remained of her dignity, Mariah kept her shoulders back and her gate measured. After what had just occurred, it would be too horrible to run from the room like a frightened rabbit.

Her raw senses screamed for her to look back at the earl. But she could not bear to chance what she might see in his eyes, now that the momentary spell that had held them was broken.

Without a backward glance she walked out of the library.

Chapter Ten

"*T*hat's all right, Sally. You may clean up the tea later," Stone instructed calmly. The little maid looked devastated for a moment, then quickly rose, gave a hasty curtsy, and scurried out of the room.

His expression grim, Stone stayed motionless. For a moment he could not dismiss from his mind the image of a pair of beautiful hazel eyes filled with dawning passion.

Finally he crossed the room and sat in the chair he had vacated only moments earlier. Running his fingers through his hair, he looked down at the leather case with the sketches resting on top. Miss Thorncroft had left it behind when she had stalked out of the room.

What just happened? he asked himself, loosening his neckcloth.

Admittedly, when he had walked by the library the sight of her practically curled up in the chair and concentrating so intently on her sketches had charmed him. Her alluring figure and lovely face framed by the bow window had caused his blood to stir. However, his curiosity about her drawings had intrigued him, and learning of her prodigious talent had impressed him greatly.

Just as it had in the gallery and last night, an air of palpable intimacy seemed to effortlessly envelop them. Determined to play the gentleman, he used the excuse of looking for books on art instruction to put some distance between them before he forgot that she was an innocent young woman.

When she joined him by the bookshelves, he had been taken aback by the banked sensuality in the depths of her beautiful eyes.

He really could not recall the last time a woman had so thoroughly jarred his senses. He shook his head in wonderment. This young woman—one step away from being a mere country girl, albeit keenly intelligent—had flummoxed him.

In spite of her transparent innocence, or perhaps because of it, Miss Thorncroft was proving to be a disturbing mystery.

Today was not the first time he had noticed a subtle, unconscious sensuality in Miss Thorncroft's manner. When he had watched her dance, he had found it difficult to keep his gaze from the sinuous movements of her body. He recalled the way her delicate fingers lingered caressingly on her wineglass during dinner. The need to feel her touching him in the same way hit him with unexpected intensity.

This last thought caught him up short.

He had played passion's game much too long not to know that Miss Thorncroft was the last woman to pursue for pure physical pleasure. No. A gentleman never took advantage of a woman who was not aware of the rules of desire. Despite the untapped sensuality he sensed in Miss Thorncroft, he could not attempt to seduce her.

Gad. The fact that this thought could have even crossed his mind showed what an astounding effect she had upon him. *I must take hold,* he told himself roughly. Miss Thorncroft was not only an innocent young woman; she was a guest in his home.

Besides, Mama Thorncroft would catch on in an instant if he started showing her daughter any amorous attention.

Coming to a decision, he rose from the chair. The simplest way to avoid trouble would be to steer well clear of all personal conversation with Miss Thorncroft for the rest of her stay. It should be easy now that he made up his mind. After all, he had held her lithe, firm body against his own for only a moment or two. And it had been only the briefest of kisses—nothing of import to a man of his tastes and experience. For some reason his frown deepened as he stalked from the room.

Halting several steps down the hall, he turned back, picked up Miss Thorncroft's sketches and leather case, and tucked them under his arm before leaving the library again.

As soon as she had walked—in a perfectly sedate manner—far enough from the library, Mariah picked up her skirts and ran down the hall until she reached the staircase. Cheeks burning, she flew up the stairs and down the corridor to her bedchamber. Closing the door, she crossed the room and threw herself onto the bed, hiding her face in the soft down pillow.

I must be mad!

An instant later, unable to tolerate her thoughts for another moment, she jumped from the bed and retrieved her moss green redingote and matching bonnet from the dressing room. Within minutes she found herself walking briskly along the graveled path through the formal gardens.

It took a few yards to realize that she could not walk fast enough to keep ahead of her chaotic thoughts.

The earl had kissed her! Even worse, she had kissed the earl! Had she turned into a wanton in an instant? She was utterly dismayed. She could not even comfort herself with the lie that the earl had taken her by surprise. No, she had not only anticipated the kiss, she had practically thrown herself at his head!

She quickened her steps and soon came to a bank of yew hedges. Had he somehow mesmerized her? There was no point now in denying that everything about him had fascinated her since her arrival at Heaton. Her cheeks flamed at how often her thoughts and attention focused on him.

It was pointless to deny that she found him exceedingly attractive—especially the way he looked at her. Recalling the expression in his eyes as they had stood together by the bookshelves renewed the shiver that had traveled over her body while in his arms.

How had this happened? How had she *let* this happen?

Did Lady Walgrave feel this way about the earl? At this devastating thought Mariah stopped dead on the path. Squeezing her eyes shut, she fought against the sickening sensation that washed over her. How could she have forgotten Lady Walgrave even for a moment?

Unable to stay still, she opened her eyes and continued to walk aimlessly through the parkland.

With every step she derided herself until, finally, anger came to rescue her from the mortification of her own shocking behavior.

How dared he! She clenched her fists. His practiced skills as a seducer may have fleetingly beguiled her, but he should have known better. After all, he was involved with Lady Walgrave. Did he think to have two dalliances going on at once? He probably thought it too good an opportunity to pass up, she thought bitterly.

"You unmitigated, unabashed, debauched, iniquitous blackguard," she whispered aloud, wishing that he stood before her so she could curse him to his face.

Then, just as soon as it had appeared, her anger vanished. Desolation swelled in her throat as she folded her arms across her chest against the cold. Desperately, she tried to think of what to do next. Everything had turned into such a tangle she could hardly think straight.

She knew only that she could not bear to face the earl again.

"Miss Thorncroft! I see that you, too, do not mind

a walk in this bracing weather. May I join you, or do you prefer a bit of solitude?"

Mariah's heart jumped. Turning swiftly, she saw Lady Davinia walking up the path behind her.

Smiling at the young woman, Mariah felt relieved that a friendly face had come to interrupt her from such distressing thoughts. "Not at all. Please join me, Lady Davinia." She hoped the petite blonde would assume that the chafing wind had caused the fierce blush still warming her cheeks.

Lady Davinia reached her side, and Mariah could not help admiring the way her high-crowned bonnet framed her lovely face. Her coat of sapphire blue serge, with its matching chinchilla collar and muff, evidenced the practiced artistry of one of London's most skilled modistes.

Their feet crunched along the graveled path as a bird sang heartily in the barren branches overhead. In silent accord, the two young ladies took a path that wended around the lake. Mariah's heart swelled at the beautiful surroundings. This outdoor world shimmered in shades of silver, blue, and gray, creating an almost ethereal beauty to the countryside.

After some minutes of companionable silence, Lady Davinia, in a tone that conveyed more than mere politeness, asked, "Have you been enjoying your visit to Heaton, Miss Thorncroft?"

Mariah almost laughed aloud at the question. "Yes, very much," she said instead. "It is a magnificent yet exceedingly comfortable home. Have you had the pleasure of staying at Heaton before, Lady Davinia?"

"Oh, lud, yes," Lady Davinia replied in a chatty tone. "My family has been friends with the Morleys for eons. Stone and my cousin, Mr. Spence-Jones, were at school together. Our families have visited back and forth over the years."

"What a lovely way to grow up," Mariah said softly.

"I suppose it was," Lady Davinia said, shrugging. "As a child, I used to love our visits to Heaton. But after my come-out it became rather awkward, so I

declined to join my family when they came for our
yearly visits."

Mariah could not hide her curiosity. "Goodness!
Why? I should never tire coming to Heaton."

"Well, my parents had always hoped that Stone and
I would make a match of it. Suddenly I no longer felt
at ease with the young man I had always thought of
as a dashing, if rather intimidating, older brother. My
parents made their disappointment at his lack of interest quite clear."

Starting in surprise, Mariah stooped to pick up a
bright orange leaf that had fluttered down to the
ground from a nearby maple.

"I can see why you would feel uncomfortable," Mariah said cautiously, thinking her words quite the un-
derstatement considering her own circumstances.

Evidently the daughter of a tradesman could have
something in common with the daughter of an earl,
Mariah thought with some surprise. Even so, she
never would have thought someone as polished and
confident as Lady Davinia could feel awkward about
anything. This realization gave Mariah a new perspec-
tive on the differences between the classes.

"It was more uncomfortable for me than it was for
Stone," Lady Davinia confided in a conversational
tone. "I am sure that he never noticed a thing. He has
always treated me—whenever he deigned to notice me
at all—with a sort of amiable kindness. Thank goodness my parents no longer expect Stone to suddenly
see me as his future bride."

"That must be a relief," Mariah replied.

"Yes. Now things are much as they used to be. This
time, when I learned that my cousins had also received
an invitation to Heaton, I did not hesitate to accept.
Stone's parties are always exceedingly diverting."

"So I have discovered," Mariah said softly, watching
the breeze whip up waves on the surface of the lake.

"I am even more pleased to be visiting at this time,
for it has been a pleasure to meet you and your
family."

Mariah turned her curious gaze to Lady Davinia. The sincerity in the other woman's voice could not be denied. But considering that they had hardly had a chance to converse, Mariah wondered if Lady Davinia might be referring to Steven when she expressed her pleasure at meeting the Thorncrofts.

"You are exceedingly kind, Lady Davinia. I can speak for my entire family when I say that we are most pleased to have made your acquaintance."

Lady Davinia blushed prettily beneath her fashionable blue bonnet. They continued to walk the path encircling the lake, and after some time Mariah felt her equilibrium begin to return. Despite her confusion about kissing the earl, she determined to take herself in hand. Now that she understood the full power of the earl's mesmerism, she could arm herself against her own attraction to him.

A niggling inner voice scoffed at her resolve. If only she could somehow persuade Mama that they should go home, all would be well. But Mariah could not think of how to persuade her mother to leave without explaining the reason why. No, she would just have to avoid the earl as much as possible until they could return home in a few weeks.

"Have you been acquainted with the earl's other guests for long?" she asked Lady Davinia a little while later.

"Oh yes, I have known Mattonly and Stothart most of my life, as well as Mr. Woburn and Mr. Elbridge. I have known Lady Charlotte and Mrs. Ingram from being in London for the last few Seasons. As for Lord and Lady Walgrave, they are quite a bit older than I am, but we have mutual friends."

Mariah wished she had a closer relationship with Lady Davinia so that she could ask her about the earl and Lady Walgrave. But what could Lady Davinia tell her that she did not already know? Scolding herself for forgetting her resolution to put thoughts of the earl out of her mind, Mariah tried to concentrate on

Lady Davinia's description of her plans for the upcoming holiday season.

"And Lady Haverstone visits with us shortly after Christmas, usually arriving on Epiphany. She and my mother have been friends since their girlhood."

Mariah was curious about the earl's parents. "I just viewed a portrait the late earl painted of the countess. Do you remember him at all?"

They took a turn in the path, and a breeze picked up to chill their cheeks before Lady Davinia spoke.

"I was a very little girl when he passed away, but he made quite an impression on me. Stone is very much like his father. Not only physically, but in character as well."

"How so?" Mariah could not resist asking.

"Well, like his father, Stone is both wild and devil-take-it brave yet very attentive to duty and protective of his property and tenants. Stone angered half the House of Lords with his progressive views on farming and animal husbandry. Then he shocks half of Society with his behavior in London. Everyone knows he inherited his contrariness from his father. I do remember being fascinated by how in love the earl and the countess were. Lady Haverstone was much younger than the earl, but it did not seem to matter. He was so handsome and vital, with thick, silver white hair that looked wonderful because he was rather tan from being outdoors so much. He was very tall, did not stoop, and did not have even a hint of a paunch. He had that same air of excitement around him that Stone does. Everyone was quite devastated when the old earl died after falling from his horse."

Mariah recalled the earl's expression of mingled sadness and black humor when he had described his father's death. Her sympathy deepened. "It was indeed a tragedy."

"Yes. I believe that Stone will emulate his father by enjoying bachelorhood for a good many years to come. However, my mother thinks that underneath his rakish exterior, Stone is rather romantic and would give up his wild ways the moment the right woman comes along, just as his father did. You know—reformed rakes make the best husbands and all that."

Mariah thought about this for a moment, her curiosity regarding the earl even more piqued. "But you do not agree with your mother's assessment?"

Tucking her hand deeper into her muff, Lady Davinia shook her head. "I have watched Stone for several Seasons now. He never looks at any of the misses in white muslin. He spends his time gaming, sporting, and making clandestine assignations with some of the most attractive married ladies in the *ton*."

Taken aback, Mariah stumbled over a rock in the path. Regaining her balance, she sent a startled glance to Lady Davinia.

"Don't tell me I put you to the blush!" Lady Davinia said with a laugh. "I had the impression that you are not the least bit missish. Was I wrong?"

"No, not at all," Mariah hurriedly replied. "Few things astonish me anymore, and I quite prefer plain speaking."

Lady Davinia sent her an impish grin. "I can be a bit of a gossip when it comes to some of the nonpareils. It's fascinating to watch all the ladies fawning and batting their lashes when they walk into a room. But I could be wrong about Stone. After all, I never thought his closest friend, the Duke of Kelbourne, would wed as early as he did. By all accounts he is blissfully happy with your dear friend."

Mariah nodded her agreement. "I can attest that I have never met two people who seem so wholly suited to each other. It is so lovely and romantic."

"There! You see, there is hope for all the confirmed bachelors."

Mariah laughed at Lady Davinia's jaunty tone, quite liking her even more than she had thought she would.

Eventually, as the weak sun began its descent, they meandered back to the house. Upon entering the great hall, Lady Davinia turned to Mariah with a pleased expression. "What an unexpected treat, Miss Thorncroft. I do hope we can continue to get to know each other."

"I, too, would like that," Mariah said, returning Lady Davinia's smile with a warm one of her own.

When they parted with the promise to see each other at dinner, Mariah sent up a quick prayer that she would not encounter the earl before reaching her bedchamber.

Chapter Eleven

*L*ater that evening, Mariah stood in the middle of her floor, dressed in a stunning gown of gleaming rose-colored silk and feeling too emotionally distraught to leave the bedchamber.

Once she had gained the privacy of her room after her walk with Lady Davinia, there had been nothing to distract her thoughts from the earl.

With mounting anxiety, she wondered how she could face him. This situation was beyond her experience, and she wondered how people behaved under such circumstances. The trembling in her limbs started anew as she again relived the moment when he put his hand on her waist and drew her unresistant body to his.

Her first kiss, she thought in wonderment, lifting her fingers to touch her lips. It had been nothing like she had imagined it would be. She had always dreamed that her first kiss would be with the man she loved—and that he would be her fiancé. She imagined him taking her gently into his arms, and in a sort of pastel haze their lips would softly meet in a romanticized expression of the joining of their hearts.

Nothing in her past had prepared her for the devastating intensity of being in the earl's arms. No pastel haze softened the burning feeling that had risen from the pit of her stomach as his glinting, sensual gaze had held hers. Nothing had prepared her for the yearning to run her hands across his chest and down his back.

As hard as she tried, she had not been able to rid herself of the feelings his touch had evoked. Something told her that he would sense this the moment they met again. Rogues probably developed some sort of instinct about these things, she thought cynically. This was why her feet felt rooted to the plush Persian rug.

Her nerves, so tightly strung, caused her to jump at the sound of a knock on her door.

"C-come in," she finally managed to say.

The door opened and a maid entered, carrying a salver with a note upon it. A footman followed and placed her leather case, as well as several books, on the bench at the foot of her bed.

"With his lordship's compliments, miss," the maid said, bobbing a curtsy.

"Er—thank you." Mariah hurriedly accepted the note and moved to the desk as the servants left the room.

As she broke the seal, her fingers shook so much she could hardly make out the words. Taking a deep breath, she noted the firm, upright penmanship before actually reading the brief missive. The note read:

> *Thank you for generously allowing me to enjoy your artistic talent.*
> *With my apologies,*
> *Haverstone*

She reread the note three times. A frustrated noise escaped her at the brevity of the note. *With my apologies.* What did that mean? Did he regret the kiss? Could the most profound moment of her life not have affected him in the least? With a sick, sinking feeling, she dropped the note on the desk and stared into the crackling flames of the cheery little fire.

She could not even put a name to the emotions rushing through her at that moment. She should be touched that he would be so gentlemanly as to apologize, and yet . . .

Putting her hands to her cheeks, she closed her eyes.

The thought of spending an evening in the earl's company was untenable. Maybe she could feign some sort of illness and avoid going down altogether.

At another knock at the door, she jumped up, quickly shoving the note into the top drawer of the desk. Before she could direct the person to enter, the door opened and her mother stepped in.

"Are you ready?"

Speechless, Mariah gazed at Mama, who looked resplendent in a gown of pumpkin silk with an ecru-colored shawl. Her ecru turban was fashionable to the last stare.

A frown began to pucker her mother's brow. "Is something amiss, Mariah, dear?"

Alarm flashed through Mariah. The surest way to make a difficult situation worse was to make her mother suspicious. Cautioning herself to be careful, she said in a nearly normal tone, "No. I am ready to go down with you."

Mama did not move and kept her gaze on Mariah's face. "Are you sure? You are not falling ill, are you? You look a bit strange."

Turning from her mother's perceptive blue gaze, Mariah went to the bed and picked up her shawl. "Lady Davinia and I took a long walk this afternoon. Perhaps I am a little tired."

Thankfully, the mention of Lady Davinia distracted Mrs. Thorncroft from her daughter's odd behavior.

"I vow, I have rarely met such a sweet and generous creature as Lady Davinia Harwich," Mrs. Thorncroft said as they left Mariah's room.

"I completely agree," Mariah said, feeling her panic escalate as each step brought her closer to the earl.

As her mother's ceaseless chatter flowed over her, Mariah told herself that everything would be fine if she could just maintain her composure. She must make sure to do nothing, by expression or action, to cause her mother to notice anything strange between herself and the earl.

"Have you heard what amusements are planned for

the evening?" Mrs. Thorncroft's question shook Mariah out of her reverie.

"No, I have not. Not more dancing, I hope."

"Oh no. We are to be treated to a musical evening. Lady Charlotte and Mrs. Ingram are evidently quite accomplished. They have offered to play and sing for us. I do wish you could sing and play the pianoforte so that you could exhibit your talents as well."

Mariah shuddered. "I can think of few things worse than having to perform in front of these people."

"Be that as it may, you must endeavor to sit near Lord Stothart or Mr. Elbridge."

Mariah sighed. "If I must sit next to either of them, it shall be Mr. Elbridge. He is the lesser of the two evils."

Mrs. Thorncroft waved her ivory fan at Mariah impatiently. "Why must you always speak so foolishly? They are both extremely fine gentlemen. However, I shall not complain if you choose Mr. Elbridge. He will do nicely. I just hope he inherits soon."

"Oh, Mama." Mariah shook her head, knowing that it was futile to start this old argument again.

They reached the salon, and the footmen on either side of the doors opened them at their approach. Mama immediately hurried toward Steven, leaving a relieved Mariah trailing behind to catch her breath.

At first she did not see the earl among the mingling guests and was grateful for it. A servant circulating with a tray of wineglasses approached, and Mariah accepted one with gratitude.

Unfortunately, her reprieve was short-lived, for she noticed the earl weaving his way through the guests toward her. With her heart racing at a gallop, she fought to keep her expression serene, though his tall, broad-shouldered frame and gleaming dark hair made this task difficult.

Lifting her chin, she forced herself to meet his gaze when he stopped before her. Inclining his head in the merest bow, his expression unperturbed, he said, "Good evening, Miss Thorncroft."

At his faint smile, Mariah felt some of the heat in her cheeks cool.

With my apologies. Now, gazing into his unreadable eyes, Mariah thought the meaning of those words could not be clearer—their kiss had meant less than nothing to him. She felt some of the warmth leave her heart as well.

What did she expect? she asked herself with bitter scorn at her foolishness. Kissing his female house-guests was probably only a momentary diversion for him.

Whipping up her pride, she told herself she did not care and squared her shoulders. Lifting her chin, she forced her features to impassivity. "Thank you for returning my case and for sending along the art books." She knew she sounded stiff and strange, but could not help it.

"My pleasure. Talent such as yours should be nurtured," he said, his rich, deep voice sending a faint shiver through her body.

"You are very kind, my lord."

She could not look away from his disturbing gaze, and several seconds passed in a strangely tense silence.

Vaguely, she was aware of the scent of fragrant wood burning in the enormous fireplace. The swirl of vibrantly colored silks worn by the other ladies melded around her into a riotous kaleidoscope, and the low hum of conversation seemed to recede.

She felt oddly removed from the happy, festive scene. The only thing that held her attention was the enigmatic expression in the earl's eyes.

This urbane, composed man bore little resemblance to the man she had kissed in the library. That man had seemed so intently, passionately absorbed by her that her heart fluttered at the memory.

Finally she could not bear another moment of the silence stretching so tightly between them, and she blinked, her tilted hazel gaze unconsciously revealing her confusion. "I accept your apology, my lord," she said softly.

Just for an instant she saw something flare in the depths of his unreadable gaze.

A second later the look was gone, and a sardonic smile twisted his lips. "I was rather hoping you wouldn't," he drawled.

With a half-bow, he turned away from her and began to circulate among the other guests. Staring after him in utter surprise, Mariah tried to discern his meaning.

Thankfully, Mr. and Mrs. Spence-Jones joined her at that moment. Smiling at the couple, Mariah wondered desperately how she would manage to get through the rest of the evening.

If I have to sit here and endure one more dueling aria, I shall grow cross-eyed, Mariah thought, doing her utmost to keep a pleasant expression on her face.

They had all entered the formal music room an hour ago. Since then they had been listening to Lady Charlotte and Mrs. Ingram—with an unexpectedly proficient Mr. Woburn on the pianoforte—trying to outsing each other, one exceedingly difficult piece following another. If she had been in a better mood, she would have found the whole thing rather comical.

At least she did not have to try to converse with anyone, she thought with a measure of relief.

Mrs. Ingram, who had a pleasing soprano voice, took her turn next and attempted a popular libretto.

As the pretty redhead's voice filled the room, Mariah, with an effort to appear offhand, allowed her gaze to sweep the guests. They all sat on ornately gilded chairs, arranged in several rows facing the performers. Mariah had taken a chair at the end of the second row. The earl sat in front of her, several chairs down.

Unable to stop herself, she found her attention lingering on his strong, angled profile for a few seconds. What had he meant when he said that he'd rather hoped she would not accept his apology? The question had tortured her all through dinner. She finally concluded, with an odd pang in her heart, that it meant nothing. The earl was an expert flirt, and she was a silly green girl for paying any attention to him.

The way he leaned his head toward Lady Walgrave, who sat next to him, caught her attention. Her heart clenched sharply at the sight of his dark head so near her fair hair. What a lovely couple they made, she thought bitterly. Whatever he was saying raised a smile to the elegant blonde's classic features.

Forcing herself to look away, Mariah wondered if the earl, despite his rakish behavior, could be in love with the married baroness.

She stared at the front of the room while Lady Charlotte joined Mrs. Ingram in warbling something in Italian, with mixed results.

Mariah's thoughts continued in this vein, and she wondered if Lady Walgrave was in love with the earl. After considering the possibility for a moment, Mariah had to concede that she probably was. Mariah wondered how it would feel to love a man she could never have. It would be quite dreadful, she concluded, almost feeling some sympathy for Lady Walgrave. Almost.

Mariah pitied whomever the earl did finally marry. The poor woman would have his name and position in Society, but she would never have his heart. Inexplicably, the ache near her own heart seemed to deepen.

She allowed her gaze to wander back to the earl before moving to some of the other guests. Lord Stothart, who was several seats down from the earl, met her glance with an almost leering expression on his pudgy features.

Affronted, she lifted her chin and looked away. His manner made her even more determined to avoid his company in the future.

Lady Charlotte and Mrs. Ingram continued to try to show each other up with their musical talents until the guests became noticeably restive.

Without her realizing it, Mariah's gaze traveled back to the earl's chiseled profile. Why did her heart thump whenever she looked at him? Why did that tingly feeling travel up her arms and down her spine when they spoke? Why had she responded in such an uncharacteristic manner when he took her into his arms?

A rather horrible thought came to her mind. What if she were falling in love with the earl?

The music seemed to stop. No! Only someone who did not have a care for her own heart could be so foolish as to fall in love with a man like the Earl of Haverstone.

I must stop this nonsense! she told herself firmly. *This foolishness can only lead to pain. I am not falling in love with him,* she repeated to herself several times. The thought was much too horrid to entertain. She tried to tell herself that she was only confused because his charm put an attractive façade on his true nature.

Clenching her hands in her lap, she thought of how desperately she wanted to go home. Maybe she could write to Papa and tell him Mama was losing money at piquet. That should spur him into demanding their immediate return.

However, that would take days, and she had a desperate desire to leave as soon as Harris could pack her bags.

Until she could convince Mama to leave—and she had not the vaguest notion of how to accomplish that—she would have to steel herself to behave normally.

"We were certainly given a rare performance tonight, do not you agree, Miss Thorncroft?"

Mariah turned startled eyes up to Lady Walgrave before allowing her confused gaze to sweep the rest of the room. Evidently, while she had been lost in her thoughts Lady Charlotte and Mrs. Ingram had ended their concert. The other guests had risen, and Mariah heard someone mention retiring to the salon to play cards.

She quickly stood up, retrieving the trailing end of her shawl. "Yes, my lady. A most enjoyable concert."

Watching the earl lead the way out of the music

room, Mariah and Lady Walgrave trailed a little behind the other chattering guests as they walked down the candlelit hallway.

"Miss Thorncroft, I desire a private word with you."

Turning to Lady Walgrave with surprise, Mariah saw the older woman gesture to the open door of a small withdrawing room adjacent the salon. Though Mariah was hesitant, sheer politeness forced her to follow.

Lady Walgrave moved to a pair of chairs by the fireplace and indicated with a graceful gesture that Mariah should be seated. Silently, Mariah sat down in the opposite wing chair.

"Yes, my lady?" Mariah gazed at the other woman curiously. Her golden gown revealed an elegant expanse of bosom, and her hair surrounded her face in a riot of pale gold ringlets. Mariah thought her face would seem rather angelic if not for the coldness in her sparkling blue eyes.

Lady Walgrave folded her hands on her lap, and a sweet smile curved her lips. "There is no use in pretending that you did not see Stone and me together the other night. I would like you to know that we do appreciate that you have been such a good girl and have not made any mischief for us."

Feeling as if the wind had been knocked from her chest, Mariah could say nothing. Had it really been only the other night that she stumbled across the earl and Lady Walgrave embracing in the garden? It seemed impossible, for a lifetime of events and emotions had occurred since then.

Lady Walgrave did not seem to notice her silence and continued in the same calm, kindly tone. "These situations are complicated and I am sure much too sophisticated for someone"—she paused as if searching for the right word—"well, someone from Chippenham to comprehend. But because of my friendship with Stone, I am very sensitive to everything that affects his happiness."

Clearing her throat, she fixed her narrowed gaze on

Mariah and continued. "I believe it would be best to speak plainly. I have seen the way you look at him. I sincerely caution you to spare yourself the humiliation of hoping he could ever notice you. You and your family may have a high opinion of yourselves because of your wealth, but that has no significance in our circles. After all, no one knows who you are, where your people come from, or your history."

Mariah felt her jaw drop. Lady Walgrave's words, though spoken in a kindly and calm voice, were the most insulting Mariah had ever heard. With her spine as straight as a ramrod, she felt a hot, humiliated flush rising up her neck and into her cheeks. *I have seen the way you look at him.* Despite her efforts, could she have been so utterly obvious? Mariah wondered as her mortification intensified. She loathed the thought of Lady Walgrave finding her behavior so transparent.

Lady Walgrave, her expression haughty despite the lingering smile, continued. "I intend no offense, of course. I just thought to save you from any more embarrassment."

Swallowing hard, Mariah forced herself to speak clearly. "You have made yourself extremely clear, my lady."

"Good." Lady Walgrave nodded approvingly. "I do not mind telling you that all of Stone's friends have been wondering what he could have been thinking in inviting you and your family here. You must admit it has been rather awkward. But I feel better now that we have had this chat."

She feels better! Mariah felt her mortification fade, and her anger began to seethe. Lifting her chin, she leveled her glinting gaze at the other woman.

"I am so glad you feel better, Lady Walgrave," she said, her tone icy with sarcasm. "You are correct on one point. My family does not have an illustrious name. But *we* at least have manners."

Gasping, the lady drew her light brown brows together in anger. "Such impudence! What do people like you know of manners? You only mimic your betters without any real understanding of how to conduct yourselves among Society. Make no mistake, you insolent chit, Stone shall hear of your impertinence. I should not have bothered to stoop to help you." She rose, twitching the skirt of her golden gown into place, and said in the tone of a queen carrying out a judgment, "I had intended to recognize you if we met again during the Season, but now I shall not."

Mariah remained seated, gripping the arms of the chair tightly. "Thank you."

Looming over Mariah with a look of wrath in her eyes, Lady Walgrave said, "Oh! You insolent mushroom. I shall not address you again."

Knowing that she could easily say something even more vexing, Mariah forced herself to stay silent.

Lady Walgrave swept out of the room and shut the door behind her sharply. Mariah, her heart-shaped face frozen in a look of forced composure and her hands still gripping the chair arms, remained by the fireplace for quite some time.

Chapter Twelve

After a dreadful night, full of fitful dreams of the earl and Lady Walgrave, Mariah awakened to a clear, bright morning with a bereft feeling weighing heavily upon her heart.

Harris had brought in her breakfast tray some time ago, but Mariah had not touched the food. Pushing her long braid off her shoulder, she turned over onto her side and again tried to drive Lady Walgrave's ugly words from her mind. At that moment, she saw a letter on the breakfast tray nestled between a delicate porcelain chocolate cup and the toast caddy. At the sight of the familiar handwriting on the front, Mariah pushed herself up onto her elbow and reached for the missive. After scanning the seal on the back, a smile came to her lips. The letter was from her friend Julia, the Duchess of Kelbourne. With a feeling of utter relief at having an excuse not to go downstairs, Mariah decided that she would dress quickly and go into the sitting room next to her mother's bedchamber to read the long missive. After tossing and turning most of the night, she longed for a distraction from her own befuddled thoughts.

A short time later, upon entering the pretty room, she was relieved to find it unoccupied. She had just settled into the comfortable sofa and unfolded the pages of the letter when Steven walked in.

"Here you are. Did you already have your breakfast?"

Mariah looked up from her letter and smiled at her brother. She thought he looked quite handsome in his brown cutaway coat that nearly matched his smiling hazel eyes. For an instant she was tempted to share the details of the ugly confrontation with Lady Walgrave last night, but she dismissed the urge quickly. It would only hurt him and probably make him defensive among his new friends.

"Good morning. Yes, I had breakfast in my room. I have just received a lovely long letter from Julia and am about to devour it."

"I shall not disturb you. I see that the weekly village paper has been left on the table over there. I shall peruse it while you enjoy the news from Kelbourne Keep."

"All right," Mariah said, sending him another smile before returning her attention to the letter. Steven settled in a wing chair across from her and picked up the newspaper. Mariah had just read past Julia's salutation when Steven spoke again.

"Is Lady Davinia not lovely?" he asked in a casual tone.

Mariah lifted her gaze to his. "Very lovely."

Setting aside the paper, Steven arose and walked to gaze pensively out of the bow window. "Such elegant yet easy manners," he added.

"Indeed." She was beginning to wonder where his observations were leading.

He turned from the window and looked at her with a serious expression. "And she is good-humored without being sharp or acerbic."

At his earnest tone, Mariah had a little difficulty suppressing a smile. "A true paragon."

"Yes, and a diamond of the first water. I have never met such an elegant and accomplished young lady in my life." His tone remained serious as he ran his fingers through his hair.

Mariah could no longer contain her gentle laughter. "Oh, Steven, I believe you are a fair way to becoming completely smitten."

He sent her a frown and began to pace the room. "Not a bit of it. Cannot a man admire an exceptional young lady without having everyone think that he is ready for the parson's mousetrap?"

Shaking her head, she laid Julia's letter aside. "You do not fool me."

Steven threw up his hands in an impatient gesture. "It does not signify if I fool you or not, Mariah. I know very well that someone like Lady Davinia would never look at someone like me. It only highlights her excellent breeding that she has been kind to me these last few days."

The uncharacteristically defeated tone in her brother's voice tugged at her heart. A feeling of protective concern surged through her as she shook her head in disagreement. "Do not sell yourself so cheaply, Steven. I do think Lady Davinia is an exceptional young lady, and she cannot help but see your innumerable fine qualities."

Steven continued to pace. "She is a member of the aristocracy. She is related to some of the most illustrious families in the country. Her father would never even consider the suit of a son of a woolen mill owner." A bitter note had crept into his voice.

"You do not know that for sure," Mariah said firmly.

Steven laughed without humor. "Give over, Mariah. You know as well as I do that we will always be considered parvenus. If we were not rich and if you were not friends with the Duchess of Kelbourne, no one would give us any notice. I received an invitation from the earl only because I was just foxed enough to be bold and he was in an odd humor. But to the beau monde we will always be inferior."

Her brother sounded as hopeless as she felt, Mariah thought as Lady Walgrave's stinging words replayed in her mind. She could think of no argument to rebut Steven's statement. Unfortunately, they both knew this was the way their world worked.

Despite her desire to leave Heaton, she wanted to

say something to rally his spirits. "That may be, but we *are* here, and we'd might as well behave as if we belong. Truly, who says we do not? You have nothing to be ashamed of, and I think Lady Davinia would be an exceedingly lucky girl to have you."

Before Steven could reply, the door opened and Mama walked in, looking rested and happy in a morning gown of ochre serge. "Here you are. Why are you not in the salon with the rest of the guests? I do not wish the others to think you are unsociable."

"We are hoping that absence will make the heart grow fonder," Mariah replied, tossing her brother an impish smile. He smiled back with a look that told her they would resume this conversation later.

"I suppose it's just as well to be here," Mama sniffed, moving to join Mariah on the sofa. "Lord Mattonly, though an interesting gentleman, can be a veritable chatterbox."

Steven took his seat again and sent Mariah a conspiratorial smile before responding to their mother.

"Lord Mattonly's attention toward you is beginning to cause whispers, Mama."

The look of astonishment Mrs. Thorncroft sent her son caused both her children to fight back their mirth. "What nonsense are you speaking, silly boy?"

"He's right," Mariah said quickly, following Steven's lead. "If you are not careful, you will find yourself saddled with a cicisbeo. I certainly hope Papa does not get wind of this." She fought to keep her features composed.

"Someday your wretched sense of humor will get you into trouble, my dear girl. I just hope I am there to witness your comeuppance."

Mariah smiled across to Steven, for her mother did not sound truly angry.

"You cannot deny that Lord Mattonly behaves like a mooncalf whenever you are near," Steven said, evidently unable to leave well enough alone.

Mama dismissed the notion with a wave of her

hand. "Tosh! I am twenty years older than he, if I am a day."

"It is common gossip that the Regent fancies mature ladies," Steven continued. "Maybe Lord Mattonly is just following the fashion."

Mama was beginning to look a touch vexed. "I will not listen to another word of your nonsense. I will change this ridiculous subject by asking if either of you has seen George in the last hour."

"Yes, he headed to the stables about then. Evidently he has made fast friends with the head groom," Steven offered.

Mrs. Thorncroft's brow cleared. "Well, I suppose he cannot get into much mischief there. I hope he tires himself out before bedtime."

"Why don't we bundle up and take a turn around the grounds?" Steven suggested. "At dinner your new beau will admire the roses in your cheeks."

"You are as incorrigible as your sister. I have no desire to go out in this weather, but do not allow that to stop you if you wish to walk."

"I am not averse to a stroll in the garden," Mariah said to Steven. Refolding her letter, she decided to save it for later. "Shall I meet you downstairs in ten minutes?"

Half an hour later, Mariah and Steven reached the edge of the formal garden, then took another path that led to a charming arbor Mariah had discovered on a previous walk. They had exhausted the topic of Steven's admiration for the seemingly unattainable Lady Davinia. Mariah's best efforts to encourage him met with little success. She shook her head at how he seemed to concede the race for her hand before it had truly begun.

"Enough of me, Mariah. Though I appreciate your support and encouragement, we shall not solve my dilemma today."

"I suppose not," Mariah agreed, stuffing her cold hands deeper into her otter-skin muff.

"Speaking of admirers," Steven began, his tone changing dramatically, "you certainly are leading a couple of gentlemen on a merry chase."

Sensing the beginnings of a tease, Mariah sent him a mock scathing look. "Just because I have danced. with Mr. Elbridge and Lord Stothart does not mean I am leading them anywhere, or that they would follow if I did."

"I am not numbering Mr. Elbridge among your admirers—he never talks of anything but his dogs. No, our host is the other gentleman I am speaking of."

Reaching the arbor of birch trees and witch hazel hedges, they both sat on the wide stone bench. Mariah turned to look at her brother in wide-eyed surprise. "What are you speaking of?"

Steven flicked some dust off his Hessian boots before sending Mariah a pointed look. "Oh please, Mariah. False innocence does you no credit. It has not escaped anyone's notice that you and the earl seem to have developed an instant . . . er . . . camaraderie, shall we say."

Mariah bit her lip. Lady Walgrave's words came back to echo Steven's—*I have seen the way you look at him.* Mariah sputtered a few false starts before she felt capable of responding to her brother's alarming assertion. "That is the most ridiculous thing I have ever heard!"

Ignoring her protest, Steven continued. "I am surprised that Mama is not panting over the fact that the earl singled you out during the dancing for a tête-à-tête on the other side of the room. And if she could have seen the two of you in the gallery the other day she would be ready to have the banns read."

Even though Steven's tone was light and teasing, his words sent a frisson of alarm up her spine. If Mama knew what had occurred in the library yesterday— The thought was too mortifying to complete!

"Mama believes the earl and Lady Charlotte have an understanding. Besides, the earl and I have discussed only the most mundane subjects." She felt the instant flush come to her cheeks at the lie. Kissing the earl, albeit for only the briefest of moments, could not be considered mundane by any stretch of the imagination.

"It's not the words. It's the expressions on your faces that have caused so much comment."

Truly shaken, Mariah jumped up from the bench and began to pace along the graveled path in front of her brother. "What a packet of nonsensical twaddle! I cannot believe you have given it any heed," she retorted sharply.

Steven looked doubtful. "Is it nonsensical? You cannot deny that Stone has rather singled you out. You should be beyond pleased. He is of the first consequence and a dashed handsome devil."

Mariah looked at her brother in horrified shock. The other guests had actually discussed her and the earl! How mortifying. It would be the height of folly to allow such gossip to continue. If Mama heard, she might reverse her decision to set aside her hope for the earl as a prospective son-in-law—and begin her heavy-handed matchmaking schemes all over again.

"I do not care!" With mounting agitation she threw down her muff on the bench next to Steven and continued to pace. "The earl may be handsome and charming, but there is nothing to recommend him to any self-respecting young woman. I would be in constant fear of having to sell the silver to cover his gambling debts. And who would wish to live with the possibility of stumbling over his latest mistress around every corner? I could never entrust my heart to such an unabashed, unmitigated rakehell."

Steven, looking up at her from the bench, held up his hands in surrender. "Goodness, Mariah, don't get into such a pet. I was just teasing you about the gossip circulating among the guests. You've certainly lost your sense of humor since coming to Heaton."

She continued to pace. "Well, I can do without that kind of gossip." The words came out more waspishly than she intended.

Steven rose from the bench. "It's getting colder. Are you coming back with me or are you staying here, Miss Grumpy?"

With her anger abruptly spent, she smiled sheepishly up at her brother. "I shall stay out for a while. Mayhap the bracing weather will improve my mood," she said by way of apology for her prickly tone.

"I hope so," he said, grinning. "I will see you at dinner."

She watched her brother stride off, confusion furrowing her brow. Telling herself Steven must have been exaggerating, she felt her alarm begin to subside. After all, one or two conversations with the earl could not really have everyone speculating about them. Could it?

Deciding to walk down to the lake, she picked up her muff and left the bench. She rounded the end of the hedge—and ran straight into something solid.

Staggering back in surprise, she looked up into a pair of ice-cold blue eyes. The earl stood before her in a heavy black overcoat, hatless, with feet braced slightly apart.

Swallowing hard, she glanced back to the hedge and then to the bench she had just left. A cold wave of shock washed over her as she realized that he must have overheard her scathing comments about him to Steven. Her distraught gaze flew back to his.

They stared at each other for an immeasurable length of time, his grim expression and pale gaze chilling her to the heart. Every harsh insult she had just uttered against him repeated itself in her mind as mortification washed over her in waves. She groped in vain for something to say.

Finally, when she could no longer stand the tension vibrating between them, he sent her a smile as bitter as the look in his eyes. "I assure you, Miss Thorncroft, your vehemence is completely unwarranted."

He then performed a courtly bow and stalked off, leaving her staring after him with a veil of tears shimmering in her eyes.

Chapter Thirteen

$\mathcal{A}$fter staying out in the garden for some time, Mariah finally returned to the house, still fighting tears.

Once inside Heaton, she pulled open the first door she came to and swiftly stepped into an antechamber. Shutting the door behind her, she leaned back against it, taking great gulping breaths. Several minutes passed before she felt her heart begin to beat normally.

"What am I going to do?" she said aloud.

Pushing away from the door, she scarcely noticed the elegant blue-and-cream room as she removed her coat and bonnet. Laying them on a chair, she began to pace the floor, her hands clenched together tightly.

Could anything be more utterly horrid than what had just happened? A fresh wave of embarrassment caused her to halt her pacing. She stood stock-still, cringing at the memory of the earl's cold gaze searing into hers.

Fighting more tears, she tried to think clearly, to come up with a way to extricate herself from this awful predicament.

A thought suddenly presented itself. She ran back to the door and stepped into the hallway.

A footman walking down the hall turned at the sound of her call.

"Please, will you find my brother Mr. Thorncroft, and send him here to me?" She knew her voice sounded anxious, but that could not be helped.

"Right away, miss," the young man said, then moved swiftly down the hall.

Mariah stepped back into the room and shut the door. Resuming her pacing, she waited impatiently for her brother to come to her.

There was nothing else for it, she thought with sudden resolution. She would have to tell Steven what had happened. He would, she prayed, be able to help her unravel this horrible tangle.

Finally she heard the door open. Relief flooded over her when her brother came in.

Looking concerned, Steven strode toward her. "Are you ill, Mariah? You look terribly pale."

Reaching out, she took his hands, her anxious gaze seeking his. "Steven, the earl was walking near the arbor when we were there."

He looked baffled. "Yes?"

Dropping his hands, she said in alarm, "Do not tell me you have forgotten what we were talking about."

After another moment's contemplation, understanding dawned on her brother's features. "I hope you don't believe he heard what you said. You called him an unabashed, unmitigated rakehell!" An ashen pall settled on his face.

"I know what I called him," Mariah said through gritted teeth. "And I do not believe he heard—I *know* he did."

Steven stood very still. "How?"

"Because I literally ran into him, and he told me my vehemence was completely unnecessary." She could barely get the words out over the tears clogging her throat.

"I cannot believe this, Mariah! What are we going to do?"

Clasping her hands before her, Mariah met Steven's distraught gaze. "As much as I know he would like to, the earl is much too well-mannered to ask us to leave. We will just have to convince Mama that we must go."

Steven instantly nodded his agreement. "Her

screams will be heard from one end of the house to the other," he said with gallows humor.

Mariah shook her head despairingly. "I know. But if you are with me when I tell her, it might not be so bad. It really does not matter if she rolls on the floor kicking—we must leave."

"Yes, we must."

Hearing the flat disappointment in his voice, Mariah reached out and grasped his arm. "I am so sorry, Steven. I know how much you have been enjoying yourself."

"Do not fret. I goaded you into saying what you did with my teasing. Besides, who could have imagined that he would be there at that moment?"

Mariah sighed, dejected. "How do we tell Mama?"

Steven thought for a moment. "She is resting right now, so I would not disturb her just yet. But this must be dealt with well before dinner. I will go up and direct the servants to start packing our trunks. We will stay at the inn in the village tonight and leave for home in the morning."

Mariah nodded, grateful for his decisiveness. "Thank you, Steven. I will remain here for a little while before we go up to face Mama."

"I understand. This room has the added appeal of not being much in use, does it not?"

She smiled a little at his understanding. "Yes, it does. I shall try to compose myself in the next little while."

He leaned down and kissed her on the cheek. "Very good. I will meet you in your room later. Do not worry. Mama will see reason. But for now there is much to do." With that, he swiftly left the room.

Moving wearily to the sofa, she sank into it with an intense feeling of despair. Now she would have to confess everything to Mama. As much as she loathed the thought of this, she could think of no other way to leave Heaton before the house party ended. Surely Mama would see that they had no choice.

Tears welled again, and a bitter shame scorched her.

Why had she said those dreadful things about the earl aloud? She knew she would never be able to forget the harsh look in his eyes—so different from the way he had looked at her before their kiss.

Her heart clenched in despair at the memory of that brief but intensely beautiful moment—now gone forever.

At the sound of the door opening, she turned, expecting to see that Steven had returned for some reason. To her surprise Lord Stothart stood in the doorway.

"Miss Thorncroft. I have found you at last. The footman said I would find you here."

With a start, Mariah looked at him in dismay.

Shutting the door behind him, Lord Stothart approached. Stiffening, Mariah frowned at his cat-that-got-the-cream smile. She liked the fact that he had closed the door even less.

He was almost upon her before she stood up slowly and sent a pointed look at the closed door. "I shall leave you to enjoy the solitude of the salon, sir."

"Actually, Miss Thorncroft, I desire a word with you. You will be pleased when you understand why I have bent the rules of propriety." He chuckled, his second chin quivering like aspic.

A feeling of alarm spurred Mariah to take several steps to the side in an attempt to move past the grinning baron. He slid in front of her. Frowning, Mariah realized that unless she wished to walk on the sofa she would have to stay still for the nonce.

Remaining silent, she looked at him coldly with a brow raised in query.

Clearing his throat, he steepled his fingers together and pressed them to his lips. His eyes swept her figure in a furtive manner she found disgusting.

"Well then. I have been keeping my eye on you these last few days and have come to the conclusion that we will suit each other quite well. Normally I would approach your father first, but I decided there was no need to be so formal with people like—"

Watching the unattractive red flush at what he had

almost said stain his cheeks, Mariah stared at him in astonishment, scarcely believing she had heard him aright.

Running a finger along the inside of his cravat, Lord Stothart swallowed hard before resuming his speech.

"That is to say, I shall call upon your father as soon as it is convenient, to work out the details of our betrothal."

Mariah knew she was gaping at him, but she could not help it. Taking a step back, she felt the backs of her legs pressing against the sofa.

As he continued to send her that self-satisfied grin, she felt a searing anger and contempt suddenly rise up within her. She did not think that she was any more vain than other young women her age, but she wondered what nerve made this repulsive toad, title or no, think that he could aspire to her hand.

"Do you, perchance, consider what you have just said to be a proposal of marriage? If so, I must tell you that I decline your offer. Please step aside, sir."

It was Lord Stothart's turn to gape. His hands dropped limply to his side as he sputtered, his face turning an odd shade of purple.

"I cannot believe you are fully cognizant of the honor I am bestowing upon you, Miss Thorncroft. I will ignore your insulting behavior and suggest that you take on a more respectful tone toward me in the future."

Enough! Mariah thought, anger sparking in her eyes. Heedless of his bulk over her, Mariah pushed past Lord Stothart and headed for the door.

Within a few feet of the door handle, she felt his hot, fleshy fingers grab her upper arm.

Outraged, she tried to shake off his grasp as he swung her around to face him, placing himself in front of the door. Fury distorted his features, and if she had not been so angry, the look in his eyes might have frightened her.

"Let go of me! How dare you behave in such a boorish manner!"

Dropping her arm, he said, "And how dare you act as if you are too good to accept me. Are you so foolish that you believe you have the chance of a better offer? You may be an attractive chit, but without your dowry you are one step above a scullery maid. Who are your people? Where do you come from? Anyone would consider that I am being quite generous to overlook such flaws and offer you my family name. Yet you insult me," Lord Stothart sneered, his tone scathing.

Mariah had never felt so deeply shocked. Could this be how the earl felt as well? After all, he and Lord Stothart had been friends since childhood. Perhaps beneath the thin veneer of highly polished politeness, all the earl's guests thought as Lord Stothart and Lady Walgrave did—that anyone not born in their world must be a less worthy creature. *How sad and disturbing,* she thought. She dismissed her concern an instant later, for her immediate problem was Lord Stothart standing between her and the door.

Clasping her hands together, Mariah strove for composure. She said in a clear if unsteady tone, "My family name may not be as illustrious as yours, but *you* have nothing to recommend yourself to *me*."

The anger that twisted his features caused her a jolt of fear. Swiftly, she tried to dart past him and reach the door again. He grabbed her wrist and jerked her body back around, pulling her against him.

As a feeling of horror swept over her, Mariah gasped for breath. "Stop! Let go of me at once!"

Ignoring her demand, Lord Stothart lowered his face to hers. Feeling almost ill with shock and revulsion, Mariah pummeled his shoulder with her free hand, shouting for him to stop. Desperately, she turned her face away from his.

"You think you're too good for me," he sneered as his fleshy lips began to press hard, damp kisses against her neck.

Feeling faint, Mariah fought for air as he squeezed her tighter.

"Stop!" She heard the panic in her own voice as if from a distance.

Still straining to keep her face turned away, Mariah suddenly heard the door open behind her.

"What the hell—"

Hearing the familiar voice, she felt heady relief flood over her.

The arms tightly embracing her abruptly loosened, and Mariah staggered back, putting several feet between her and the baron. Regaining her balance, she swiftly looked up to see the earl standing before them, a frown as black as thunder marring his brow.

Glancing back to Lord Stothart, Mariah saw his flushed, sweaty face, and another shudder of revulsion went through her body.

At the sight of the earl Lord Stothart's eyes seemed to bulge from his head. "Stone!" he blustered, looking ashamed and defiant at once. "Miss Thorncroft and I were having a private conversation."

Mariah gasped in outrage, and her gaze flew to the earl. It would be too horrible if he believed that she had willingly embraced Lord Stothart.

Hands clenched at his sides, the earl stepped forward and Lord Stothart took a quick step back.

"If I did not hesitate to distress Miss Thorncroft any further, you would now be naming your second, Stothart. As it stands, you will leave my home immediately."

At the hard edge in the earl's voice, Mariah quickly shifted her wide-eyed gaze to Lord Stothart.

He darted Mariah a contemptuous look before turning back to the earl. "Come now, Stone. Surely you are not going to let a nobody cause a rift in our friendship," he said with a feigned laugh.

With a look of disgust, the earl slowly shook his head, drew back his right fist, and landed a fierce punch to Lord Stothart's jaw.

Cringing at the sickening noise made by the contact, Mariah raised her hands to her face. "Oh my!" she gasped.

Lord Stothart stumbled backward, landing in a sprawl on the wing chair behind him.

"What friendship?" the earl said calmly. "Get out. Now."

Clutching his chin, Lord Stothart scrambled to his feet. Mariah could not find any sympathy for the shock and pain on his face.

Without another word the dazed man scrambled past Mariah and the earl. He yanked the door shut behind him with a crash, and the noise reverberated through the room. Staring at the door, Mariah realized that her shaking hands were still on her cheeks and that her heart was pounding.

With great effort she lowered her hands and smoothed her skirts, aware of the earl's eyes upon her.

"Are you all right, Miss Thorncroft?"

She marveled at the calm composure in his deep voice.

Looking up into his eyes, which expressed a combination of anger and concern, she said, "I think so, my lord. I . . . It happened so quickly. I cannot thank you enough—" To her mortification, her voice broke and unexpected tears choked her words.

An instant later she felt his strong arms come around her in a gentle embrace.

Unresisting, Mariah rested her head against his solid shoulder and shut her eyes to keep the tears from spilling.

"Do not thank me, my dear. I am ashamed that you were subjected to such ugliness in my home."

Sensing the depth of his sincerity, Mariah felt soothed. She took a shuddering breath, and some of the fear and tension left her still-trembling body.

She stood silently in his light embrace, eyes closed, as his firm hand stroked her upper arm reassuringly. Soon the anxiety ebbed away as she allowed herself to sink trustingly against him. Thank goodness he had entered the room when he did! He had actually punched Lord Stothart—his friend—and demanded that he leave, she marveled.

Suddenly she became keenly aware of her cheek pressing against the exquisite fabric of his coat and the firm chest beneath it. The faint, heady scent of bay rum and tobacco teased her senses. She found it odd that even though the shock of Lord Stothart's attack receded quickly, her heart had not slowed its quick pace.

"Mariah, I am very sorry."

The softly spoken words vibrated over her body. Some deep intuition told her that he was not just referring to what had occurred with Lord Stothart. The rapid tattoo of her heart skipped a beat.

Opening her eyes, she lifted her head to look up at him and met his serious, somber gaze.

The expression in his intensely blue eyes caused an inexplicable tingle to travel up the insides of her arms and settle in her chest.

His arms did not tighten around her. He remained motionless, his gaze not leaving hers. Mariah's lips parted. She needed to speak to him but did not know what to say.

At a sound of the salon door opening, they both turned their heads.

Mariah's heart sank to her slippers at the sight of her mama's shocked face.

"Mariah! My lord!"

Chapter Fourteen

*F*eeling stunned on top of her shock, Mariah watched her mother step quickly into the room and close the door behind her. A feeling of cold dread crept over Mariah.

The earl dropped his arms from around her but not before he gave her arm one last squeeze. She was vaguely aware that he did not step away.

Beneath the surprise on her mother's face, Mariah suspected calculation lurking in her gaze as well.

Of course! Mariah thought with growing bitterness. No matter how much her mother loved her, Mariah knew her first instinct would be to determine how best to take advantage of this excellent opportunity.

Mrs. Thorncroft stepped farther into the room. "My lord! I am astounded! I am sure I do not overstep myself by demanding to know your intentions toward my daughter."

Mariah's heart sank past her slippers, down to the dungeon George had informed her existed beneath the oldest part of Heaton. The silence hung between the three of them until Mariah's nerves stretched past her bearing.

If only she was the delicate kind of female who fainted easily, she thought with rising desperation. Fainting would be a lovely escape from this mortifying scene.

Unfortunately, she stayed upright and her mother

continued to look at the earl expectantly, obviously
waiting for him to make an offer for Mariah.

What must he be thinking at this moment? she
thought, her heart clenching with a sickening pang.

She could not bring herself to look at him. After
their kiss in the library, then the awful scene after he
overheard her insulting him, he had saved her from
the disgusting advances of Lord Stothart. If that was
not bad enough, he was now forced to answer her
mother's ridiculous question.

Mariah doubted that it would be possible to recover
from the devastating feeling of shame and mortification draining the color from her face.

Feeling helpless, she watched the avid expression
on her mother's face, and without warning a bubble
of mirth rose in her throat.

"Mrs. Thorncroft, I—"

At the sound of the earl's firm voice, her unexpected laughter suddenly burst forth, cutting off what
he had been about to say.

To her increasing humiliation, laughter shook her
frame as the earl and her mother turned to look at
her in surprise.

Try as she would, Mariah could not gain control of
her wayward mirth. At the look of baffled anger her
mother sent her, Mariah clutched her sides as a wave
of inexplicable hilarity sent her into another gale of
trilling laughter.

"Mariah! Have you taken leave of your senses?"
Mrs. Thorncroft asked sharply. She turned her wide-
eyed gaze to the earl. "I assure you, my lord, my
daughter is normally the most sober-minded of
young ladies."

At the nervous, almost pleading tone in her mother's voice, Mariah laughed even harder.

She knew she must appear mad, but she did not
care. The culmination of the past few days' tensions
and strange events were obviously having a bizarre
effect upon her, but somehow this half-hysterical

laughter was better than breaking down in tears in front of the earl.

"Mariah, I insist that you catch hold of yourself. Go to your room at once. I will come to you after the earl and I have had a chance to discuss this shocking matter."

"N-n-no!" With the greatest of efforts, Mariah gained a semblance of control over herself.

Moving away from the earl's side, she approached her mother, placing her hand on her arm.

"Mother, I *must* have a private word with you." The firmness of her tone was somewhat diluted by her fading hiccups of laughter.

"No," Mrs. Thorncroft said, looking determined. "Now do as I say."

Mariah did not intend to be put off by her mother's unyielding tone. Gripping her arm, Mariah said, "Mama, please. I *must* speak to you before this goes any further."

Meeting her mother's gaze, Mariah silently, and desperately, willed her to come away.

The instant she saw the slight softening in her mother's expression, Mariah sighed in relief and her helpless laughter finally subsided. Nevertheless, she did not release her mother's arm.

"Excuse us, my lord. We shall have to delay our discussion," Mrs. Thorncroft stated as she turned to the door with Mariah.

"At your convenience, ma'am," the earl replied.

Mariah glanced back at the earl and met his quizzical gaze.

Something in the way he stood in the middle of the room clutched at her heart. He seemed utterly unperturbed by what had just occurred—completely confident and at his ease.

How she envied him his composure! And yet . . . And yet something deep within her wished that he did not seem so unaffected by what had happened—not just what had happened today but over the last few days as well.

He stood there, still gazing at her with an enigmatic expression.

A wry, defeated smile came to her lips. "I think we should just blame all this mischief on the moonlight, my lord."

Before he could respond, she followed her mother out of the salon.

Once in her room, Mariah thanked heaven they had not encountered any of the other guests on the way. Turning to her mother, she stated without preamble, "We must leave at once."

Mama looked as if Mariah had just suggested they jump off the roof. "What nonsense is this? I saw you in the earl's arms as plain as the nose on my face. We are staying and arranging for your betrothal to him. Why are you behaving so oddly? Although I am surprised, this is above wonderful. Why did you not tell me that you and the earl had developed an understanding?"

Mariah clasped her hands together in mounting frustration. "Because we have not! You have no idea what occurred between the earl and me. Come sit down and let me reason with you, Mama."

Although Mama frowned, they moved to the chairs in front of the fireplace. Once seated, Mariah took a deep breath before launching into her story, deliberately leaving out the kiss and the encounter with the earl by the hedgerow after insulting him to Steven—she would rather not have to mention that unless it was absolutely necessary.

After explaining how Lord Stothart had insulted and accosted her, she told her mother how the earl had offered her comfort.

"So you see, Mama, nothing of a truly intimate nature happened. He was just being chivalrous after Lord Stothart's shocking behavior."

Mrs. Thorncroft looked quite crestfallen for a moment. "Lord Stothart is certainly worse than a lout and a bounder. I am shocked that a gentleman by birth would behave so boorishly. You must not tell Steven of this or he will call Lord Stothart out. Oh, Mariah, this is a horrible turn of events," she said with anguish, and then suddenly her expression brightened. "All may not be lost. The earl may still be able to be worked upon. He is a gentleman after all—"

"Mama!" Mariah jumped up, anger vibrating through her being and determination glinting in her hazel gaze. "I will not have the earl trapped into marriage. No matter how badly you want me to marry a peer, I will not stand for this. I have always done my best to be a good and respectful daughter. I have always tried to understand your desire for a titled son-in-law. But enough is enough. If you wish me to throw the biggest fit seen by this rarefied segment of the *ton*, then you will press me on this."

"Mariah!" Mrs. Thorncroft raised her hands to her bosom, her expression revealing genuine shock.

"I mean it, Mama. I intend to be in a carriage within the hour."

Watching the play of conflicting emotions cross her mother's features, Mariah waited. She felt the blood pounding through her veins. Never before had she felt so steadfast in her resolve. She could not tolerate the idea of her mother trying to force the earl to offer for her. In fact, the thought of ever seeing the earl again was unbearable, and if she had to sneak out of Heaton and walk all the way to Chippenham then that was exactly what she intended to do.

Mrs. Thorncroft must have seen the determination in her daughter's eyes, for she leaned back in the chair with a defeated huff.

"Very well, Mariah. You are rarely so stubborn, but when you are like this I know there is little I can do to change your mind."

Sagging with relief, Mariah closed her eyes and lowered her head. "Thank you, Mama," she whispered, wondering why this rare taste of victory held no sweetness.

Chapter Fifteen

As her booted feet crunched through the thick layer of frost covering the ground, Mariah kept her head down against the damp chill. After several more minutes of striding across a field in a purposeful manner, she finally paused to catch her breath and look around.

To her surprise, she had almost reached the causeway that led from Chippenham to Langley Burrell without even realizing she had walked so far. She had been so lost in her thoughts that she had given little notice to her surroundings until she found herself miles from home.

Pausing, she gazed at the beginning of the causeway for some minutes. At this spot the stone structure was really only a raised path; it would not incline to a proper causeway for several more miles.

She remembered the first time her mother had told her of how the causeway had come to be. More than three hundred years ago, the turn in this area was very different. There were very few roads, and those that did exist were nothing more than rutted cart paths, low-lying and prone to flooding. In the neighboring village of East Tytherton lived a good woman, a widow of independent means who desired to create the causeway so that all could "walk dry shod." Mariah had always loved hearing about Maud Heath, finding it amazing that a woman who had lived so

long ago could make her own decisions about how to
distribute her monies.

By Deed of Gift, Maud made a bequest large
enough to have the five-mile-long causeway built. Mariah marveled at the fact that the remaining money
was still held in trust to this day, almost three hundred
and fifty years later, for maintenance on the structure.

Walking along the causeway, especially where it
crossed the river Avon, always gave Mariah a sense
of pride in her village and a sense of history. She
would imagine her ancestors using the causeway to
take their eggs or livestock to market, grateful to the
good widow for easing their way.

Maud Heath had been an amazing woman, just as
Alice of Surrey had been, she thought, wishing she
could emulate these two strong women.

Curling her fingers deeper into her ermine-lined velvet muff, Mariah made a wide arc across the rolling
countryside to return home from a slightly different
direction.

The gray day, the sky low and dark with the threat
of rain, seemed to match her mood. Despite the cold
nipping at her nose, she was glad she had walked so
far. The distance would keep her from home that
much longer. Glancing down, she noticed how damp
her boots had gotten and how the chill had seeped in
to her toes. Shifting her direction, she walked to an
old lane that took a circuitous route back to the
manor. She knew her feet would stay dryer on the
path and that it had the added benefit of taking even
longer to return home.

Not that home was awful, she mused. She just sorely
needed a reprieve from her family. To leave behind
all the concerned faces she would gladly walk for miles
in the autumn chill.

Hunching her shoulders, she recalled how just this
morning Mama had clucked and shaken her head in
concern over Mariah's subdued demeanor at breakfast.

In truth, she could blame only herself for her parents' smothering concern for her. The night they had

returned to the manor from Heaton, Mama had immediately pulled Papa into his library and closed the door. Lord only knew what she had told him, but he never mentioned the visit to Heaton and only watched her with an uneasy expression on his handsome features whenever they took a meal together. Sometimes Mariah felt that if Papa patted her shoulder in that sad way one more time she could easily break something.

Sighing as she sidestepped a puddle, she chided herself for not behaving normally. She really did try to act as if nothing was wrong, but the more she tried to force cheerfulness for her family's sake, the more they clucked and patted.

Thank goodness Steven did not behave in the same exasperating way. She had seen little of him since their return from Heaton a few days ago. Although he did not stare at her in the woeful way their parents did, she did think him unusually quiet at mealtimes. It was obvious to her that he had changed since meeting Lady Davinia, and Mariah's heart went out to him, though she could think of nothing to say that would help the situation.

George was the only member of the Thorncroft family who seemed to behave as if all was fine. George would chatter happily about the marvels of Heaton and would often wonder aloud if they could go back someday.

His childish ramblings made Mariah cringe—in fact, any reminder of Heaton seemed to cause such a reaction.

She walked along the path, a faint breeze pulling tendrils of wavy hair from beneath her bonnet, and suddenly realized that there was no use hiding from the truth any longer. She missed Heaton.

Even after so short a time at the magnificent estate, the contrasting clutter of the manor oppressed her even more. She recalled Heaton's main salon, with its expansive view of the rolling parkland and lake, and wished she could empty her home of half its contents.

Despite the grandness of the formal rooms, there

had been a feeling of lightness and spaciousness about Heaton that Mariah had quickly grown to love. Everything about the earl's estate had delighted her senses. It was a place where she could spend a lifetime exploring and sketching.

It was quite strange, but it seemed to her, during those few days, that her life suddenly had so many possibilities. It was as if Heaton had uncovered depths of emotions and thoughts that she had not realized existed—depths she could not seem to examine here in Chippenham.

A vision of light blue eyes, dark hair, and broad shoulders came to her mind. Maybe it was not Heaton that had enchanted her so thoroughly, her heart whispered.

Stopping dead on the path, she scolded herself for her wayward thoughts. Days ago, she had vowed that she would cease thinking of the earl. Why would her thoughts keep returning to him when doing so only caused a sharp pain in her heart? She hardly knew herself anymore. It made no sense to think about a man so wanting in morals that he could carry on an affair with the wife of his friend, practically under that friend's nose.

Yet she could not seem to muster her previous shock over such behavior. No, what came to mind more often was how she had been able converse with the earl so easily and how he had admired her drawings without even a hint of condescension. She recalled how they had teased each other and talked together and how he had given George fencing lessons on the lawn. She remembered the way he studied her sketches as if he were interested and, then, the barely leashed passion of their kiss.

These were the memories that caught at her heart, causing her to walk and walk until she returned home so tired that her sleep would not be disturbed by thoughts of the earl.

She reminded herself that leaving Heaton had been for the best; to stay would have just caused her more confusion regarding the earl. No, best to forget the earl and Heaton altogether. Besides, despite his gallantry concerning Lord Stothart, the earl had told her that her "vehemence was completely unnecessary."

Again, as she had done almost every day since returning home, she vowed that from this moment on, she would have control over her emotions and forget that she had ever met the contradictory Earl of Haverstone.

By the time she returned home Mariah was tired and chilled to the bone. Passing several urns and chests and chairs and any number of sculptures, she made her way wearily upstairs, wondering if she could beg off dinner. A moment later, she thought better of it, knowing her parents would only cluck and pat all the more if she did not join them at mealtimes.

Opening her bedroom door, she saw Harris laying out her dinner clothes on the bed.

"There you are, Miss Mariah. I was just about to send a groom out to look for you. If you don't hurry you will be late for dinner, and you know how that annoys the master."

Mariah began to unbutton her coat, sending her maid a wan smile. "There is plenty of time, Harris."

"A letter arrived for you, miss," Harris said, placing a shawl next to the gown. "By messenger."

Mariah's hands ceased their activity. "A letter? Where?"

"On your desk. I've never seen anything as fancy as the seal."

Mariah rushed across the room, knowing whom the letter must be from before reaching the desk.

Picking up the thick, folded parchment, she needed only the swiftest glance to recognize the handwriting.

"Julia!" she said with a heartfelt whisper. Breaking the seal, she sat down in the desk chair, unable to wait a moment longer.

"Miss, you will be late!" Harris cautioned.

"Oh, bother dinner. Julia's letter cannot wait."

Harris shook her head disapprovingly but left her mistress to read in peace.

Unfolding the letter quickly, Mariah read:

> *Dearest Mariah,*
> *I shall dispense with the pleasantries and tell you that I am on tenterhooks as to why you left Heaton in such a precipitous manner. Your last letter was much too brief and mysterious for my liking, but I have a very clever plan to bring you to my side.*
> *I have been redecorating a number of the rooms here at Kelbourne Keep and find that I can no longer do without your exquisite eye for color and detail. I will send a coach for you and insist that you stay until shortly before Christmas. I am sure that your parents would not wish you to stay through the holiday, anyway. My dearest husband entreats you to come, and looks forward to seeing you again. Do say yes, Mariah dear. I will have the coach made ready so that it can leave the moment you respond to this letter. See, I take it for granted that I shall be seeing you within the fortnight.*
> *Give your parents my regards, and tell them that I know they can do without you for a month. Is Steven still breaking the ladies' hearts? I shall close now so that you may direct your maid to pack your trunks.*
> *With my love,*
> *Julia*

With tears shining in her eyes, Mariah felt a wave of gratitude and relief wash over her. This letter from her dear friend felt like a gift from God. To see Julia would be too wonderful, and the time away from home would be more than welcome. Now she needed only to convince Mama and Papa to let her go.

Impulsively, she left her room and ran down the

stairs. Rushing through the house, practically knocking over delicate tables around every corner, Mariah finally found her mother seated at her desk in the little drawing room off the long gallery.

"Mama, I must speak to you!"

"Goodness!" Mrs. Thorncroft said as she looked up at her daughter's flushed cheeks and shining eyes. "Such a flurry! I have been wondering where you had gotten off to. At least take off your redingote and sit down like a civilized young lady before you tell me why you are so excited." Her smile softened her words as she set aside her quill and household ledger book.

"I've received a letter from Julia!" Mariah's fingers flew over the dozen jet buttons down her deep cranberry coat. Flinging the garment over the sofa arm, Mariah pulled a chair close to her mother's. "She wants me to come for a visit. She and the duke would like me to stay until almost Christmas. Please, Mama, will you speak to Papa? I would dearly love to go."

With a look of surprise, Mrs. Thorncroft sucked in her breath. "Gracious! The Duke and Duchess of Kelbourne. I still find it hard to fathom that Julia Allard—always so unfashionably tall—has reached the zenith of the social world."

"Never mind that." Mariah waved away her mother's oft-repeated lament. The whole family knew that Mama would never recover from her disappointment and envy over what she deemed Julia's "good luck."

"I would love above all things right now to visit Julia at Kelbourne Keep."

Mama smiled, reached forward, and patted Mariah's arm reassuringly. "Of course we may go. Will there be other guests as well? Perhaps some of the duke's friends may be visiting? It would only be fitting that your oldest friend should use her connections to help you—"

The excitement froze in Mariah's heart. "No, Mama! I do not believe that there will be other guests. I will let you read Julia's letter—she specifically invited me. I do not wish to start an argument, but is there any reason I could not go alone? I would take Harris, of course, but I would love to visit Julia. . . ." She did not know how to explain to her mother how she felt without sounding disrespectful.

"You would like to visit Julia without me?"

With a pleading gaze, Mariah said, "That's not what I mean at all. It's just that . . ."

As she groped for the right words, her eyes clouded with distress. How could she say, right out loud, that if she did not get away from this house and away from the oppressive expectations of her parents she would run mad?

Mrs. Thorncroft leaned forward, a frown marring her youthful features. "What is it, Mariah? You may speak plainly. Your papa and I have noticed how unhappy you seem of late—since coming home from Heaton. Are you still upset over Lord Stothart's insult?"

"No, Mama," she said flatly. "I have not given Lord Stothart another thought."

"Then what is so wrong? We have never seen you this way. You have always been rather quiet, but not like this. I do not believe you have sketched anything since our return. You spend all your time at the parish school or walking all over the countryside. We are becoming quite worried."

Touched by her parent's concern, Mariah marshaled a reassuring smile. "Maybe this dismal weather has put me in the doldrums. As for Julia's invitation, it is not that I do not wish for you to come, but Julia made no mention of anyone else accompanying me. She wants my help choosing fabrics and paint for some of the redecorating that she is planning for her home."

Mrs. Thorncroft continued to contemplate her daughter with a concerned frown. "In truth, it would be a most inconvenient time for me to leave. As you know, we shall be having a house full of relatives over the holidays. I had thought to do a little rearranging myself. Heaton has inspired me to make a few changes around here."

Mariah raised a brow in surprise, distracted for a moment from the subject at hand. "Indeed? What have you planned?"

"Well, I may store some of the furniture and—and things. Heaton, despite its grandness, seemed so open and airy. The lack of fussiness has given me a few ideas."

Mariah could scarce believe it. Evidently Heaton had worked a spell over her mother as well.

"But that is unimportant," Mama continued. "Maybe a change of scenery will do you good. But promise me if an eligible friend of the duke's—"

The powerful yet indefinable emotion that had been growing inside her since leaving Heaton suddenly burst from Mariah so quickly that she could do nothing to stop it.

"Mama, please! Does it not make any difference to you what happened at Heaton? Can you not forget your desire to see me married to a title? Everyone there sees us as parvenus, as mushrooms! I would rather spend the rest of my life alone than ever again place myself in the position of having a man like Lord Stothart insult me so grievously. He believed I should be *grateful* for his disgusting attention because he perceived me as a grasping nobody."

Seeing the look of stunned surprise on her mother's face only spurred her passionate outburst. She continued, her voice trembling with the intensity of her emotion. "It would have been a future too mortifying to contemplate to have the Earl of Haverstone marry me because my dowry proved too much of a temptation against his gambling debts. And it would have been just as bad to have taken advantage of his kindness toward me after Lord Stothart's loutish behavior. Mama, I beg you to set aside this ridiculous pursuit of a title at the price of my dignity. Our time at Heaton taught me something I shall never forget—I may not have any chance of happiness in the future, but I refuse to let go of my chance for peace." Spent, Mariah leaned back in the chair and turned from her mother's astounded gaze to stare into the flames leaping in the fireplace.

Uncaring that her mother was about to ring a peal over her head for such impertinence, Mariah felt an odd sense of relief wash through her body at finally verbalizing some of the frustration that had been building within her for so long.

A tense silence hung between mother and daughter for some moments. When she could no longer tolerate the silence, Mariah sent an anxious glance to her mother. The look of surprise and concern on her face took Mariah aback.

"I had no idea that you felt this strongly about my desire for you to marry well," her mother said softly.

Mariah shrugged and held her hands up in a defeated gesture. "I was never happy about it, but I never wanted to quarrel with you. Now I can no longer be silent. The earl's house party changed everything."

"Yes, I believe it did," Mrs. Thorncroft said, nodding her head slowly. "I never meant to hurt you, my dear, but I see now that I pushed too hard. It is just that you are so beautiful and sweet and intelligent, I could not bear to see you marry a mere mister."

"Oh, Mama." She did not know what to say as tears clogged her throat.

Mrs. Thorncroft bit her lip and looked very near to tears herself. "Now no need to cry after you have stated your piece so well. 'Tis all very simple, my love—you shall visit Julia and have a lovely time, and I will not mention your marrying a peer again."

A look of stunned surprise came to Mariah's face as her mother opened her arms.

"Oh, Mama," Mariah said again, hardly believing this turn of events. Slipping from the chair to her knees, Mariah wrapped her arms around her mother's waist and laid her head on her lap. She did not fight back her tears any longer.

"There, there," Mrs. Thorncroft said right before Mariah felt a kiss on the top of her head.

For some time, the heavy tears flowed in a healing

stream down her cheeks as her mother continued to murmur soothingly and stroke her back.

Mariah fully realized what this concession cost her mother, and the gratitude for their new understanding swelled within her heart.

"Thank you, Mama."

"I just wish you had told me about Stothart before we left Heaton," Steven said in an angry tone as they both sat in the salon the next afternoon.

"There really was no point to it," Mariah replied. Steven still had not forgiven her for waiting until they had returned home to tell him of Lord Stothart's perfidy.

"No point? I think defending my sister's honor would be the point." Rising, he crossed the room to look upon the rain-dulled scenery outside. He slapped his clenched fist into his palm. "Dash it, Mariah, I would have liked to flatten that jackanapes."

Smiling at her brother's protectiveness, Mariah tried to soothe his annoyance. "There was no need. The earl flattened him quite nicely."

"I know," Steven said glumly. "But I should have had a chance at him as well. I will tell you this—if I ever see him in Town I shall challenge him."

Mariah's eyes opened wide with concern. "Don't be a goose. If you meet Lord Stothart in London, you must give him the cut direct. He is beneath your notice."

Steven frowned for a few moments. "Maybe that would be the best way to deal with him. After all, Stone will certainly no longer address him, and therefore Stothart will never be fully accepted by Society again."

At the mention of Stone, Mariah felt a fresh pang of despair. Since leaving Heaton, an ache seemed to lurk in places within her heart she had not known existed before meeting the earl. She wondered what he was doing at this moment. Imagining him hunting or painting was infinitely preferable to envisioning him with Lady Walgrave. Halting her painful thoughts, she reminded herself that it did not matter what he was doing, because she would probably never see him again. At this realization, the pain in her heart intensified.

"So you shall be visiting the Duke and Duchess of Kelbourne?"

Mariah nodded at her brother's question, for her upcoming trip had been the main topic of conversation at the manor since yesterday.

"You shall enjoy yourself," he continued.

"I always have a wonderful time with Julia. What plans have you made for the next month or two?"

He turned from the window to look at her with grave hazel eyes, his square jaw set firmly. "I have come to a decision. I know our parents want me to live the life of a gentleman, but I am bored with this idleness. Watching Stone deal with his estate matters showed me that even fine gentlemen are not always idle."

This was something new indeed, she thought, looking at her brother with keen curiosity. "I like the sound of this. What are you going to do?"

"The foundry in East Tytherton is facing foreclosure. I intend to buy it. I have many ideas for improvements and expanding its operations."

"You have already investigated this? You have discussed this with Papa?" she asked in surprise.

"Yes. Over a year ago I heard the foundry was in trouble and began to look into what it would take to manage it. Father says that he trusts my judgment."

"I don't know what to say, Steven. You never mentioned your interest in the foundry. Are you sure this is what you want to do?"

He turned back to her, and she thought a new air of maturity had suddenly settled over his handsome features.

"Yes. I did not completely commit to the idea until we returned from Heaton, but now I am sure."

Mariah looked down at her hands for a moment. "Our visit to Heaton seems to have had a profound effect on all of us. But I must ask you about Lady Davinia."

"What about Lady Davinia?" he replied gruffly.

Sending him a gentle, understanding smile, she said, "I will not press you, but you must know that you cannot gammon me. It was as plain as the nose on my face that you were smitten by her. Can you just set that aside so easily?"

"I have no choice."

The grimness in his tone made Mariah realize how deeply her brother cared for the lovely Lady Davinia.

"We always have a choice," she stated with a new-found maturity of her own. "Besides, I believe Lady Davinia was developing feelings for you as well."

Steven shook his head, a look of pain crossing his features. "Don't be so naive, Mariah. You know very well that we could never truly be accepted into Society, no matter how rich we are. Lady Davinia may have enjoyed my company, but looking at me as a potential husband is a completely different matter. She can marry any man she wants—why would she marry one who sullies his hands in trade?"

"What if she wants you? I am not so foolish as to believe that everyone would see your marriage as completely advantageous to Lady Davinia, but if she loves you what would it matter?"

He pressed his lips together in a grim line. "There was nothing in her manner toward me that suggested anything other than kindness. I must not pine for what cannot be if I am to move forward. The foundry is the kind of challenge I want. I intend to make a success of it on my own."

"I have no doubt that you will make a great success of whatever endeavor you involve yourself in. But I intend to write Lady Davinia before I depart for Kelbourne Keep. I will send her your regards."

Steven opened his mouth to protest, then closed it a moment later and sent her a sheepish look. "Do as you see fit."

"From now on I shall attempt to do just that," she said with a glint of resolve in her eyes.

Chapter Sixteen

"*W*here is everybody?"

Stone had just left his office after his monthly meeting with the mayor of Morley Green and had intended to join his guests in the grand salon, only to discover the room empty.

The footman he questioned bowed and said, "Her ladyship took everyone to have tea in the conservatory, my lord."

Of course. He should have known, he thought with a smile before heading down the hall. "Thank you, Thomas."

The conservatory had always been his mother's favorite place in Heaton. During his boyhood, the conservatory had been a place filled with laughter from the extended Morley family. He had watched his parents enjoying themselves as they pored over plans to improve and expand the room. Now he rarely entered the impressive octagonal space with its exotic flora, Grecian urns, and friezes, unless he had company.

The footfalls from his tasseled Hessian boots echoed along the lengthy corridor as he walked to the other side of the house.

He would have liked to show Miss Thorncroft the conservatory. No doubt, with her keen artistic eye, she would have had an interesting opinion of the unusual room.

His steps slowed, and he came to a halt beneath

one of his favorite paintings—a portrait of his father by Ramsey.

However, he was not gazing at the painting, only staring through it with a frown. Why would he want the high opinion of an unsophisticated young woman who thought of him as an unabashed, unmitigated rakehell? he wondered, feeling annoyed with himself for allowing Mariah to enter his thoughts again. *Well, aren't you all those things and more?* came the unbidden thought.

He resumed walking, telling himself that he was relieved to be shed of the Thorncrofts. If Miss Thorncroft had not shown the good sense to convince her mother to leave Heaton, he would now be contending with an extremely awkward and potentially embarrassing situation.

Impatient fingers raked his thick dark hair as he turned the corner and stepped through the wide, arched entry to the conservatory.

Before him, beneath the domed glass ceiling, the remainder of the earl's original houseguests mingled with the new. His mother, who had arrived yesterday with his Aunt Elizabeth and several cousins, sat with Lord and Lady Walgrave, Lady Davinia, Mr. and Mrs. Spence-Jones, Lady Charlotte, and Mr. Woburn. Mrs. Ingram, Lord Mattonly, and Mr. Elbridge had departed that morning, bound for other amusements.

He paused just within the entryway and scanned the group. His mother, regal in a purple-and-gray tea gown, held court beneath the glossy, draping fronds of a banana tree. She never wore a mobcap, and her dark hair looked extremely fashionable piled high on her head.

By the hum of voices, the conversation certainly seemed lively. A hint of a smile curved his mouth until he heard the gist of the discussion.

His smile disappeared, replaced by a grim set to his jaw as Jane Longmarch, a cousin on his mother's side, spoke in a complaining voice. "My lady, I thought there would be a young gentleman Percy's age staying at Heaton. Percy's now terribly disappointed and bored."

His mother set her teacup down and turned to her niece. "Yes, Stone mentioned in his letter that a family by the name of Thorncroft was staying. Evidently, they left rather unexpectedly. Percy will just have to entertain himself."

Stone had indeed encouraged Jane to bring her son, but that was when he thought the Thorncrofts would be staying for several more weeks. He would have liked Percy to meet George, he thought with a hint of regret. Stone had found master Thorncroft to be an engaging and intelligent youngster—and the boy was definitely more rough-and-tumble than the coddled Percy.

Stone now recalled with some amusement how he had at first been against George's joining the men during the grouse shoots. The boy had not been shy in proclaiming that he had been hunting since he was "little" and that he knew how to behave. That had started an instant friendship of sorts between them. George had chattered about the excitement of the yearly sheep shearing and about the frogs he collected from the banks of the river Avon. Stone had also learned of how George fished with his sister and how she had come to his defense when some bigger boys had tried to bully him away from his favorite fishing spot. This had piqued Stone's curiosity about Miss Thorncroft even more.

Shamelessly, he had taken full advantage of George's trusting, garrulous nature and asked him any number of questions about his intriguing sister, all of which the boy answered in unhesitating and full detail.

Felicity Walgrave's voice carried through the room, pulling him back to the conversation taking place before him.

"Oh, la! Thank goodness the Thorncrofts departed a few days ago. I fear I found them much too coming. They were a rather pushy family, my lady, and I hate to say it, but they took advantage of your son's generous nature."

The dowager Countess of Haverstone raised her dark brows in surprise at Lady Walgrave's description. "This is the family referred to as 'charming'?"

Stone noticed the Spence-Joneses and Lady Davinia shifting a little uncomfortably as Felicity set her cup down, leaning forward eagerly to answer his mother's question.

"Charming? I never saw any evidence of it," Felicity said, gazing at the others for confirmation. Before anyone else had a chance to comment, however, she continued, "Oh, and Mrs. Thorncroft! What an oddity. Always hinting about their wealth—as if anyone of breeding cares about such things. The family, I understand, is in *trade*."

Stone frowned, thinking of Mrs. Thorncroft. Yes, she did have a rather uncomfortable habit of hinting at the enormity of her daughter's dowry. And she tended to bandy about how much she paid for things, but for all that, he rather liked her. He had found her willingness to please and be pleased an engaging attribute. He also could not deny that for a woman of a certain age she was quite pretty. What was the old adage? The mother was a good indication of how the daughter would look at the same age? If that were true, then Miss Thorncroft would only grow lovelier in the years to come.

"I know what you mean," Lady Charlotte said, her golden ringlets bouncing as she agreed with Felicity. "I will say that Mr. Steven Thorncroft was not such a bad sort, but he lacked a certain refinement that true gentlemen possess."

Crossing his arms over his chest, Stone deepened his frown. In his opinion, Steven Thorncroft did not lack refinement—he lacked worldly experience and was hungry for it. Steven had a solid character, was an excellent shot, held his liquor, and had the same slightly sarcastic sense of humor as his sister.

"And Miss Thorncroft!" Lady Walgrave said, adding another offering to the bonfire of the Thorncrofts. "Such a unique creature. She told me she dislikes London! Can you imagine? I found her to have an unseemly independence and an unsociable nature that was sadly bereft of amiability."

"Gracious me!" Stone's mother said as she poured tea for Lord Walgrave. "They sound a queer lot. Here is Stone now," she said with a smile, peering at him through the bank of ferns. "Tell me, have you rusticated so long that you believed we would find such people charming?"

He strode forward, a tight smile on his face, his eyes cold. "They are a charming family."

Though he spoke softly, something in his voice halted the movement of everyone in the room. This was all he intended to say on the matter, for he knew that once he made his position clear, no one would have the temerity to criticize his former guests again.

He caught the exchanged glances between Mr. and Mrs. Spence-Jones and Lady Davinia. The latter's usually serene expression was tense. His mother, his aunt Elizabeth, and his cousins looked on with curious expressions, sensing the undercurrent but not understanding the cause.

A mirthless smile briefly touched his lips. It amused him now that he had invited his family—weeks before their usual time to visit—only so that the Thorncrofts would feel more comfortable.

Felicity sent him an angry, bitter glance, causing him an inward sigh of annoyance. When he had terminated their affair, the day after Mariah stumbled upon them, he assumed all was well. After all, when they began their relationship last Season it had been with the clear understanding that the affair would last only so long as it amused them both.

When he presented her with an emerald brooch and thanked her for their time together, she had accepted the gift with all the sophisticated good nature she was noted for. The parting had gone smoothly, seemingly with no hard feelings from Felicity. Apparently, he had been quite mistaken.

His mother, always the diplomat, evidently sensed something amiss, for she said with a bright smile, "How unfortunate that they had to leave. I would have enjoyed meeting them."

"I believe you would have," he said evenly. Moving forward, he took the seat next to Roger Spence-Jones.

The easy conversation of earlier had ceased, but Stone was in no humor to help it along.

Lady Davinia filled the breach of silence with a delicate cough that brought all eyes to her. "I—I, too, found the Thorncrofts to be a charming family and was most disappointed that they were called away."

Lady Walgrave sniffed derisively. Stone's mother and Aunt Elizabeth exchanged glances, and Stone felt his temper rise. Even so, he sent Lady Davinia a smile. He had always looked upon Davinia as a younger sister, and now he owned he was proud of her for defending the Thorncrofts.

"I would agree," Roger put in. "They may have lacked a little polish, but Amelia and I found them delightful."

"Yes. We intend to have them at Wick Hill as soon as may be," Amelia Spence-Jones stated, with a quick pointed glance at Felicity.

Stone caught his mother's intense blue gaze. She raised one delicately arched brow questioningly. He knew that look well—it meant that they would be discussing this subject later.

"If we are done with the Thorncrofts, I am wondering if anyone is still interested in taking a gallop to the village. I am out of snuff," Mr. Woburn complained, deftly changing the subject through a half-suppressed yawn.

It did not surprise him in the least when late that evening he found his mother sitting by the fire in his library, a brandy warming in her hand.

"What an interesting day," she stated dryly as he poured himself a drink and sat next to her.

"You thought so? I found it rather dull." He tossed back most of the contents of his snifter.

Tilting her head to the side, she sent her son a half-amused, half-concerned look. "Hmmm. Could that be because the mysterious and controversial Thorncroft family is no longer in residence?"

Shrugging in reply, he kept his gaze on the fire. He should have known that his mother, with her keen perception, would make the connection.

As strange as it seemed, the spark had gone out of life in the last few days. He usually enjoyed this time of year immensely. The hunting and the harvesting—fall was always a busy time at the estate. But now the excitement vibrating in the air had gone flat. And he strongly suspected that it was because a certain pair of intelligent, mischievous, alluring hazel eyes was absent.

"Nicholas, if you become taciturn with me I shall scream. Since you turned eighteen, I have never interfered with your personal affairs—though Lord knows I have been tempted to—but this is different. I saw the look on your face in the conservatory and later at dinner, when the Thorncrofts were mentioned again. I have a notion that Miss Thorncroft is someone that should be made known to me."

He turned from the fire to meet his mother's concerned gaze. The amber firelight softened her regal features, reminding him of all the times they had sat together in front of a fire during his childhood.

"It is a rather complicated situation." As close as they were, he had no desire to explain to his mother how Mariah had caught him with Felicity and the events that followed.

His mother affixed him with an assessing gaze. "If it is important, then un-complicate it."

He sent her a mirthless smile. "Is life as simple as that, *Maman*?"

"When it comes to matters of the heart, I have

learned that it is best to be as uncomplicated as possible."

At the grimace of chagrin that crossed his face, a knowing look came to her handsome features. "Or is it too late for that?"

At her words he froze, his drink halfway to his lips. Was it too late? A moment ago he was trying to deny that there was anything to un-complicate. Now he felt galvanized by a sudden uneasy feeling.

They sat in silence as he stared into the fire, frowning fiercely, for some minutes. His mother's words repeated themselves—*if it is important, then un-complicate it.*

"*Maman,* I have an important matter to attend to at one of my other estates." He finished the brandy in a gulp.

"Is that so? Which one?"

He shrugged lightly. "I am not sure yet. I will explain to everyone that I must leave. However, I hope they will all feel free to stay at Heaton. Would you be so kind as to act as hostess for me in my absence?"

"Certainly," she said with an impish smile. "We will have a lovely time speculating about what you are really doing."

Stone gave a burst of laughter. "How have you always been able to see right through me?"

His mother's smile softened to a nostalgic curve. "Because you are so very like your father, my love."

Chapter Seventeen

As each lurching, swaying mile brought her closer to Kelbourne Keep, Mariah could feel her excitement increasing, despite the odd, lingering sadness that now seemed to be with her constantly. Unfortunately, the pain, buried in the secret passages of her heart, had only intensified since her precipitous departure from Heaton.

Why this should be she refused to examine. The only thing that could not be ignored was that the strange ache was directly connected to Stone.

Being of a logical temperament, Mariah concluded that if she could only get thoughts of him out of her mind, then the pain would depart.

She reached over and lifted the blind covering the coach window and watched the stark countryside passing by.

A group of children, all bundled against the bleak day, stood shouting and waving on the side of the road.

Leaning forward, Mariah lowered the window. Disregarding the frigid blast of air, she extended her gloved hand and waved her kerchief at the children.

Hearing their cheers, she waved more vigorously before closing the window and leaning back in the luxurious interior of the Duke of Kelbourne's traveling coach.

She could well imagine how exciting children would

find the sight of two shiny coaches, each pulled by six matched bays, and four outriders with the colorful ducal banners rippling in the wind. She herself had been more than impressed at the sight the other morning when they had thundered up the drive at home.

Snuggling deeper under the heavy fur rug, Mariah wondered how Harris fared in the other coach with the maid and footman Julia had so thoughtfully sent along for the journey. Though why Julia thought Mariah would need three personal servants, Mariah did not know.

Mariah was excited about seeing her old friend again, but she was also extremely curious about Julia's new life. From her letters, Julia sounded the same as she always had: warm, generous, and witty. But Mariah could not believe that becoming a duchess had not affected her friend in some way.

Well, she would find out shortly, she told herself. Leaning into the corner, Mariah closed her eyes, hoping to nap. Even though she had been traveling since early morning, she would not reach the Keep until late. If she could manage to sleep in the moving coach, it would help to pass the time.

As she relaxed into the warm leather squabs, her mind drifted to her family's farewell early that morning.

The day before, her family had taken her as far as the inn near Tenterden and had spent the night to see her off the next morning. It was the merriest time they had all spent together in a very long time.

Early this morning they had stood on the inn's wide front steps, their breath white in the morning chill. Papa had embraced her closely, telling her to enjoy herself—he had even surprised her by giving her a good deal more money than he ever had before. Steven had kissed her cheek and teased her about the grand traveling coaches and liveried outriders, saying everyone would mistake her for Princess Charlotte. George had scurried around the horses, exclaiming that they were just as prime as the earl's horseflesh. She had smiled at them all, sad to leave them even though she was very glad to be visiting her friend.

To her surprise, Mama had looked near to tears as Mariah climbed into the coach's opulent interior.

"I shall miss you, Mariah, dear," she had said through the open door. "But you must promise me that you will enjoy yourself."

"I will miss you, too, Mama. I will write to you very soon," Mariah had replied, choking back her own tears.

After waving out the window until the coach rounded the curve at the end of the drive, Mariah was suddenly struck with the thought that her mother had made no mention of finding a titled husband since their heartfelt discussion some days ago. It touched her deeply that she and her mother now had a much better understanding of each other than they had had in years.

Maybe things could change for the better if Mama and Papa really would give up their hope of her marrying for a title, she mused within the quiet sway of the coach. She fervently hoped so. Mariah wanted nothing more than for her parents to find contentment. They had worked so hard for so many years to be free from any material want that it seemed a shame to waste so much time and energy chasing something so pointless.

She prayed that all this nonsense about titles and court presentations would truly be forgotten and that perhaps someday she would find a worthy, respectable man to wed and her parents would find some joy in that.

This thought did not give her the sense of satisfaction and relief that she needed.

Pulling the rug up to her chin, Mariah settled into a more comfortable position and tried to ignore the occasional jarring movements of the coach.

Some time later she awoke with the lingering vision of broad shoulders, nearly black hair, and piercing blue eyes. Disoriented, she looked sleepily around the darkened coach for Stone.

Rubbing her eyes, Mariah tried to clear the sleep-fuddled thoughts from her head. Of late, so many of her dreams were inhabited by his disturbing image that she should have been used to it by now.

Unfortunately she was not.

Despite how hard she tried to rid herself of thoughts about Stone during the day, he filled her dreams at night. Her cheeks warmed. Would she ever cease wincing over the memory of the look on his face after he overheard her insult him so viciously to Steven?

The slowing of the coach and the distinct sensation of going uphill pulled her—gratefully—back to the present.

Nothing but blackness met her gaze as she peeked out the window, and she suddenly felt very alone and bereft.

Shivering from the cold—for the rug had slipped to the coach floor—Mariah judged that they must be nearing Kelbourne Keep. She hoped so, for she had been alone with her thoughts for much too long.

Moments later, the coach slowed to a stop and the door opened. Standing on the steps in front of a pair of the largest, heaviest-looking wooden doors Mariah had ever seen, stood the Duke and Duchess of Kelbourne, surrounded by a throng of servants holding torches aloft.

An instant after she alighted from the coach, she found herself in the warm embrace of her oldest friend.

"Mariah! I thought you would never arrive!"

Half an hour later, as quick as mercury, Mariah changed from her traveling clothes to a shimmering russet evening gown.

After the warm but all too brief reunion with Julia, Mariah had been shown to a beautiful bedchamber to freshen up before joining Julia and the duke for a late supper.

She gazed admiringly around the room, particularly impressed with the immense canopy bed hung with brocaded burgundy-and-gold draperies.

Promising herself that she would explore her surroundings tomorrow, she finished tidying her hair, then left the bedroom.

A footman led her through a long stone corridor and down a massive staircase to a drawing room. The footman opened the door, and Mariah was glad that he did not formally announce her.

She entered the large room and saw the Duke and Duchess of Kelbourne standing in front of a massive fireplace drinking champagne. Evidently there would be only the three of them for dinner, Mariah noticed with some relief.

"Miss Thorncroft." The duke's warm deep voice rumbled over her as he stepped forward to greet her. "Welcome to our home. I trust your journey did not prove too arduous?"

Feeling somewhat shy before someone so grand, Mariah performed her best curtsy, sending Julia a quick glance on the way up.

Looking radiant in a gown of burnished gold silk that flattered her pale blond hair and gray eyes, Julia beamed a smile from Mariah to her husband and back again.

"I thank you, Your Grace," Mariah stated simply, smiling into his warm gaze while thinking that his dark evening clothes only accentuated his tall, broad frame. "Your coach is so comfortable, the journey seemed to take no time at all."

Julia stepped forward and handed Mariah a glass of champagne, and the three of them chatted for a few moments about the weather and their families' health. As Julia stood next to her imposing husband, Mariah thought her friend did not look quite as tall as she usually did.

As he stood smiling tenderly down at his wife, the duke's regard for her could not be mistaken. This pleased Mariah deeply, for Julia's happiness was extremely important to her. She still found it somewhat hard to comprehend that just half a year ago Julia had been convinced that the Duke of Kelbourne was the most loathsome man in the world. Now, however, Mariah felt profoundly reassured by witnessing their loving expressions.

Sweeping the duke with a glance, Mariah judged him to be an inch or so taller than Stone. The Duke of Kelbourne, with his wavy dark brown hair and light brown eyes, could possibly be considered by some as handsome as his good friend the Earl of Haverstone, but Mariah would not be numbered among them.

Why does everything turn my thoughts to the earl? she chided herself in frustration.

"How fitting that Mariah should be our first guest, for who better to practice my hostess skills upon than my oldest and dearest friend? So I would like to toast our guest," Julia said as the duke gallantly refilled their champagne glasses.

Julia's warm gaze met Mariah's as she continued, "To Miss Mariah Thorncroft, the dearest, most loyal and supportive friend anyone could ever have." She and the duke raised their glasses, bringing a blush to Mariah's cheeks.

"To Miss Mariah Thorncroft," the duke echoed, lifting his glass a little higher before he and Julia took a sip of champagne.

Tears came to Mariah's eyes at her friends' lovely words. "Thank you," she whispered. "I am so happy to be here."

Supper proved to be extremely enjoyable and much less formal than Mariah had anticipated. At first she had found the duke rather intimidating as the three of them dined at one end of an enormously long table. Soon, because of Julia's innate ability to put anyone at ease, Mariah found herself laughing a lot as she and Julia told the duke stories of some of the scrapes they had gotten into over the years.

For his part, the duke showed a keen interest in

their tales and encouraged them to keep talking, re-filling their wineglasses himself. Mariah felt warm, welcomed, and not just a little charmed by Julia's handsome, sophisticated husband.

After they finished the sweet, the duke pushed back his chair. Rising, he gestured to both ladies to remain seated.

"I shall twist convention slightly and say that I will leave you ladies to your port—and conversation," he said, grinning slightly at the surprise on their faces.

Recovering her manners, Mariah looked up at him in dismay. "Please do not leave on my account, Your Grace."

"Not at all, Miss Thorncroft. I know Julia has been longing to have a coze with you. She told me just this morning that these last five months have been the longest time she has been away from you since both of you were about five years of age. I bid you good evening." He smiled and turned to Julia. "I won't wait up for you, my love."

Julia laughed and sent her husband a loving smile as he kissed her hand tenderly.

After he strode from the room, Julia turned to Mariah. "He is correct about my longing to talk with you, but are you too tired after your journey?"

"Not at all. I slept a good deal in the coach. I would love to sit up and talk the way we used to."

"Good." Julia nodded her pale blond head in pleasure. "Then let us go into the drawing room and settle in. I am going to keep you up quite late."

Leaving the dining room, they walked down a short hall to Julia's private sitting room.

"You are obviously exceedingly happy," Mariah said, smiling at Julia as they settled into a plush settee.

"I confess that I am happier than I ever thought it possible to be. I have become one of those tiresome creatures who expound the benefits of marriage."

Mariah laughed. "You need not expound, for your

expression gives your joy away. I am very happy for you, Julia. It is clear the duke adores you."

"Thank you. I feel adored," she said with a serene expression crossing her features. "But enough of me. I have been eager to hear what has been happening with you. There is something different about you, Mariah. I cannot put my finger upon it just yet, but I will."

"I do feel different, so it is not a wonder that you see it as well."

"Then tell me how you have changed and what has caused it. From your letter, I suspect that it has something to do with your time at Heaton with the Earl of Haverstone."

Settling more comfortably into the corner of the settee, Mariah met Julia's perceptive gray gaze. "My time at Heaton affected me in a most profound way."

"Start from the beginning and leave nothing out," Julia charged.

The entire story came pouring out, and Julia listened in attentive silence, interjecting only a few comments during the narrative. The first was when Mariah told her of finding the earl with Lady Walgrave.

"Gracious! I have heard that Stone does not care a fig what people think of him, and this proves it. You certainly handled that much better than I would have. Your composure is to be admired."

"Thank you." Mariah inclined her head with a slight smile before continuing.

When she came to the kiss, she fumbled over her words a little, hardly able to look at her friend. Julia, seeing Mariah's distress, said softly, "His charm is legendary, Mariah. I can understand perfectly why you did not resist."

"Resist? I welcomed his kiss," she said, her voice full of scorn for her wanton behavior. She then told Julia of her confrontation with Lady Walgrave, bringing a fierce scowl to Julia's brow.

"Truly? She will not address you if she meets you

again? Humph. *I* shall not address *her* when next we meet in London," Julia said with newfound hauteur. Then she spoiled it with a laugh, saying, "It's rather fun to be a duchess."

"No doubt," Mariah agreed with an answering smile.

Mariah finally came to the end of her story, and Julia was silent for a few moments, shaking her head.

"My gracious, Mariah! All this happened in a matter of a few days?" Julia's pale gray eyes were wide with wonder.

Mariah sighed. "Yes, but it seemed like so much longer."

"How difficult it all must have been for you. I have a thousand questions. But your story does explain something."

"It explains something?" Mariah looked baffled.

"Kel told me he received a missive from Stone the other day. It was brief—and he did not explain why—but in it Stone stated that he would no longer acknowledge Lord Stothart."

Mariah looked dumbstruck. "He did?"

"I am certainly not surprised, now that I know what occurred. Since my marriage I have discovered that the nobility are a strange lot. They are above the laws of the land, and the most nefarious behavior hardly raises an eyebrow. But if one of their own shows himself to have behaved as less than a gentleman by their strange code, then he is ostracized by Society. It is quite an effective way to keep the beau monde terribly exclusive."

Mariah did not know what to think about what Julia just said. She only remembered how safe she felt when Stone had taken her into his arms after Lord Stothart's attack.

"So what now?"

Mariah pulled her attention back to Julia, a confused frown furrowing her brow. "What now?"

"Yes. What about Stone?"

"What do you mean, 'what about Stone?' " Mariah

felt unable to hold her friend's direct and perceptive gaze, so she looked down at her hands resting in her lap.

Julia made a half-impatient, half-amused noise. "Do not cut up stiff with me. You know exactly what I mean. What about Stone?"

Mariah shrugged. "Nothing. I do not flatter myself that the kiss meant anything. If I did, the look on his face after he overheard my horrid comments to Steven about him would dispel that notion."

"But Mariah, I suspect that you were developing a regard for the earl—especially after Stothart's insult."

Eyes wide with shock and dismay, Mariah quickly tried to correct her friend's assumption. "No! I own that he is attractive and—and interesting, but how could I truly care for such an unrepentant rake?"

Julia frowned at this. "I have come to know the earl a little through his close friendship with my husband. Though I did find him rather daunting, and he is famously wild in some ways, nevertheless I found I quite liked him. I have no doubt that he has dallied with numerous women and has probably gambled away several fortunes—but he is a gentleman underneath it all."

Mariah shook her head, but Julia continued, "I shall say right out that I believe he behaved the way he did because you snared some part of his heart. And I know you too well, Mariah. You would never let him kiss you if you did not have a *tendre* for him."

Mariah continued to shake her head vehemently, her confusion growing. "Even if that were true it doesn't matter."

"Then what does?" Julia questioned softly.

Mariah hesitated before answering. "I believe Heaton cast a spell over me," she finally said with a self-deprecating smile. "Instead of the usual kind of spell where the maiden falls asleep, this spell has awakened me."

"How do you mean?"

"Heaton made me realize that I have been asleep

most of my life. Oh, I have always kept busy. There is always plenty to do at home and at church. The parish school has taken up a great deal of my time—most happily. But I have been in a state of *waiting* since I was old enough to put my hair up."

Julia listened with a look of awe at her friend's maturity. "I cannot tell you how much I have missed you, Mariah. This is vastly interesting. What do you mean by 'state of waiting'?"

Mariah pulled a plush indigo velvet-and-silk pillow onto her lap before going on. "As busy as I was—as happy as I was—I was always waiting for my life to begin. Always waiting for something to happen, but I never knew exactly what. Oh, Julia, it is so difficult to put into words, but I am utterly weary of waiting. Heaton has opened my eyes, and I see everything so differently now. And I intend, to the best of my ability, to live my life without waiting for something to happen. I must make the best of this moment and each moment that follows. Am I making any sense at all?" she asked on a forlorn little laugh.

"Yes—yes, you are. But what of your parents' desire for you to wed a peer?"

Mariah smiled a little. "Mama and I have come to a new understanding. The fact that I could speak so frankly with her tells me that the change I feel within is real. I see now that some of the tension between Mama and me was my fault. I had grown so tired of arguing over the years that I let her think that I would be docile if a plum title wanted my dowry. Now everything is so much better between us."

"I am glad your mama will no longer put so much pressure on you. But do you really think that you can forget what happened with Stone so easily?"

"Yes," Mariah said with a desperate firmness that she suspected Julia did not believe. "I must. Besides, there is no reason for me to be so vehement about him. I was never in danger of attracting his interest."

Julia's frown revealed her deep concern for Mariah,

and she wondered at the new shadows of sadness lurking in her friend's eyes.

They sat in silence for a while—each considering what had just been said.

The essence that made their friendship what it was felt just as strong as if they had never been apart. Because of this, Julia could not set aside her concern.

"Is your heart broken, Mariah?" Julia asked the question gently, compassion vibrating through her voice.

Mariah turned away from Julia's gently probing gaze and watched a massive cedar log, as big as her body, burning in the huge hearth.

"Can a heart be broken in a matter of days?" Despite reaching for a light, careless tone, Mariah knew she did not sound very convincing.

"I assure you, from my own experience, it may only take a matter of moments under the right circumstances."

Evidently Julia was not going to let her avoid the subject. Mariah turned back to her friend with a wry smile.

"Until now I have refused to contemplate such a question because I suspected I would not like the answer. I would be more than a fool to allow my heart to be broken by a man like the Earl of Haverstone. But I will not deny that somehow he charmed me as no one else ever has."

"Only charmed?"

Shifting uncomfortably, Mariah shrugged at the softly asked question. "There may be a very slight crack in my heart, but I do not think that it is truly broken." Mariah hoped—rather than believed—that this was true.

Again silence held them for a moment before Julia said, "I shall plague you no more with questions. You will rest here in my home, and I will keep you so busy that you will not have time to worry about that crack in your heart. Tomorrow the upholsterer is bringing a cart full of fabric and such to redecorate my bedchamber, sitting room, and salon. I shall depend on your artistic eye to help guide my taste."

"You have been to my home so many times that I am surprised that you would trust me with so much as choosing a pillow for this magnificent place," Mariah said, relieved at the change of subject.

Julia laughed. "I do not fear that you have your mother's taste. But you are right when you say that Kelbourne Keep is magnificent. I could scarce believe my eyes when Kel first brought me here. I was so daunted that I could not see myself as mistress of this imposing place. But now, because of Kel, this is home."

This simple explanation brought tears to Mariah's eyes, leaving her with a poignant ache in her heart for Heaton.

Sitting next to her, Julia frowned at the quick flash of pain that crossed Mariah's features. She could not stop herself from asking, "Mariah, how do you propose to live your life from now on?"

Lifting her chin to a stubborn angle, Mariah said, "Well, that is the part I am not exactly sure of, but I know that I can never go back to the way I was before."

Chapter Eighteen

*T*hree days later, the Earl of Haverstone strolled into the White Hart, an inn situated on a busy merchant street in the village of Chippenham.

The innkeeper, a shrewd little man, took one look at the earl's fine clothes, powerful build, and expression of natural hauteur and instantly recognized him as a member of the Quality. As he approached the gentleman, the innkeeper mentally raised his prices by half.

Removing his gloves, Stone glanced around the common room, finding it as quaint as the village he had just ridden through. Though it was the middle of the day, several men sat around the rough-hewn table with full tankards of ale. All conversation had stopped at his entry, but Stone paid no heed, taking their curious stares as a matter of course.

The proprietor shuffled up, pulling his forelock. "Would you be wantin' the use of the private parlor, sir?"

"Yes, good man. I will also need three adjacent rooms for the next night or two. I will be occupying the middle room. For now, I will have a pint of ale and ask you how far it is to Thorncroft Manor."

The innkeeper rubbed his hands together. "Several miles east of here, sir. You take High Street to Cocklebury Road, then take that to the end, and you will come to a long drive that leads to the Thorncroft place. I'll get your ale. Would you be wantin' a tab, sir?" He knew there was no need to ask for payment up front from this fine gentleman.

"Yes. I'm Haverstone."

Just then his head groom, Crenshaw, entered. Stone signaled him over as the innkeeper shuffled off.

"In half an hour I will need a message sent to Thorncroft Manor."

"Very good, my lord. I will send Robby. He's a fast rider and knows how to behave himself."

"Excellent." Stone smiled slightly at the groom's description of the lad. "Are the horses and carriages in good repair?"

"Aye, my lord, especially considering the time we made."

Stone nodded in satisfaction. "I'll have the note ready shortly."

In his room an hour later, Stone stood gazing out the second-story window overlooking the front of the inn. Behind him, Stolt bustled around arranging the earl's things and tidying the simple, clean room.

Despite his seemingly relaxed stance, Stone felt his patience becoming strained. It had been well more than an hour since Robby had been sent to Thorncroft Manor with the note—more than enough time to return with a response.

Not that Stone doubted his welcome by the Thorncrofts; he was just growing impatient to see Mariah again. Now that he saw things clearly, it was imperative to settle the tension and confusion of their parting.

Stolt finished laying out the earl's clothes and said, "Will you be dining here, my lord?"

Stone glanced at his valet over his shoulder, a faint frown crossing his features. "I am not sure yet," he said, turning back to the window.

Just then he saw his young groom, riding low in the saddle, gallop into the inn yard on one of his fastest dappled gray mares.

"Robby's returned," he said, unable to keep the edge of excitement from his voice.

"I'll go down, my lord," Stolt said.

The valet returned in minutes. Handing a folded and sealed piece of vellum to the earl, Stolt bowed and left the room.

Staying by the window, Stone broke the seal and scanned the brief message, a look of satisfaction coming to his face.

> *My Lord Haverstone,*
> *We are most pleased to hear that you are*
> *visiting the area. My wife and I would be*
> *most honored to have you dine with us this*
> *evening if you have no other engagement.*
> *We will be expecting you, at your convenience,*
> *this evening.*
> *Your most humble servant,*
> *Edmund Thorncroft*

Loosening the knot in his neckcloth, Stone felt his mood elevate instantly. He wondered how Mariah had reacted to discovering he'd traveled to her village. He would know soon, he thought, with a feeling of pleasurable anticipation.

Several hours later, as his carriage swept up the long drive to Thorncroft Manor, Stone felt oddly tense about the impending meeting with Mariah. The thought of seeing her mischievous hazel eyes and lovely heart-shaped face caused his heart to race.

The coach slowed, pulling up to the front steps. Before Stone alighted, he saw from the coach window that the front doors were open and Mrs. Thorncroft and a man he assumed to be Mr. Thorncroft had stepped out onto the wide marble front steps.

As he ascended the steps, he looked at Mariah's father and saw the resemblance to his daughter in his sparkling, intelligent eyes.

"Welcome to Thorncroft Manor, my lord Haverstone," Mrs. Thorncroft called in a delighted tone as she curtsied. "Never did I think that we would be seeing you again . . . so soon." Her smile faltered as she turned to the bowing man at her side. "My lord, may I present my husband, Mr. Edmund Thorncroft."

"Good evening, Mr. Thorncroft. I am pleased to meet you." He put out his hand and grasped Mr. Thorncroft's, impressed by the man's direct gaze and firm handshake.

"The honor is mine, my lord. I would like to thank you for your kind hospitality toward my family."

Meeting Mr. Thorncroft's unflinching eyes, Stone wondered how much he knew of what had occurred during his daughter's stay at Heaton.

"You are always welcome at Heaton, sir. Your family brightened the halls."

Mr. Thorncroft responded with a slight bow.

"And Mrs. Thorncroft." Stone turned back to her, noticing the look of alarm in her eyes despite her smile. "You are looking exceedingly lovely this evening."

Mrs. Thorncroft gave a delighted laugh as they moved into the foyer. As the butler closed the doors behind them, Stone glanced around, almost giving a start at the prodigious number of gilded art objects and decorations covering every square inch of wall space and crammed onto tabletops and into corners.

"Please come into the salon, my lord. We will go in to supper shortly, but my husband is proud of his cellar and can offer you something I am sure you will enjoy."

They walked down a long hall—just as overwhelmed with gilded objects as the foyer—until they reached a pair of double doors. Mr. Thorncroft opened them himself, and Stone strode forward to see Steven Thorncroft rise from a chair, a strained smile upon his features.

A moment later Stone realized that, save for Steven, the busy room held no other occupants. Swallowing his disappointment, he greeted the young man, who did not seem nearly as at ease as he had at Heaton.

"It is very good to see you again, my lord," Steven said, bowing.

Not a hint of his disappointment showed as Stone greeted the young man, then turned back to Mr. and Mrs. Thorncroft. "I trust the rest of your family is well?" he asked with exquisite politeness.

He did not miss their hesitation as the three of them exchanged quick glances. Suddenly he became aware of a palpable tension and was instantly concerned as to its cause.

"We are all quite well. Thank you for asking, my lord." Mrs. Thorncroft spoke quickly, filling the awkward silence.

As he was about to ask directly about Mariah, the door flew open, cutting off his words. A small boy came running toward him.

"My lord Stone!" George shouted excitedly, skidding to stop a second before he ran into the earl. Performing a hasty bow, the boy cried, "You are here!"

"George!" Mr. and Mrs. Thorncroft shouted in unison, horrified at their son's forwardness.

Stone smiled down at the boy with great pleasure, thinking him a handsome little replica of his lovely sister.

"How are you, young George? I hope you are practicing your fencing."

"Oh yes, sir," George said breathlessly, his eyes shining with hero worship. "But I think I have forgotten a few things. Would you show me again while you are here?"

"That is enough, young man," Mr. Thorncroft said sternly.

Stone's smile was indulgent. "It is a perfectly reasonable request, Mr. Thorncroft. I did agree to instruct your son in the art of fencing. If George is not otherwise occupied tomorrow, we can have another lesson."

"My lord! That's much too generous—" Mr.

Thorncroft began before George shouted his acceptance over the top of him.

"Thank you, Lord Stone!"

"Now, George, your father has said that is enough. Do not pester his lordship." Mrs. Thorncroft's pretty features were flushed with embarrassment.

"Off to your room, George," Mr. Thorncroft instructed in a tone Stone surmised his children never disobeyed.

Slightly crestfallen, George bowed again and walked slowly back to the door. As he pulled the door open, he turned back and said, "Too bad Mariah is visiting Miss Allard—I mean, the duchess. She won't be able to watch us fence." Then he left the room.

At George's words Stone felt a sharp stab of disappointment, for it had never occurred to him that Mariah would not be at home.

Keeping his expression carefully bland, Stone turned to Mariah's parents. "Evidently Miss Thorncroft will not be joining us this evening. I trust she has been well since she left Heaton?"

Silence met his question. Suddenly Mrs. Thorncroft seemed to find her fan very interesting, and Steven tugged at his neckcloth.

"Yes, quite well. Thank you, my lord," said Mr. Thorncroft. "Mariah shall be in Kent for a month and is no doubt enjoying her visit with her childhood friend, the new Duchess of Kelbourne." He walked to a carved and gilded cabinet. "May I interest you in a glass of very fine Burgundy that I have recently acquired?"

"Certainly, Mr. Thorncroft," Stone said cordially, wondering with barely concealed frustration how soon after supper he could have a private word with Mr. Thorncroft and how soon he could leave Chippenham after his fencing lesson tomorrow with George.

Accepting the drink from Mr. Thorncroft, he realized with rising frustration that he was still at least two days away from seeing Mariah again.

Chapter Nineteen

Almost a week after arriving at Kelbourne Keep, Mariah sat in the cheery drawing room, admiring the overstuffed furniture covered in claret-colored velvet. A brace of beeswax candles stood in each corner, casting a mellow amber glow over Julia's guests.

Across from her, the duchess sat with the Honorable Mrs. Wilfred Francis and Mrs. Phillips, the vicar's wife, by the fireplace.

Although Julia had done her best to bring Mariah into the conversation, Mrs. Francis and Mrs. Phillips, both quite a bit older than Mariah and Julia, were determined to keep the topic on local affairs and gossip, which Mariah had no knowledge of, and therefore she had nothing to contribute. Neither lady found anything amiss in her silence.

Pinning a serene smile on her face, Mariah rose from her chair and excused herself from the ladies, explaining that she desired a bit of fresh air. As she passed them, she saw the thinly veiled concern in Julia's eyes.

With a reassuring smile Mariah said, "It's such a clear night, I thought I would take a turn around the terrace."

"Mercy, you young people are hardier than I am," Mrs. Phillips offered from her seat next to Julia's. "Much too chilly to be traipsing around terraces at night. I hope you do not catch your death of cold."

Mariah and Julia exchanged amused glances at Mrs.

Phillips' dire warnings. Julia had told Mariah before
dinner that the vicar's wife was as cantankerous as the
vicar was cheerful.

Mrs. Phillips' negativity had not been so noticeable
during dinner, but since leaving the gentlemen to their
port, she had grown increasingly irascible. As the
woman went off on one tangent after another, Mariah
and Julia had avoided looking at each other, lest they
spark each other's laughter.

Pulling her violet paisley shawl over her shoulders,
Mariah dismissed the weather, feeling that her indigo
velvet gown and shawl were sufficient protection.
Smiling, she said to the older woman, "I shall not stay
out long enough to catch a chill—but thank you for
your concern."

Mrs. Phillips only sniffed irritably in reply, turning
back to her hostess and Mrs. Francis.

"It should be a beautiful night," Mrs. Francis
opined.

Julia, her gray eyes alight with laughter, said, "Do
not stay out too late."

Mariah slipped through the French doors and
walked out onto the stone terrace that spanned half
the width of the house.

A cool breeze ruffled her hair as she moved to the
edge and rested her hands on the cold marble balustrade. The moon, full and luminescent in the sky,
bathed the terrace and the garden below in silver blue
light. In the inky black distance, she could make out
the glow from the cottages and farms in the village.

Inhaling deeply of the fresh night air, she released
her breath with a sigh.

The memory of another night like this one came
back in a rush of intense, painful emotion. Why did
she have to find him kissing that dreadful Lady Walgrave in the moonlight? Suddenly she realized that
she was angry with Stone. Foolishly, pointlessly angry.

If only she had not seen them, then it would not
hurt so terribly bad to love him. Her breathing stilled
at this thought. The admission she had fought so hard

to suppress had slipped out in an instant. With a pang in her heart, she knew she could not stuff the truth back down again.

She loved Stone.

And hated him. Clenching her fists, she pounded them once on the balustrade. Anger flared through her as she wished him to feel the pain she was now experiencing.

Had she fallen in love with him that first night, a night so like this one? Yes, that was when it had begun, she realized—when he had teased and talked to her as if they were friends.

Raising her eyes to the sky, she thanked heaven that she had left Heaton before making a fool of herself over him. Well, before making a *complete* fool of herself, she amended dejectedly.

"It would seem that neither one of us can resist a full moon."

At the sound of the familiar, slightly amused voice behind her, she whirled around with a stunned gasp.

Staring in shock, Mariah could not stop her exclamation as she saw Stone's familiar build silhouetted against a set of French windows on the other side of the terrace.

Eyes wide with astonishment and disbelief, Mariah watched him stroll toward her until he stepped into a pool of crystalline moonlight, revealing his piercing blue gaze.

"Why—when did you arrive?" she whispered, hardly comprehending that he was actually standing in front of her.

"Just moments ago," he said, his eyes searching her face.

With a mounting sense of unreality, Mariah stared at him, her incredulous gaze sweeping his face and form. He was not dressed for dinner. In fact, he was wearing riding clothes, the buttons on his dark double-breasted coat glinting in the moonlight. Her heart caught at how incredibly handsome he looked.

"Did you know that I was here?" Instantly she

wished she could take back the question. Why should he not be here? She knew that he and the duke were friends. Clasping her hands together, she chided herself for being so gauche and forward.

"Yes," he began in a conversational tone that belied the intense expression in his eyes. "After I was shown into the dining room I saw you on the terrace from the window."

"No, I mean, did you know that I was at Kelbourne Keep?" *Why can I not keep my mouth shut?* Her befuddled brain continued to struggle with his sudden, disarming appearance.

"Of course. You are the reason I am here, Mariah."

At the tenderness lacing his deep voice, Mariah felt almost dizzy. Just a moment ago she had been thinking of him with anger and longing clutching her heart. Now he was here, looking unbearably handsome and intensely masculine, and saying impossible things.

His nearness in the moonlight made her head spin. *He is here,* her heart whispered. Their gazes locked, and with slow deliberation, he stepped closer. She remained where she was, her shivering having nothing to do with the cool night air. A deep, unexpected feeling of joy began to spread through her being.

His arms came around her and pulled her gently yet firmly against the solid length of his body. She inhaled deeply, savoring the familiar, intoxicating scent of him and the feel of his arms encircling her unresistant body. She felt his warm lips against her temple. "I have missed you, Mariah."

With a sense of wonderment, she felt his huskily spoken words melt into her body and touch her soul. She raised her lips to his, and his warm mouth descended. Muscular arms tightened around her body as she clung to his broad shoulders, returning his tender kiss with all the longing she'd been suppressing since that first dinner at Heaton. As her heart thudded in her chest, his lips moved over hers, caressing and insistent. His hands moved down her back to her waist, pulling her with him into a sensual moonlit whirlpool where she was past caring about anything but the feel of his lips and body.

As his kiss deepened, a sudden inner voice, belated but persistent, cautioned her to be careful.

Unable to trust her feelings and overwhelmed by his sudden appearance and the sensual barrage upon her senses, she pushed at his chest. Immediately, he set her free.

She dragged a deep breath into her lungs, took a step back, and saw the passion blazing in his eyes.

Pulling her shawl back up to her shoulders, she tried to gather her composure. She had spent the last few days working very hard to put him out of her thoughts. How could he just appear out of nowhere and destroy her hard-won peace of mind? She must not allow his sudden and overwhelming presence to impair her judgment, she decided. From experience she knew he had the frightening ability to affect her heart quite effortlessly, and her newfound sense of independence screamed within her to be careful.

"What are you doing here?" she said, her tone angry and defensive. "I don't understand any of this."

He remained motionless, his cool eyes meeting her cautious, troubled gaze. "I didn't either until you had been gone for a few days." His deep voice created a coiling tension within her that made her want to return to his embrace. Forcing herself to stay still, she gazed up at him, her distraught eyes sparkling in the moonlight.

Something in the way he stood, so tense and alert, seemed to stop her heart for an instant.

"Marry me, Mariah," he said, his voice rough with passion.

"What?" she whispered, believing that she must be dreaming.

"Marry me."

Stunned, she fought to keep her mind clear. It took a moment for the fog of passion and longing to lift enough for his words to sink in. When they did, the hint of burgeoning joy froze within her breast. Her spinning senses began to settle, and harsh reality returned with a sickening jolt.

"Marry you?" She took a half step back. "What is wrong with me?" she said more to herself than to him. "Why do I lose all self-control when you are near?"

Gazing down, he studied her distraught features with tender amusement. "I am certainly not going to say that is bad news."

Ignoring the familiar gentle tease in his voice, she said with an edge of desperation, "I must be wise. Considering a life with you would be foolish." She was too frightened to be anything but blunt.

She sensed him wince as if she had dealt him a blow.

"What do you mean?" he questioned, his tone unemotional.

"I mean, my lord, that it would be the height of folly to trust you," she stated shakily.

He did not move. "Of course you have reason to feel that way. But anything that has happened in my life before you is exactly that—before you."

Unable to hold his gaze, she looked away and swallowed nervously, desperately trying to hold on to what she knew to be true at this moment: that if she did choose to trust him and he betrayed her, it would destroy her. And there would be no one to blame but her own foolish self.

"Mariah, I know you believe that I am an unabashed, unmitigated rakehell. But you must know—you must feel because of what has passed between us—that this feeling we share is real."

She met his intense gaze, her eyes filled with confusion. "I no longer know what is real."

"You are frightened."

"Of course I am frightened. If I married you, I would just be reverting back to the way I was."

He made an impatient gesture. "I don't understand."

Without any real idea of how to explain, she plunged ahead. "I used to just wait for things to happen. I waited for circumstances to dictate how I lived.

If I married you, the waiting would start all over again. After my time at Heaton, I promised myself never to live that way again."

He spread his hands wide, and she could see by his frown that he was trying to understand what she was saying. "How would marrying me make you revert back to something you don't like?"

Shaking her head helplessly, she struggled to put her feelings into words. "I would always be waiting for one of your friends to sneer at my family because we are beneath you. I would always be waiting for one of your mistresses to insult me. I would always be waiting for you to break my heart. I cannot live like that. I—I want to be like Alice of Surrey." Her beseeching gaze silently begged him to understand and tempt her no more.

"Marry me and you can do and be whatever you want," he said, his voice low and forceful.

The words hung between them, and for a moment she almost succumbed to the heady seduction in his voice.

Feeling her resolve weakening, she turned away. "Please don't," she said in a choked whisper before whirling away and running back to the French door, leaving him to stare after her with a grim expression on his moonlit face.

Chapter Twenty

"*H*e's gone."

At the sound of Julia's soft voice, Mariah rolled over onto her back and pulled the covers up to her chin against the cold morning.

A moment later she felt Julia's weight lowering onto the bed. "I have brought you some chocolate and some pears from our hothouse."

Opening her eyes, Mariah squinted up at her old friend and saw that Julia wore a dressing gown in an exquisite shade of ecru mixed with pink.

"Thank you, Julia," she said, pushing herself up against her pillows.

"I hope you are not too upset to talk. If you are, I will apologize in advance for plaguing you with questions, but I positively cannot resist."

Mariah looked at the beautifully arranged tray resting next to them on the bed. "Did Stone really arrive here yesterday evening?" she asked, only half joking.

"Oh, yes. When the gentlemen rejoined the ladies in the dining room, I own that I was quite astounded to see him. Evidently Jeffries did not see fit to tell me that a new guest had arrived. Stone certainly gave Mrs. Francis and Mrs. Phillips a thrill. He had them giggling like schoolgirls."

"Yes, he has that effect on women." Mariah leaned forward and picked up her cup of chocolate, trying to avoid meeting Julia's perceptive gaze.

"Mariah! Your hand is shaking! Tell me at once

what is amiss. Did Stone insult you? Though it would be beyond odd to come all this way to do so."

Placing the cup and saucer in her lap to steady her hand, she quickly shook her head. "No, he did not insult me. In fact, he paid me a great compliment—he asked me to marry him."

Julia's own cup rattled in its saucer as she almost dropped it. "He did? My gracious, Mariah, what happened?"

The encounter with Stone was too recent, her emotions too raw for her to reveal all the details to Julia. Nonetheless, when she finished giving the most important points, Julia stared at her with wide-eyed concern.

"But why did you reject him? You cannot humbug me. You care for him."

"That is precisely why! Because I care for him, he could crush my heart with so little effort. How could I ever trust him? I must be wise."

"You are frightened."

"That is what he said." Mariah sat her cup back down and pushed her braid off her shoulder.

"Well, he is right. Mariah, love is a risk. You cannot give your heart to someone with any guarantee that it will never be hurt. But I assure you that the rewards are worth the risk."

"But he does not love me!" Struggling to suppress her pain and confusion, she spoke more sharply than she intended.

Julia made an impatient gesture. "How can you say so? How many women do you think the Earl of Haverstone has followed across country to ask to marry him? I'd wager everything except my husband that the answer is none."

Mariah's frown was doubtful. "But he did not say he loved me."

Julia sent her a look of understanding. "Oh, Mariah, don't you know anything about men? You used to be the wise one. What has happened to you?"

"You did not know much about men before about six months ago," Mariah said with a wan smile.

"You have a point, but if Stone is anything like Kel—and I believe he is, since they are the best of friends—then actions speak much louder than words."

Mariah digested this for a moment while Julia curled up at the end of the bed and leaned against the post.

Mariah hardly knew what to think. She found it quite astounding that Stone had come all this way to see her. That he could have come because of her dowry did not fit with everything she had come to know of him, and yet she simply could not believe that he loved her and that he would give up Lady Walgrave and other women in the future.

"Even if he does love me, I am not sure it is enough," she whispered.

"As I said, there are no guarantees when it comes to matters of the heart. Look at it another way—he came all this way and if you had said yes, what assurance would he have that you loved him and did not desire him for his title?"

"But I do not care about his title!"

"How would he know that?" Julia reasoned. "He could not know for sure. He would have to trust you."

Maria frowned, considering Julia's words. She had not looked at the situation from this vantage point. She put her hand to her throbbing head. The feeling that she had made the most dreadful mistake of her life warred with her desperate need to protect herself from further hurt.

"Mariah, we have been friends for so very long that I cannot but speak frankly to you."

"Of course, Julia. It has always been so between us."

Mariah saw her friend take a deep breath before she continued. "As we grew up and started going to assembly balls and parties, and the young men started to flock to your side, I observed a change in your personality."

Mariah frowned, trying to recall a time that seemed an eon ago. "What do you mean?"

"Most young women would feel flattered and care-free, leading any number of beaux on a merry chase. Not you. You grew more cautious and shy. Because of our friendship, I understood what was happening. You found it difficult to believe that any young man could be interested in you for you alone. Your dowry has hung over your head for so long that you can no longer see past it."

The simple truth of the words hit Mariah so hard that she could not halt the sudden flood of tears that came to her eyes. Julia's words were true. Mariah had never listened to a compliment without wondering if the gentleman paying it knew of the thirty thousand pounds her father had settled upon her.

Suddenly she recalled the night she had danced at Heaton, when Stone told her that he could empathize with her concern about fortune hunters. "My title is often the attraction, instead of my sterling character," he had said. At the time his tone had been so satirical she had not taken him seriously. After all, there was so much more to him than his pedigree that any woman would be lucky to have him, coronet or not.

But what if there had been more truth to his off-hand statement than he had let on? she wondered with growing unease.

"If it is true," she whispered aloud, "then he came here risking that I would say yes just because of his title."

"It would seem so," Julia gently agreed.

"You said he is gone?"

"He left after an early breakfast."

"Then that settles that." Mariah choked back the words. "My rejection has put him off or he would not have left so soon."

Julia smiled, reaching over to pat Mariah's blanket covered leg. "You must be in love. That is the only thing that would explain your extremely uncharacteristic vacillation."

A new thought suddenly struck Mariah. Dashing away an escaped tear, she looked at her friend eagerly.

"Julia, has the post left yet? I need to send a letter immediately." She had no idea what she intended to write, but that did not matter right now.

"Not to worry. I will have it sent by messenger. As I told you before, it's rather fun to be a duchess," she said with an impish smile as Mariah jumped out of bed and ran to the Hepplewhite escritoire on the other side of the room.

Ten days later, wrapped in a pale lilac robe, Mariah sat in her bedchamber gazing out the window that overlooked the famed vale of Kelbourne.

Next to her chair a breakfast tray sat on a delicate pear-wood table, the food untouched. She stared out the window, watching the late-morning light break over the vale below and the picturesque village nestled in the distant downs.

Turning her head at the light tap on the door, Mariah saw Julia, dressed in a raspberry-colored morning gown, her pale hair twisted in an elegant coif, step into the room.

"Goodness, you are usually such an early riser," Julia said as she crossed the room to sit next to Mariah.

"Yes, I'm feeling a touch lazy this morning," Mariah replied, summoning a smile.

Since sending her brief missive to Heaton—politely requesting that she and the earl continue their discussion at the earl's leisure—Mariah had not spoken of Stone to Julia. Instead, during the day they had kept very busy with all the things that interest a new bride, and in the evening they were entertained by the very urbane and amusing duke, who made no mention of Stone's brief visit.

As each day passed, Mariah had grown more bereft and dejected. If Stone had been interested he would have responded to her note days ago. Valiantly, she had tried to ignore the dull ache in her heart and behave as normally as possible in front of Julia.

Julia took the seat across from Mariah and looked at her with a queer expression. "Well, I hate to disrupt your restful morning, but there are three gentlemen in the drawing room with a letter of introduction from the Prince Regent, of all people, wishing an audience with you."

Mariah's mouth dropped open, and then she laughed at Julia's rather odd joke. "What nonsense is this?"

" 'Tis not nonsense. Kel is having a lovely chat with them. They do not seem in the least bit of a hurry."

Sitting bolt upright, Mariah said, "Julia! You are hoaxing me! Why would there be gentlemen wishing to speak to me?"

"I haven't a clue, though I suspect if you give it a moment's thought you might figure out who is behind their being here. They are an interesting-looking lot. I believe Kel is rather enjoying himself."

Mariah jumped up, pulling her robe tight around her. "What are you prattling about? Who is here to see me?"

"The Reverend Mr. John Petersham, Mr. Reginald Tracy, and Mr. Cecil Harding all arrived a half an hour ago."

"But *who* are they and *why* do they want to see me?"

"Lord knows," Julia said breezily. "But with a letter from the Regent, I am rabid to find out."

"Julia, I am about to have a fit! What is going on?"

"Get dressed and find out," Julia said with a laugh.

"There are really three gentlemen waiting downstairs for me?" Mariah said as she moved to the bell-pull to summon Harris.

"That's what I have been telling you for the last five minutes."

After pulling the rope, she turned back to her friend. "Well, I suppose I must go see what this is about," she said with a baffled shrug.

* * *

Less than an hour later, Mariah found herself downstairs seated in the splendor of the Duke of Kelbourne's formal drawing room.

On her lap rested a letter from the Prince Regent. *The Prince Regent!* she marveled. With a supreme effort she resisted the urge to glance down and read it again. Having read it three times already, she knew that the brief note, with its thick wax seal and silk cord, simply requested that she be so kind as to attend the good gentlemen there to see her. It was signed with a distinctive flourishing scrawl. *When Mama sees it, she will no doubt have a paroxysm,* she thought distractedly.

Seated across from her was Mr. Reginald Tracy, a distinguished-looking gentleman with thinning gray hair and sharp brown eyes.

"As the papers I gave you indicate, I have a position as consultant with the Royal Academy of Arts. During my tenure, I have had the privilege of instructing Thomas Lawrence and a few other notable artists. Since going into partial retirement some years ago I have devoted myself to the instruction of only the most gifted students," he said in the clipped, precise tones of a schoolmaster. "And I must say, Miss Thorncroft, when I first saw examples of your work I was ignorant to the fact that you are a woman. I was even more surprised to learn that you have never received any formal instruction in art. That is accurate, is it not?"

Mariah stared at him in utter astonishment for a few moments. "Er—yes, it is," she finally recovered herself enough to reply.

He nodded curtly and continued. "Miss Thorncroft, I am prepared to spend whatever time you are willing to devote to the development of your considerable talent. In fact, I would deem it a great honor."

Mariah could not speak. In the back of her mind she wondered how this man had gotten hold of some of her sketches. More than that, she felt stunned and rather humbled that a man of Mr. Tracy's credentials could find her talented.

"I do not expect a decision right now, Miss Thorncroft. I will leave my direction so that you may write to me if what I have said is of interest to you." Rising, he bowed and handed her his card before moving toward the door.

"Thank you, Mr. Tracy," she said, hastily recovering her manners despite her shock. "Thank you very much."

Bowing again, he smiled for the first time since entering the room. "It is my pleasure, Miss Thorncroft."

She did not have a moment to digest what Mr. Tracy had said before the butler announced Mr. Harding. Rising, she greeted the thin, well-dressed man and indicated that he should be seated.

Bowing, he placed a large portfolio and leather satchel next to his chair. Once they were both seated, he began to speak to her in a respectful, businesslike manner.

"Miss Thorncroft, I am one of the Earl of Haverstone's solicitors. I am with the firm Harding and Harding, and we have proudly and devotedly served his lordship for more than twenty years. I thank you for allowing me to speak with you on such short notice." Reaching down into the portfolio, he pulled a stack of papers out and spread them on the tea table between them.

Mariah looked at them in surprise. Obviously they were some sort of legal documents.

"I will leave these for you and your own solicitor to review. In essence, they state that your entire dowry is to be set aside for your sole and exclusive use. You will also find that there is a provision for an extremely generous monthly allowance." He used his quill to point to a section in the papers. "There is also a codicil stipulating that a certain amount of the Earl of Haverstone's capital would be set aside and invested for your sole and exclusive use. If he should predecease you, none of the monies or real estate belonging to you would return to the earl's estate, and the allowance would continue for your lifetime."

He paused, obviously waiting for some sort of response from her. Mariah, mute with astonishment, could only stare at the documents spread before her.

When it became apparent to Mr. Harding that she was not going to speak, he pulled from the satchel several leather-bound books and placed them on the table. "Here are the earl's accounting ledgers. They list all his holdings, investments, speculations, and etcetera. I can explain in depth where the bulk of his lordship's wealth resides, but it will take some time."

This offer finally pushed her out of her speechless shock. "No, Mr. Harding! Thank you, but that will not be necessary!"

His eyebrows arched, and he looked a bit flabbergasted. "Miss Thorncroft, I have been instructed to explain that the earl is one of the wealthiest men in the Kingdom and to show you—" He opened one of the accounting books and pointed to several places.

Mariah held up her hands in protest. "Please, Mr. Harding. I certainly believe you. Truly, there is no need to go any further with this."

Mr. Harding frowned and began flipping through the ledger pages. "May I at least show you the column that shows his gambling wins and losses? You will see that, averaged out over the last several years, his lordship is well in the black."

With the cold, bereft feeling melting from her heart at every word, a slight smile began to curve her lips. "I am sure he is, Mr. Harding."

The Reverend Mr. Petersham paced in front of Mariah as she stared at him with wonderment. *What next?* she mused as a delicious thrill went down her spine.

She waited for the tall gentleman to speak, thinking he looked very distinguished with his black clothes and his shock of white hair.

"Miss Thorncroft, I am keenly aware that this is a

matter of the utmost delicacy. Though we do not know each other, I would beg you to feel free to ask me any question you deem necessary. I have been instructed to give you my candid opinion on the Earl of Haverstone's character—in all respects."

Clasping her hands together in her lap, Mariah inclined her head. "I appreciate your frankness, Mr. Petersham."

Smiling, he finally seated himself in the wing chair opposite her. "I have known the earl since he was a baby. Of course, he was Viscount Morley until the death of his father. As a child and young man, he was high-spirited, curious, extremely quick-witted, and keenly intelligent. He has always exhibited a natural ability to lead that I believe has enabled him to be an excellent steward of his holdings." He paused for a sip of tea.

By the sincere eagerness in his voice, it was apparent to Mariah that Mr. Petersham very much liked and respected Stone.

Setting his cup down, he went on, his tone growing more serious. "At rather too young an age, he inherited all the rights and privileges of his rank. Although he has always put his responsibilities first, he has reveled just as hard as he has worked. It is a fact, Miss Thorncroft, that men of such power and privilege are often sophisticated when it comes to—shall we say—worldly matters."

He paused, watching for her reaction.

"I do understand," she said evenly.

Evidently satisfied that she was not about to turn missish, he resumed his narrative. "The earl has met and tested all the temptations men of his rank invariably face. Quite beyond anything we mere mortals contend with, I assure you," he said with a smile. "Through our frequent and frank discussions over the years, I believe there are few temptations that the earl cannot resist, if only by the simple fact that he has given in to most of them at one time or another. Forbidden fruit holds no allure for the earl. I can say without reservation that I believe the earl would make a committed, devoted, and faithful husband.

"Furthermore, though his father died when the earl was only seventeen, he had his father's excellent example for those years, and I believe he would strive to emulate his parents' happiness in his own marriage. Do you have any questions for me, Miss Thorncroft?"

For a moment Mariah's heart was too full for her to speak. "Just three. How did the earl look when last you saw him?"

Mr. Petersham thought for a moment. "He looked extremely tired and rather grim."

"And are you going to be seeing him soon?"

"Yes," he said with a smile.

"When you see his lordship, would you be so kind as to inform him that I am leaving for my home in the morning?"

"Certainly, Miss Thorncroft."

Mariah took a very deep breath and held her hand out to him. "Thank you so very much, Mr. Petersham. You will never know what our time together has meant to me."

Chapter Twenty-one

M ariah arrived at Thorncroft Manor late in the afternoon. She felt bone-tired, and her moss green traveling ensemble looked a bit disheveled from riding in the coach since last night.

The sight of George running down the front drive to meet her brought a weary smile to her face.

By the time the coach rolled to a stop at the front door she saw the rest of her family waiting for her on the steps.

Alighting, she looked from her mother to her father, too weary to read their expressions. Had it really been more than a fortnight since she had departed for Kelbourne Keep? she wondered as she glanced up at the handsome half-timbered Tudor house.

Her mother stepped forward and opened her arms. "Come up to your room, Mariah, love. You look too tired to talk right now." Without a word she stepped into her mother's warm embrace, feeling very happy to be home for the first time in a long while.

As her mother held her, she felt her father pat her back and she heard Steven say, "Welcome home, Mariah."

They all trooped in, leaving George chattering to the coachmen. Stopping in the middle of the foyer, Mariah looked around, surprise coming to her tired features. "Mama! The foyer looks so different!" she exclaimed.

"Do you like it?" Mama queried as they moved toward the staircase.

"Very much. It is so elegant." Her gazed traveled around the room, admiring the new spacious feeling and the noticeable lack of gilding.

"I decided to start with the foyer. I will work on the salon next. Your father is ever so pleased with my new decorating scheme."

As she walked up the staircase, Mariah thought about how much her life had changed. It seemed only fitting that the house should change as well.

As much as she wanted to tell her mother what had occurred during her stay at Kelbourne Keep, she also wanted to keep it close to her heart for a little while longer, to savor this wonderful feeling until everything was settled between her and Stone. She was also too tired to think, certainly too tired to answer any questions.

"I think I would like to go to bed now," she said, sending her mother a weary smile.

"Of course. Would you like something brought up on a tray?"

"No, thank you, Mama." Turning to her father and brother, she said, "I will see you both in the morning."

They bid her good night, and her mother continued to walk with her to her room. When they had reached the door, Mama turned troubled eyes to Mariah. "I hope you will not be angry when I tell you what I have done."

A frisson of alarm halted Mariah's hand on the banister. "What has happened?"

Mrs. Thorncroft's smooth brow puckered. "Well, I received the loveliest invitation from Mr. and Mrs. Spence-Jones asking us to join them at their home, Wick Hill, in the new year. I accepted. I do not wish for you to think that I am disregarding the discussion we had before you left for Kelbourne Keep. I only accepted because I found the Spence-Joneses delightful, not because I believe there will be any eligible gentlemen attending the house party."

At the concern on her mother's face, Mariah threw her arms around her, hugging her close and laughing with delight and relief. "I would love to visit Mr. and Mrs. Spence-Jones!"

Mrs. Thorncroft returned her daughter's embrace warmly. "That's all right, then. Now sleep well so you will be bright enough tomorrow to tell us of your visit to Kelbourne Keep."

The next morning, right after breakfast, Yale, the butler, informed Mariah that her father wished to see her in the library. Thanking him, Mariah immediately set aside her napkin and left the room.

"Well, my dear, we have much to discuss," her father said as soon as she walked into his library.

"Yes, Papa," she said quietly, taking the seat next to him.

Mariah wondered how much her father knew about her and the earl. She had concluded days ago that Stone must have come here first. How else would he have known that she had been visiting Kelbourne Keep, or the terms of her dowry? Even so, for Mama not to have mentioned the earl's visit seemed rather astonishing.

Holding her breath, she waited for her father to speak.

"He's an imperious sort, isn't he?" he said without the least hint of annoyance in his voice.

"Yes, he is rather," she agreed with a tentative smile, knowing exactly who "he" was.

Papa sent her a curious look, then continued. "The earl, to my utter shock and surprise, made known to me his intention to pay court to you. I am not ashamed to admit that I was a touch flummoxed by this pronouncement—I say pronouncement because it certainly could not be characterized as a request for my permission. It took me a moment to recover myself, because I had gathered from your mother that you wanted nothing to do with the earl."

Mariah swallowed, completely unprepared to explain to her father how she had fallen in love with

Stone. "What did you say then, Papa?" Mariah asked instead of responding to his implied question.

"I made it very clear to him that your mother and I would not put any pressure on you to accept his suit."

Mariah's jaw dropped. "You did?" Her voice almost squeaked.

He nodded emphatically. "Your mother and I had a long talk after you left for Kelbourne Keep. Your unhappiness since coming home from your visit to Heaton was unmistakable and very concerning. We have never seen you so melancholy. If the earl had anything to do with your depressed spirits, then I was not going to make any arrangement with him without first discussing it with you."

Mariah stared at her father, unable to speak for a moment. His unexpected words so touched her that tears instantly pooled in her hazel eyes as she gazed up at his troubled features.

"Thank you, Papa. That you would set aside your long-hoped-for desire for me to marry a title has made my heart whole," she said, her voice breaking on a little sob as she leaned into his arms to hug him.

He returned her embrace, patting her back reassuringly. "So you do not mean to have him, then?"

With a big sniff, Mariah pulled back and looked up at her father, smiling through her tears. "Not at all. I mean to have the Earl of Haverstone or no one."

Her father, looking startled and perplexed, opened his mouth to question her just as his wife stepped through the open library door.

"Here you are, Mariah. I wish to go to the village this afternoon and thought you might accompany me."

"Certainly, Mama," she said with shining eyes. "But first, I have something to share with you and Papa. Would you come in and sit with us?"

Casting a questioning glance from her daughter to her husband, Mrs. Thorncroft crossed the room to the chair opposite the settee.

Clasping her hands together, Mariah took a deep breath, hardly knowing where to begin. "I know you both think that I cut short my visit to Kelbourne Keep because I have been unhappy. Indeed, I was unhappy, but not anymore. I came home because I wanted to be with my family when the earl returns."

Mrs. Thorncroft's furrowed brows showed her confusion, "But Mariah, love, why would the earl be returning? You made it abundantly clear that you did not wish to marry him, and your father and I have respected your wishes."

"I know, Mama," she said earnestly. "And you have no idea how happy that has made me. But while I was at Kelbourne Keep, the earl did something so astonishing and wonderful that everything has changed."

Mariah then told her avidly listening parents about the three men the earl had sent to her. She barely got through the story for the tears constricting her throat. Even now, she found it a marvel that someone as proud and private as the earl would send emissaries to plead his case.

"Mariah! This is astounding," her mama cried. "I had decided not to mention the earl's visit for fear of upsetting you. Now I scarce know what to say. Are you sure? Truly, now that the moment is here, I would not wish you to wed someone you do not hold in the highest regard."

"Oh, Mama," Mariah whispered, jumping up to embrace her mother in her chair. "I do have the highest regard for the earl. He is the most wonderful man in the world. Next to Papa, of course." She cast an impish smile to her father as she pulled back from her mother.

Mr. Thorncroft stared at his daughter with a thunderstruck expression. "Do you mean to say that you could have snared an earl without the thirty thousand pounds?"

Mrs. Thorncroft shook her head at her husband's pained expression. "Too late now, Edmund," she said with a laugh.

*   *   *

The next day Mariah sat in the salon doing her best to read a book that Julia had sworn she found impossible to put down. Maybe the fact that she kept looking out the window to the front drive every few moments explained why she had not read past the third page.

When Steven strolled into the room, she gratefully set aside the book with a smile. Moving to the window, he turned to her and asked, "Mama told you of the invitation she received from Mrs. Spence-Jones?"

Mariah recognized what she had always referred to as his "offhand face," and smiling a little replied, "Yes, she did. She is beyond excited."

Slowly, he began to pace. "I received an invitation from Mrs. Spence-Jones as well. She is quite a gracious woman, and I am very gratified to be included on her guest list. She also mentioned that Lady Davinia would be visiting Wick Hill in March."

Raising a brow, Mariah shifted in her seat to get a better look at him. "Indeed? I think it is rather telling that Mrs. Spence-Jones would include such information in her letter to you. I hope you intend to accept the invitation."

"I believe I shall. The renovations and improvements on the foundry should be well under way, so being away for a couple of weeks should not cause any problems."

"Oh, Steven, being droll does you no credit," Mariah told him with a teasing laugh. "There is no doubt in my mind that Lady Davinia specifically told her cousin to include the information that she would be visiting Wick Hill."

Steven seemed to be having difficulty suppressing a grin and cast her a sheepish look. "I am much too modest to assume such a thing. But I have decided that I would not be overstepping myself to send Lady Davinia a letter—just a friendly, conversational letter—until we meet again."

"I think that is a very good idea."

"And what of you, Mariah? You have been sitting

in this room all morning, staring out the window. What are you waiting for?"

Mariah's laugh was full of delight. "All my life, I have always hated waiting. Probably because I never knew what I was waiting for. But this time I have no doubts. Steven, I know the earl came to dinner while I was away. Did Papa not tell you what transpired between them?"

"No, we were all quite surprised to get the note from the earl saying he was visiting the area. The honor rather bowled us over. I thought Mama was going to have to resort to her hartshorn."

"I would bet that she did," Mariah said dryly before he continued.

"As usual, the earl was an engaging dinner companion. You were conspicuous by the fact that you were not mentioned even once during the meal. After dinner he, father, and I enjoyed an excellent port and talked of politics and horses. After a bit, the earl, with exquisite politeness, requested a private word with Papa. They stayed closeted for more than half of an hour, and then the earl said a charming good-bye to us all and left. He came back the next morning to fence with George, but declined to stay for dinner, saying that he had another appointment. If I did not know that you think him an unabashed, unmitigated rake, I would have suspected he was making an offer for you." His jovial laugh told her that he thought this notion a complete impossibility.

Mariah decided not to share her astounding news with her brother, thinking it would be rather delicious to see the look of surprise on his face when the earl arrived.

Just then the rest of her family came into the salon. Mama, looking lovely in a celadon tea gown, smiled at her children. "Good. Now that we are all gathered in one place, I wish to discuss our guest list for Christmas. Now that we have made so many new friends we must start a new one."

All of a sudden her youngest son's excited shout cut off her words. "Look! A bang-up coach is coming up the drive." George pointed out the window, and all the family moved forward to see a large coach and four coming up the drive in the distance.

Mariah's heart stilled for a moment, then began to race at a frantic speed. Finally! Though she had waited in a high state of agitation for this moment, she was suddenly trembling with shyness.

Hastily checking her hair with shaking fingers, Mariah was glad that she had chosen to wear one of her most flattering ensembles: a heavy silk gown with fitted sleeves in a lovely shade the modiste called "ashes of lilacs," with a matching ribbon threaded through her coif. She wanted him to see her at her best—unlike most of the occasions when they had been together, she thought wryly.

Mrs. Thorncroft whirled toward her daughter. "Mariah, sit over there," she said, waving her hands toward the other side of the room. "The light is so much more flattering. Now, Edmund, Steven, you stand by the fireplace so when the earl is shown in, the first thing he sees is Mariah. George! Come away from the window at once!"

Laughing, Mariah's father did as his wife bid.

"What is happening?" Steven asked with baffled amusement at his mother's strange behavior.

"The earl is here!" Mrs. Thorncroft cried, waving him to the fireplace.

Quickly, Mariah moved to the settee, smoothing her lilac gown. Suddenly, all the things she had been longing to say to Stone vanished from her mind. Feeling a flush rising to her face, she found herself unable to look at her parents and instead stared into the fire blazing in the hearth.

"Now where will I sit?" Mama looked around the room in alarm.

With a pounding heart, Mariah listened as George described the scene outside.

Standing on his tiptoes, he pressed his nose against

the windowpane. "The horses are matched chestnuts. The coachman is taking the curve at a fast clip. They're pulling to a stop."

Fighting the urge to run downstairs to the drive to meet him, Mariah tried to compose her expression, but knew that the hot blush on her cheeks gave away the true state of her emotions.

"Oh! It's not the earl!" George called, disappointment plain in his tone.

"What?" her parents shouted.

Eyes wide with surprise and disappointment, Mariah watched George crane his neck as he strained to get a better look. "It's Lord Mattonly, Mama's beau!"

The youngster's words had the effect of a gunshot on his astonished family.

"What?" Mr. Thorncroft crossed the room to his son.

"George! Stop prattling such nonsense," Mrs. Thorncroft scolded, sending her husband a half-amused, half-alarmed look.

"He is too your beau. I heard Steven and Mariah say so at Heaton," George said over his shoulder, seeming affronted that anyone should suggest he had gotten his information wrong.

"Mary, I demand to know what George is speaking of. Who is Lord Mattonly?" Mr. Thorncroft said, looking back at his wife.

Rising, Mariah cast a quick glance to Steven, who met her gaze with barely concealed laughter.

"Papa!" Mariah said as her mother sputtered incoherently. "It is nothing. George just took our teasing about Lord Mattonly literally."

"Teasing about what? Who is this Lord Mattonly and what is he doing here?" her father demanded.

"He must be here to see Mama," George offered helpfully.

"Stop that, George!" Mrs. Thorncroft said, finally recovering her voice. "Now, Edmund, Lord Mattonly is a young gentleman barely older than Steven. We danced together at Heaton, and the children—you know their dreadful senses of humor—teased me about having a young beau. It is the most ridiculous thing on earth."

Mr. Thorncroft still frowned. "I do not like the sound of this. It does not explain why he is here."

"Mr. Elbridge!" George shouted from his post at the window.

Whipping around to look at her little brother, Mariah could hardly believe she heard him correctly. "What of Mr. Elbridge?" she said with complete shock.

"He just stepped out of the coach after Lord Mattonly."

Mariah exchanged surprised glances with Steven and Mama.

"Who is Mr. Elbridge?" Papa practically shouted.

"He was another of the earl's guests. I waltzed with him at Heaton," Mariah hastily supplied.

"Waltzed with him? Here now, what is going on?" Papa threw his hands up in an aggravated gesture.

"He is the heir to a baronetcy," Mrs. Thorncroft offered.

"Humph," Mr. Thorncroft snorted. "Looks as if we shall be entertaining enough noble blood to satisfy even you, my dear."

Exchanging another befuddled glance with her mother, Mariah wondered what Lord Mattonly and Mr. Elbridge were doing in Chippenham.

Despite her bewildered disappointment, she tried to school her expression to politeness as the butler opened the door and announced the unexpected guests.

Two exquisitely garbed gentlemen, looking as if they should be stepping out of some fashionable London club, strolled into the salon.

As they both bowed, Mama rushed forward to greet them. After the introductions were made and everyone was seated, an awkward silence hung in the room for a moment.

"We were just about to have our tea, my lord, Mr.

Elbridge. You will join us, won't you?" Mrs. Thorn-croft asked in a nervous rush of words.

"Certainly, Mrs. Thorncroft," Lord Mattonly said.

"Very kind," Mr. Elbridge mumbled quickly, rubbing his hands together in a nervous manner.

Lord Mattonly, his fair hair styled à la Caesar, turned his sky blue eyes to Mr. Thorncroft. "Elbridge and I are so glad to find you all at home. You see, we were just passing through the area and remembered that the charming Thorncroft family resided in Chippenham. We got your direction at the posting inn in the village."

"You are most welcome to Thorncroft Manor, my lord, Mr. Elbridge. We certainly hope you intend to stay for supper," Mr. Thorncroft offered.

Lord Mattonly's smile showed his elation at the offer. "You are too kind, sir."

"Indeed. Thank you," Mr. Elbridge hastily added, sending Mariah a tentative smile.

Stepping forward, George said with childish eagerness, "Lord Stone, I mean Haverstone, was also in the area not long ago. It's strange that so many of the people we met at Heaton are suddenly in Chippenham."

At this Lord Mattonly and Mr. Elbridge exchanged odd looks.

"George, dear, why don't you go look at his lordship's horses?" Mama suggested in a sweet tone.

George was delighted to do so, and after he skipped out of the room, the stilted conversation struggled along in fits and starts.

Mariah gazed at Lord Mattonly, mystified at his sudden appearance on their doorstep. She did not believe the nonsense about just happening to be in the area. No, the way Lord Mattonly looked at Mama, with the pathetic expression of a moonling, made his purpose here very clear.

It really was shockingly funny, she thought, guiltily stifling a laugh. Even though she and Steven had teased Mama about Lord Mattonly, Mariah never would have guessed that the young man would be so foolish as to go haring off across the countryside to see her again.

Shooting her father a quick glance, she was relieved to see that amusement lurked beneath his polite expression.

While Mama poured tea for everyone, keeping the conversation on mundane matters, Mariah determinedly tamped down her abject disappointment. After all, if Stone had gone all the way back to Heaton instead of staying in the village near Kelbourne Keep, then he might not return to Chippenham for days yet.

This bit of logical deduction did nothing to curb her aching desire to see him.

"Shall you be staying in Chippenham for long? This Thursday will be the local assembly ball. We cannot boast such company as we had in Heaton, but the orchestra is quite fine," Mama said as she handed Lord Mattonly his tea.

"If I may be honored again by leading you in a dance, then I have every intention of staying in this charming village," Lord Mattonly said before turning to Papa. "I am sure I do not tell you what you do not know, Mr. Thorncroft, but Mrs. Thorncroft is an extremely accomplished dancer."

Mariah caught Steven covering his laugh with a cough. Oh how she wished Stone were here to enjoy this little drama with her.

"I thank you on my wife's behalf, Lord Mattonly," Mr. Thorncroft said with a slight inclination of his head. "I believe over the near thirty years of our marriage she has only grown more accomplished."

It was Mariah's turn to choke back her laughter as Lord Mattonly looked completely lost for words.

"Er, how are your foxhounds, Mr. Elbridge?" Mariah asked hastily to fill the awkward silence.

His rather nondescript face broke into a wide smile. "Hale and hearty, Miss Thorncroft. I am readying them for the hunt in January."

"Ah, you hunt, sir?" Papa asked politely, willing to let the subject change.

"Elbridge is famous in Leicestershire for his kennels," Lord Mattonly offered.

Mr. Elbridge fairly beamed with pride at such praise. "Do you like foxhounds, Mr. Thorncroft?" he asked, leaning forward eagerly.

Considering the question, Mr. Thorncroft rubbed his chin. "I have not been around foxhounds much, but I do like dogs."

"That's wonderful! Miss Thorncroft has told me that she likes dogs, too," he said, sending her a delighted smile.

Alarm warred with Mariah's sense of the ridiculous as she returned Mr. Elbridge's smile with a courteous one of her own.

She had the sudden suspicion that because she liked dogs and had a fat dowry, Mr. Elbridge had come all this way to ask her father for her hand! Fearing she might burst out in laughter, Mariah looked away from Mr. Elbridge's grinning face.

Just then, a movement out the window caught her attention. In the distance, she saw a familiar figure on horseback riding up the drive at breakneck speed. Her heart pounded in her throat as she gripped the armrests. *Stone!*

Glancing quickly around the room, she saw that no one else seemed to be looking out the window. Unbearable love and longing forced her from her chair, cutting off another compliment from Lord Mattonly to her mother. Ignoring the proprieties, she moved swiftly toward the door.

Conversation ceased as everyone turned to look at her in surprise, the gentlemen struggling to rise. "No, please do not get up! I—there is something I must attend to. I beg you to excuse me." Dropping a curtsy, she left the room, uncaring of the astonished faces she left behind.

Chapter Twenty-two

After seeing his coach safe at the inn in Chippenham, Stone had jumped onto his fastest horse and headed for Thorncroft Manor.

With his jaw clenched and his heart pounding in his chest, Stone admitted to himself that this was one of the few times in his life when the outcome of one of his endeavors was unclear. And his hurried wooing of Mariah Thorncroft could certainly be called an endeavor, he thought with dry humor, thinking of the effort it took to get Misters Tracy, Harding, and Petersham to Kelbourne Keep.

When the Reverend Mr. Petersham, vicar of his parish church, had given him Mariah's cryptic message that she was leaving Kelbourne Keep the next morning, he had been astounded.

"What the hell does that mean?" he had asked as he paced the floor of the room he had taken in Wenlock Downs. He had waited all day for the vicar to come to him, never once conceiving that this would be her reaction to the gentlemen he had sent to her.

Petersham had not been able to enlighten him, saying only that Miss Thorncroft had seemed pleased with the information he had shared with her. "Truth be told, my lord, after four and twenty years of marriage I still find the female mind a puzzle," he had said.

Stone told himself that he would wait a week, that he would not go tearing after her again. But after a day and a half, the waiting had become intolerable, and so he directed his servants to return him to Chippenham.

Be it yes or no, he had to have her answer now or he felt he would go mad, he thought, urging his horse into a faster gallop.

In that second, around a curve in the drive, came Mariah.

Hauling back the reins, his horse came to a prancing stop. His gaze roved over her delicate features and the beauty of her eyes as they looked up into his with an unreadable expression. Hungrily, he took in the way the sun danced off the honeyed highlights in her hair and the way her exquisitely tailored gown flattered her slender figure. Resisting the urge to sweep her into his arms, he dismounted and tossed the reins to a stableboy who had come trotting up. Stone kept his gaze on her flushed face, trying to gauge her feelings.

Turning away, she directed the boy to attend to his lordship's horse.

Taken aback by her sudden appearance, Stone momentarily forgot how he had planned to greet her. "Good afternoon, Mariah," he said instead.

"Good afternoon, my lord," she replied softly. "Would you care to take a stroll around the grounds? There is a pretty arbor by the pond."

His brow rose at the obvious nervousness in her tone. "Certainly."

As they walked together through the courtyard, he noticed the stable hands unhitching a team of horses from a familiar-looking coach.

"Lord Mattonly and Mr. Elbridge are visiting," she supplied, evidently seeing him take notice of the coach.

He paused. "Matt and Elbridge? What are they doing here?" he asked, his usual politeness gone.

She sent him an impish smile. "Lord Mattonly is paying my mama the silliest compliments, for which my papa will tease her for the rest of their lives, and

Mr. Elbridge is most likely going to ask my father's permission to pay court to me."

"The devil you say?" He frowned as they strolled past the house and down a pathway that led to a stone bench beneath a leafless arbor of trees. "I never would have thought that Elbridge had it in him."

She laughed a little, gazing up at him with a look he found nearly irresistible. As she moved to the bench, the words he had been about to say fled his mind.

With growing frustration at his sudden and completely uncharacteristic inability to express himself, he watched her sit down and fold her hands in her lap. His gaze moved to her graceful, artistic fingers.

Removing his gloves, he looked at her, his heart pounding. "I was surprised that you left Kelbourne Keep so precipitously," he finally said.

He watched surprise and confusion cloud her sparkling gaze. "You were?"

Long strides took him from one end of the windswept arbor to the other as he reflexively slapped his gloves against his leg. This was not turning out how he intended at all, he thought, his heart continuing to race at an annoying pace.

He turned to her, throwing his hands up. "Enough, Mariah. In our short acquaintance, we have been nothing if not candid with one another. If the gentlemen I sent did not convince you that you can trust me, then tell me what else I need to do, or send me on my way."

He saw the confusion lift from her eyes, replaced by something he could not quite identify.

"How did Mr. Tracy come to be in possession of my sketches?" she asked softly, tilting her head to one side.

Gritting his teeth at her avoidance of his request, he turned his gaze from hers, looking into the distance across the pond to the rolling hills. "That day in the library, after you showed me what you had drawn, you left your sketchbook behind. Before returning it to you, I took two of your drawings."

"Why?"

He shrugged. "Because I rather hoped you would notice them gone and ask me about it."

For some reason this caused her to smile. "I have not looked in the case since. I wish I had."

Tossing his gloves down, he moved to sit next to her, gazing deeply into her beautiful eyes. "Mariah, quite simply, I can no longer imagine my life without you. Everything about you has captured my heart— your intelligence, your humor, your beauty. I want nothing more than to be with you. To protect you, to learn with you, to grow old with you. Only time will show you the strength of the love and respect I have for you. You hold my heart, and I have no desire to have it back."

He watched as she closed her eyes for a moment. He held his breath. When Mariah's lashes fluttered up, all that he desired was plain to see in her beautiful eyes.

In accord, they rose from the bench. "Do you really have no idea why I left Kelbourne Keep?" she whispered, drawing close to him, tears shimmering on her lashes.

"No, tell me," he said with tender solemnity.

"Because I wanted to be home, among my family, when you told me you loved me"—swiftly, his arms went around her in a fierce embrace—"and when I told you how terribly much I love you."

A little while later, as they strolled back to the house hand in hand, with her hair ever so slightly mussed, Mariah looked up at her betrothed with joy-filled eyes. She gazed tenderly at his stern, handsome features, her heart swelling with pride that this man could love her and that he would go to such lengths to show her how much.

Never again would she doubt that she was wanted

for herself, she thought as her heart soared with the
wonderful possibilities of their future.

A sudden thought stopped her steps.

"Stone," she said, looking up at him with troubled
eyes, "because of what you did, I know that you have
no interest in my dowry. But there is no way, really,
for me to prove that I care nothing for your title."

The tender amusement in his arresting blue gaze
sent a shiver of awareness down her spine. Slowly, he
raised her hand to his warm lips. "Not to worry, my
love. I knew being a countess held no interest for you
when you refused to allow your delightful and charming mama to trap me into marriage when she found
us embracing."

Laughing, he took her lips again in a warm, lingering kiss that was full of promise, and then he said,
"Let's go in and give my future mama-in-law a fit of
the vapors."